THE GIRL SHE WAS

Also By M.I. Hattersley

The Ex
The Girls' Weekend
My Daughter is Gone

THE GIRL SHE WAS

M.I. Hattersley

embla books

This edition published in the UK in 2025 by

embla books

An imprint of Bonnier Books UK
5th Floor, HYLO, 105 Bunhill Row,
London, EC1Y 8LZ

Previously published as *The Pact* by M.I. Hattersley in 2022.

A CIP catalogue record for this book is available from the British Library.

ISBN: 9781471420597

Also available as an ebook

1

Typeset by IDSUK (Data Connection) Ltd
Printed and bound in Great Britain by Clays Ltd, Elcograf S.p.A.

MIX
Paper | Supporting responsible forestry
FSC® C018072
FSC www.fsc.org

The authorised representative in the EEA is Bonnier Books UK (Ireland) Limited.
Registered office address: Floor 3, Block 3, Miesian Plaza, Dublin 2, D02 Y754, Ireland
compliance@bonnierbooks.ie
www.bonnierbooks.co.uk

For AJH

Chapter 1

It was that blasted song that had set her off. Nadia Morgan switched off the radio and leaned over her large Belfast sink unit, turning her back to the room in the hope no one had seen. A quick swipe of her hand dealt with the tears, and she opened her eyes wide to stop any more from forming and ruining her mascara. To distract herself, she peered through the window at the expansive panorama in front of her, reminding herself once again how lucky she was to live in such an idyllic setting. Luscious green fields stretched away to the horizon, topped with a rich azure blue sky. Trees and long grasses swayed lazily in the late afternoon breeze whilst birds and hedgerow insects fluttered around in casual abandon as if they knew of no predator hell-bent on eating them this fine day.

"Mummy? Are you okay?"

"Oh, God, Mum! Are you crying?"

The first question, full of confusion and concern, came from Emily, her gorgeous six-year-old girl who still thought Mummy was the best thing in the world. The second question, full of scorn and embarrassment, came from Andrew, thirteen going on thirty. Enough said. Even if you didn't have a teenager yourself, you'd been one. There was a certain age one reached when everything a parent did annoyed and embarrassed you. Although some days it seemed to Nadia that Andrew took this concept to the extreme.

"I'm fine," she said, choosing to respond to Emily. "Mummy's just been cutting onions, that's all. Sometimes they make your eyes water."

She ran her wrists under the cold water before switching off the tap and reaching for the kitchen roll. Yanking off a couple of sheets, she dried her hands before wadding up the paper and dabbing at her eyes. Job done, she turned back to the room with the biggest smile she could muster.

"See? I'm fine." Emily gave her a long stare, but Andrew offered her only a simple eye roll and returned to whatever he was doing on his iPad. She'd like to believe it was research for his English essay, but she wasn't that naïve.

"Dinner will be ready in about an hour," she continued. "Can you both go get changed and freshen up before then? And Andrew, are we going to get our homework finished before dinner? I don't want you up all night again like last week."

"Yes! All right!" He slipped off his chair and walked over to the lounge area, grabbing his blazer and school bag from the sofa before walking the full length of the open-plan kitchen-diner and into the hallway on the other side. It was rather impressive, considering he didn't take his eyes from the iPad screen once, but Nadia wasn't sure it would be a transferable skill once he became an adult. Not for the first time, Nadia had a mind to confiscate the iPad. Maybe even his Nintendo as well. At least limit his usage of both. But he needed the iPad for his schoolwork, and online gaming offered a lifeline to his friends, who all lived some distance away. That was what she told herself, at least.

"Are you going to get changed?" she asked Emily with a smile.

She regarded Nadia with those huge brown eyes of hers. "Can I finish doing this picture first? It's a space pony." She lifted the paper with a smile that would melt even her older brother's narcissistic heart.

"Wow, amazing," Nadia said, nodding eagerly at the drawing. It was actually rather good and showed some development, she thought, but she'd had the response cued up long before she'd seen the image. That was how it was being a parent. You had a plethora of stock responses saved up, which could be employed without having to engage fully with the situation.

That's amazing

Wow, that's so clever.

No! I am watching, darling!

It wasn't being a bad parent. It just meant you could fit in the million and one other tasks you needed to do each day, whilst still showing a semblance of interest.

Nadia placed the knife down and sighed. But maybe that was unfair. Being this way wasn't just about raising children whilst hanging onto your sanity. It was how all adults became, eventually. It wasn't so much about being a parent as being a human being. Life was easier when filtered through a façade of faux-delight and stock responses. Some called it having an English stiff upper lip, but being half-Bengali, half-Irish Nadia didn't subscribe to that stuffy English cliché. For her, this way of being, of always having an answer and a smile for whatever came at you, was the perfect defence mechanism. It was probably unhealthy to suppress your feelings this way, but she was English enough to suppress those thoughts, too, when they popped up. Being this way meant you kept the wolves from the door of your psyche most of the time. And that was a good thing. Nadia had a lot of wolves to deal with. Most of her memories were like dormant gremlins she'd pushed down deep inside of herself. But some days, like today, the beastly thoughts rose up and found sustenance. She could sense their spindly claws stretching out across time to invade her present.

It was that blasted song that had set her off. *Say My Name* by Destiny's Child. She hadn't heard it in years and when it came on the radio just now out of the blue, the opening bars alone had set her off.

Say my name . . .

She and her mum listened to Destiny's Child's *The Writing's On The Wall* album on every car journey they took that year. The year the album was released. Nineteen-ninety-nine. She knew that because it was the last year that they were properly together as a family. She'd always skip the CD to track twelve – *Say My Name* – much to her mum's annoyance. But she didn't seem to mind as the two of them belted out the refrain on their way to piano lessons, or swimming class. They even listened to it on the way to court, she remembered. Maybe that was why it had hit her so hard.

Say my name . . .

She always felt it strange that certain things could make you think of your past. Sometimes it was easy to understand why, but not always. She could be folding laundry or mucking out the stables and all at once an image would pop into her head. Sometimes it was a nice memory, but that was rare. Over the years, she'd grown good at deflecting these thoughts, catching them as they bubbled up through the primordial ooze of her consciousness and nipping them in the bud before they could fully form.

And it was all such a long time ago now. A different world away.

She was a different person back then . . .

"Mummy!"

Her train of thought was wiped from her mind as she emerged back into her modern-day kitchen to see little Emily looking up at her.

"Sorry, darling. What did you say?"

"You're still crying! Is it the onions?"

Nadia's hand went to her face, and she dabbed at her eyes with the crook of her index finger. "Yes. Don't worry. I'm fine."

"Are you sad, Mummy?"

"No, of course not!" She said, putting on a big smile. "What have I got to be sad about? I've got you and your brothers and daddy. I've got this lovely big house in the countryside. Why would I be sad when I'm so lucky? Now come along Emily Bunny. Get changed for dinner and tell Edward to do the same."

"But I'm not a bunny today."

"Oh? What are you?"

"A unicorn."

Without further comment, the small girl wandered out into the hallway towards the bedroom she shared with her twin brother, Edward, who was more than likely building an extensive castle with his Lego.

"And wash your hands," Nadia called after her.

She got no response, but that was okay. Sometimes, as a parent, saying it was enough. After that, it was in the lap of the gods what they did. You couldn't be with your kids twenty-four-seven. She wondered initially, when she was pregnant with Andrew, whether her own experiences would make her a strict parent – or one of those irritating 'helicopter' parents she'd read about, and then seen in the flesh in the child groups she'd attended over the years. It was true she had been much stricter with Andrew, and as he reached teenage years, she could feel herself growing more so – much to his displeasure – but she also knew how precarious life was. The best kids in the world could make mistakes. And one mistake could change everything. She wasn't dumb. She knew Andrew in particular needed space. But it was hard. The past and the future met her most nights when she was trying to sleep, and neither were pleasant bedfellows.

"Come on now, Nads," she whispered to herself. "No point going there."

She pushed her chest out and put on her smile. Because what did she have to feel sorry about? She'd been telling the truth before. She had a great life, a wonderful husband, darling children, and the most beautiful home she could ever imagine. This was paradise, and she owed it to herself to appreciate it.

She picked up the large bottle of olive oil and glugged a decent amount into the large copper casserole pan already on the stovetop. Clicking on the gas, she scooped up the onions from the chopping board and chucked them into the spitting oil. The onions were fresh and pungent and stung her eyes. Maybe they were partly to blame for the waterworks. It happened. She smiled to herself. A genuine smile this time.

Yes. She certainly was grateful. Nadia Morgan had everything she'd ever needed or wanted. But she damn well deserved it.

Chapter 2

It was Wednesday, so it was curry night in the Morgan household. Nadia had made her speciality, her take on a traditional Bengalese dish with chicken breast meat, rather than thighs, and plenty of potatoes and onions. As of a few weeks ago, she'd even begun serving the twins from the main pot rather than give them a less spicy 'kid-friendly' version and, touch wood, they were eating it without comment. That made her happy. The dish was one of the few obvious links to her heritage that she still had – except for her dark skin and that of her children – and she was pleased she could share at least some aspects of her past with her family. The curry was one of the first dishes her mother had taught her to make.

One of the first and last.

No one had spoken more than a few words since they'd all sat down to eat five minutes ago, and she took that as a good sign. The chink of cutlery on crockery and the vague noises of satisfaction and delight as everyone tucked into their food were the sounds of a job well done. Not that Nadia's role in the house was merely as the cook or even the housekeeper. She did wear both those hats – and loved looking after her family – but she also had her horses, and the glamping business as well now. And whilst the stud farm only just wiped its feet these days in terms of profit, it was hers. She loved the fact she ran two businesses, as well as being a mother and a wife. Not bad going for a shy girl from a rough part of Bradford.

"This is amazing, Nads," Laurie said, waving his fork over his plate emphatically. "One of your best. Don't you agree, kids?"

"Yeah," the twins both said in unison.

Andrew shrugged and sniffed. It was the closest you got to a response from him most of the time. Laurie caught her looking at their eldest and shook his head with a smile as their eyes met.

"Do you like it, Andrew?" he asked.

"Yeah, it's all right."

Laurie threw up his eyebrows. "Majestic praise indeed, thanks for that, Chef Ramsey."

"I said I liked it." He begrudgingly glanced Nadia's way, but still evaded eye contact. "It's nice."

"Andrew's still upset that I won't let him go to the party, aren't you, darling?" she said.

"Oh?" Laurie said. "What's this?"

Nadia waited for Andrew to reply, but when he just stared into his food, she answered for him. "Simon Burns at school is having a party in a couple of weeks. For his fourteenth. But I've found out his parents are away on holiday and his older brother is looking after him – who I imagine is also inviting friends to this party. I've told Andrew I don't think it's a good idea for him to go."

"But everyone's going," Andrew mumbled into his curry.

"Not everyone."

He tutted loudly but said nothing else on the matter. Nadia glared at Laurie, who was regarding his eldest son with kind eyes as if he was considering saying more. But he decided against it. They would discuss it later and he'd no doubt put Andrew's case forward, but it was usual for these decisions to be made by her alone and Laurie usually backed her up. She felt for her eldest son, of course she did. But he was only thirteen, and that was too young to be going to a party where there might be drink and drugs and who knows what else. She was his mother. She had to protect him from the evils of the world for as long as possible. In a few more years, he could go to whatever party he wanted. Within reason. They'd get him contact lenses too if wearing glasses was still such a bother for him. Sometimes she wished she could grab her kids and shake them, tell them not to rush growing up. It happened regardless, so stay young, for as long as possible.

"And what about you, Nadia?" Laurie asked her. "Any news from the homestead that is *Camborne Stables plus Elite Glamping Experience*?"

She reached for her glass of wine and took a sip as she thought about the question. Sometimes when Laurie spelt out the entire name of the business like that, she detected a slightly condescending tone in his voice. But today she didn't hear it. Maybe she was choosing not to.

"Not anything that fun," she said. "I did the horses, did the washing. We've got a new couple in yurt number two – the Snowdons. They're down from London. He's a writer. I'm not sure what she does. But they seem nice. They're staying until Monday."

"Great, and how's Mr Oddball in number one?"

Nadia widened her eyes at him. Sending a clear message. *Not in front of the kids.* The last thing she wanted was one of them repeating what their father had said to the guests and her getting a bad review on Trip Advisor. The right – or, rather, wrong – one-star review and the business could be over before it got going.

"*Mr Jameson* is fine," she told him. "He's a nice old man. He's just really into his birdwatching, that's all."

"I'll take your word for it."

She gave her husband another look, but she knew what Laurie meant about the guest in yurt number one. Mr Jameson had arrived last Friday and was staying at Elite Glamping for three weeks – time enough, he hoped, to catch sight of a Wilson's storm petrel. Nadia remembered the name because the old man had said it about six times in the three-minute conversation they'd had when he checked in. Nadia had never heard of the breed but, apparently, they were super-rare and a couple of them had recently been seen in this part of Cornwall. It wasn't his hobbies so much that gave the man an air of oddness, however, but the erratic way he moved his head as if he was a bird himself. Nadia had also found it disconcerting that Mr Jameson didn't converse in the way normal people did. When she'd finished saying what she had to say, rather than reply, he'd continue to stare at you with a blank expression on his face, as though he expected you to say more. Being a people-pleaser, Nadia found herself waffling on and talking absolute nonsense to cover the awkwardness.

"Don't be nasty, Laur," she whispered.

"Ah, come on, I was only messing around."

"You know I don't like name-calling."

Harpooning a large piece of chicken with her fork, she put it in her mouth before she said anything she might regret. Nadia hated being mean about people and she hated name-calling more than anything. *Sticks and stones may break my bones, but words will never hurt me.* That was how the children's rhyme went. But she'd always thought it was complete nonsense. She knew for a fact that names hurt. But so did stones.

She stared out through the glass wall that spanned the entire south side of the property. The sun was setting, and the sky was glowing a gorgeous mixture of orange and pink. Despite the view, she felt the dull but familiar spike of resentment in the back of her throat.

Say my name . . .

Leave me alone!

She'd spent a hell of a lot of time and effort pushing these memories so far down inside of herself she wouldn't ever have to look at them. Why were they haunting her all of a sudden?

"Mummy, I've not seen Marge in ages and ages."

"What's that darling?" Nadia snapped her attention to Edward, more than glad of his cute, squeaky voice drawing her out of herself.

"Marge. She's not been in my room since forever and she's not eaten her dinner for ages."

Nadia frowned. "Really? Are you sure?" Marge was the family cat, but Edward in particular had grown close to her. They'd got her as a kitten from one of Laurie's clients when Andrew was a baby and it was unusual for a cat, especially one of Marge's age, to attach itself to a human the way she had. So her bond with Edward felt even more special. Most nights, Nadia would find her curled up on the end of his bed. "Have you looked for her outside? Or in the barn?"

A frisson of panic fluttered behind her ribs. She looked at Laurie, hoping not to see anything in his eyes which might tell her he knew something bad. But he looked as nonplussed as she felt.

"A bit, but I couldn't see her," Edward said. "Can you ask people for me? Melissa and Tom and Mrs Lamb Bear?"

"I will, darling. As soon as we've finished dinner, I'll go down and ask them. I'm sure Marge is fine, though. Don't worry." She smiled at him, wishing to all the gods in the sky that she was correct, and his special friend was okay. But not coming home for food, that wasn't the Marge she knew.

Chapter 3

Once dinner was done and the dishes stacked in the dishwasher, Nadia did as promised and ventured down the long, uneven track to see if anyone had seen Marge. It was a pleasant evening, and the air quality was superb. But then it was often that way in this part of the country. It was a different world down here. Quiet. Peaceful. With hardly anyone around and just the benign sounds of nature filling the airwaves.

There were three properties in the locality, each one standing in its own sizeable grounds with forest and farmland on all sides. The houses were linked by a narrow dirt track which started at Camborne Stables and wound down the hill before bridging over a small river and rising up to the A30 that took you into Bodmin, the nearest town. Laurie and Nadia were responsible for the upkeep of the track, which could be a real pain in the neck – especially two years ago when a flood created a glut of potholes that needed attention – but it also felt good to be the ones in charge. Nadia Morgan was the queen of the homestead. This was her domain. Her safe haven.

She walked without pace, casting her eyes into the long grass on either side, calling out Marge's name whilst shaking the bag of cat treats she'd grabbed from the cupboard. Normally, the sound of treats alone would have had the old cat bounding out from the undergrowth, perhaps covered in seed buds or the like. But not today. With each step, Nadia's heart grew heavier, but she resisted the urge to play out in her head what she might say to the children about Marge. She wasn't ready for that. She wasn't ready to be the one who introduced death and pain into the lives of her babies.

She'd walked all the way to Tom and Melissa's house down by the river before she'd realised where she was. Good old Tom and Melissa. They were friendly and warm, and not being able to have children themselves, were always keen to look after the twins if Nadia needed to go into town for supplies. But as she approached the front door, she saw their lights were off. She knocked and waited, but no one was home, so she doubled back on herself and headed for the large cottage situated around the bend.

Painted pale pink and with a huge fishpond in the garden that the kids loved, the house was arguably the prettiest out of the three in the area if not the most modern. It was a beautiful two-storey Cornish cottage with dark green ivy on the walls and an enormous garage and workshop which jutted out perpendicular to the main building. From the day she moved into Camborne Stables (then simply Camborne Cottage) Nadia had always thought the pink house looked French for some reason. So it was very apt, she thought, that it now had a suitably French owner.

Mrs Lamb Bear – or Mrs *Lambert*, to those who weren't six years old – was originally from Montpellier and had bought the pink house at the end of last year. Despite being relatively young, she was already a widow and had sold up in France after her husband died. From what Nadia had picked up on from their conversation, there had been a lot of pain and sadness towards the end. So, it made sense she'd want to start again somewhere completely new.

"Good evening, Nadia, my darling." The top of the barn-style door opened wide before Nadia even had a chance to get up to it. She must have seen her marching past through the window. "Is everything all right? You look stressed."

"Do I?" she said and blew a strand of her hair out of her face. "I suppose I am. It's our cat, Marge. No one has seen her in a few days and I'm starting to worry."

"Oh no. How terrible for the children."

"Yes, Edward especially is going to take it hard if she doesn't turn up soon."

Mrs Lambert – or Elenore if you were on first-name terms like Nadia was – unbolted the bottom section of the door and eased it open. "Please, come inside. Do you want some tea? Or something stronger, maybe to help calm you? I have just opened a wonderful bottle of Chablis. It is ice cold." The way she said *Chablis* and *ice cold* prickled the hairs on the back of Nadia's neck.

"Do you know what? That would be lovely. Thank you."

"*Bon.* Come in. Please."

Elenore led Nadia into her front room and gestured for her to have a seat on the huge white couch along the nearside wall. "I'll be back in a moment with the drinks," she said, leaving her to get settled.

The front room was done out almost entirely in white. And the effect was so calming that Nadia instantly felt more grounded and able to handle the swirling thoughts cascading through her mind. Pets died. People did too. It was a fact of life. And whilst the twins were only six, they were old enough to understand the concept of death.

Because, when *was* a good time to learn of your own mortality? If the worst had happened to Marge – killed by a fox, maybe, or a car up on the road, or even just old age – they'd deal with it. As a family.

"Here we go, one small glass of wine." Elenore appeared in the doorway holding two glasses of wine, large in anyone's estimation. She sashayed over to the couch and held one out for Nadia. "This is from one of my favourite chateaux."

Nadia accepted the glass, crinkling her nose at her friend as she sat beside her. She was certainly an elegant woman. Very French. Her hair was cut short and almost entirely grey despite her being only a few years older than Nadia. They'd never discussed ages, but if she had to guess, she'd put Eleanor in her early forties, knowing she might be older. It was her skin that made it hard to age her accurately. It practically glowed and there was hardly a wrinkle in sight. She saw Nadia looking and winked.

"*Salut, mon ami.*"

They chinked glasses, and Nadia took a long drink. The wine was as cold as she'd hoped and tasted delicious. In contrast, the Chardonnay she'd opened whilst cooking dinner was lukewarm by the time she was ready for it and rather mundane compared to the crisp apple notes and slight effervescence of the Chablis.

It was obviously an expensive bottle. But maybe it was the atmosphere and the company that made the difference. At home, she was a wife, mother and cook, not to mention the owner of Elite Glamping. Here she could be a single woman with nothing to worry about but herself and the next glass of wine. For a while, anyway.

"When was it last seen?" Elenore asked.

"Sorry?"

"The cat."

"Oh, shoot. Yes. Erm . . . a few days ago, I think. She was an old cat, but the kids loved her. She might turn up, but I'm afraid I'm not holding out much hope."

"Oh, dear." Elenore smiled, but there was something in her eyes that belied the gesture.

"What is it?" Nadia asked.

"I don't know whether I should say. It is probably my overactive imagination. Or me seeing things in the shadows that aren't there."

"What did you see? When?"

Elenore rested the base of her wineglass on her knee. "Sunday night. I was getting ready for sleep and heard a sound outside my window. I opened it to look out and I swear I saw someone across the track, a dark figure in the twilight. I think it was a man, but it could have been a woman as well. Their face was shrouded in shadow. Then, as I was looking, they stepped back and disappeared into the woods. I know it sounds like maybe I had a few too many glasses of Chablis, but I am certain there was someone there. I didn't sleep well that night at all."

"No. I can imagine. That's awful."

"But you didn't see anything?"

"No." A shiver ran down Nadia's neck and the ice-cold wine wasn't the reason. "Maybe we should set up some security cameras on the track," she said. "Some lights, too."

Elenore stuck her bottom lip out. "Yes. It would deter prowlers, I think. For sure."

The way she said *prowlers* in her French accent made it sound even more sinister than it already was. But a small part of Nadia couldn't help wondering if this was Elenore manipulating her, telling her this story to get what she wanted. There had been a few other times in the last six months where she'd felt there was more to what her friend was saying than what was on the surface. But that was how most people operated, and she didn't mind. Plus, she made a good point and the track could be quite treacherous, especially in winter.

"I'll have a word with Laurie," she said. "And see what he thinks. A few security lights would be good at least."

Elenore smiled. "I am sorry. You look stressed again, and this was not my intention. I do not mean to worry you. It was probably my imagination."

Nadia drank back the rest of her wine in one gulp. It didn't taste as nice anymore. The moment had passed. "I should get going," she said. "Laurie will be wondering where I've got to." She got to her feet. "If you see Marge, will you try to grab hold of her and bring her up to the house?"

"Of course." Elenore got up too, and they walked together to the front door. Once there, she opened it before turning and placing her hand on Nadia's arm. "You're a wonderful mother, Nadia. I can see this. Those children are lucky to have you."

"I don't know about that," she replied, but her cheeks burned and she had to look away. "Thanks again for the wine. I'll have to have you up to the house one night soon. We could play cards again."

"That would be wonderful. I look forward to it. *Bonne nuit*, Nadia."

She left and wandered back to the track, waving over her shoulder as Elenore shut the door. Without the light from Elenore's kitchen, the track fell dark and Nadia felt very alone. As she walked Elenore's words echoed in her head.

A dark figure in the twilight . . . Disappeared into the woods . . .

That settled it. She was going to have a chat with Laurie about some lights. She walked a few steps and then pulled her iPhone out of her pocket and tapped on the torch app with a quivering finger. The stark light bounced out onto the track in front of her and she quickened her pace around the bend. Another thirty seconds and she could see her house up ahead. Laurie had turned off the kitchen lights, but a dull orange glow drifted out into the garden from the lounge.

"Come along now. Stop being so silly." She spoke the words out loud, surprised to hear she'd opted to say them in her mum's accent. Despite being the first generation of her family to be born in the UK, Nadia's mum had grown up in a tight Bangladeshi community and had adopted her parents' accent rather than that of the local area. When she was younger, it embarrassed Nadia whenever her mum spoke to people. She sighed. Now she'd give anything to hear her mum's voice again.

She carried on up the incline to her house, swishing the torch from side to side in case Marge was lurking somewhere.

Oh no!

At the main gate to the property, she stopped. There was a patch of something wet in the long grass.

Was it . . . blood?

She leaned down, resting her elbow on her knee and pointing the torch into the grass. It was blood, all right. She glanced around the area, ears alert for any sounds. "Marge?" she whispered. "Are you there? Are you hurt?"

She got nothing back. No mews of pain or recognition. She moved in a little closer. The red patch was dry, but there was enough blood for her to know the owner had met a grim fate. She straightened up and marched as fast as she could back to the house. It could be a rabbit, or a rat, that had fallen prey to a local fox, she told herself as she got up to the front door. It happened all the time and there was no point distressing the children unnecessarily until they knew for certain. Besides, she was exhausted and couldn't deal with anything more tonight than perhaps another glass of lukewarm Chardonnay and an early night.

Things would look better in the morning. They always did.

Chapter 4

Nadia's head felt fuzzy as she pulled on her trusty pair of wellington boots the next morning. You could probably blame the extra glasses of wine for that, but she hadn't had the best night's sleep either. She'd fallen asleep easily enough – she always did since moving to the countryside – but she'd been restless and her dreams had woken her on more than one occasion. In the cold light of 6 a.m., she couldn't remember what they were about, only that they'd been unsettling. The type of dreams that lay dormant in your soul the next day and ruined your mood.

But onwards and upwards, that was her motto. Even if it was Saturday, she had work to do. This was the life she'd created for herself, after all. Pulling on her light green Barbour jacket, she headed out the front door and down towards the stables. The horses were all awake and seemed pleased to see her, proclaiming her arrival with stamping hooves and heavy snorts as she entered. There was room for six mares along with two studs in the main block and that was the idea when she'd first convinced Laurie she could make the stud farm a going concern. But today that number had reduced to three Arabian mares, Daisy, Buttercup, and Dandelion; Tudor, a black Friesian and the only stud; and a young Arabo-Friesian colt called Heath.

"Hello, ladies," Nadia called out, giving the female horses a wave as she walked past and opened the gate on the far side of the stables which led through to the main field. "How are we all this beautiful morning?"

None of the horses replied. Which was rather rude of them, she thought. Although Buttercup – who was Nadia's favourite if you were to make her pick (which Emily constantly did) – gave her a coy, almost knowing look through her long eyelashes. Nadia opened each of the mares' stalls and ushered them out, corralling them across the stable block and through into the field beyond. As they passed between the larger stalls containing Tudor and Heath on the other side, the male horses regarded the females with passing glances, but nothing approaching lust. Tudor was old and Nadia suspected he was going a little senile. He certainly wasn't the stud he was even three years ago, and the business reflected that fact. She'd had such high dreams for the stud farm when they'd first moved here a decade earlier, but for whatever reason, it had never got off the ground the way she'd hoped. Once Heath came of age, they'd sell him but had no plans to buy more horses.

Once the mares were all safely outside and loping freely around the expansive green of the field, she locked the gate and headed for her fork and wheelbarrow, leaning against the wall. It was mucking out time, a dirty business, yet Nadia never minded this aspect of the job. Most mornings she found filling the wheelbarrow with the spoilt straw and dung almost therapeutic. Some people had yoga and meditation to help ground them. She had shovelling horse manure. There was something about the way she could switch off and just focus on the job in hand, which helped quieten her busy mind and prepared her for the day.

Today was no exception and by the time she'd dumped the last barrow load onto the manure pile outside the stable, she felt relatively settled. Although she noticed it was time to call Bob Banon, the local farmer, and have him come and collect a few tonnes of the stuff. And that was it, job done. She'd let the mares run free for the rest of the day and bring them in later, so Heath and Tudor could be mucked out and exercised before dinner. Leaning the wheelbarrow against the wall, she waved goodbye to the male horses, getting a dirty look in return from the surly Tudor, and headed back to the house.

Laurie was already awake as she entered their bedroom.

"What a sight for tired eyes," he purred in his throaty morning voice. He propped himself up on his pillow and eyed her greedily as she headed for the en-suite bathroom. "Do you fancy coming back to bed?"

She stopped and glared at him. "The twins are already awake. I could hear them chattering as I walked past their room."

"Lock the door," he said. "It'll only be a few minutes."

"A few minutes?"

"All right, half a minute." They both laughed and Laurie dropped his head back down on the pillow. "Fair enough. I've got to get to the office, anyway."

"On a Saturday?"

"I know. I'm sorry. It's this new project from Donnie Masterson. The deadline is fast approaching. It's going to be very good for us once it's finished."

"So, it's me looking after the kids on my own. Again?"

"I'll make it up to you."

"Will you?"

When Laurie flipped back the covers and tapped the bed beside him, she just glared. "You'll have to do better than that. Besides, you don't want to come anywhere near me right now. I stink."

I stink.

The words had barely left her mouth before she felt a familiar prickle of unpleasantness in her chest. It could have been shame, it could have been rage, it was probably a bit of both. At school, that had been one of the key themes of the bullying. That she stank. That she was smelly. That she should go back to her own country.

What the hell . . .?

She shook her head to dispel the unpleasant thoughts. Why was the past suddenly rushing back to hurt her this way? She hadn't thought about that time for so long. Not really. There were certain aspects of what had happened that would always stay with her, but over the years she'd learned to, if not accept them, put up with them. Like one might an unsightly wart. But for her to get caught up thinking about her past twice in two days was worrying and something she needed to explore when she had more time and energy. But for now, there was no rest for the wicked. She had chores to do.

After a brief but functional shower, she dressed in a floral dress and went through into the kitchen, where she found Laurie had made a fresh pot of coffee for the two of them. He was sitting at the island and didn't look up from his laptop as she walked over and poured herself a cup.

"I don't suppose there's been any sign of old Marge?" he asked.

"No. I'm worried. I think we need to prepare ourselves for the worst. And the kids."

He looked up finally. "It's going to destroy poor Edward."

"I know. But kids are resilient. Aren't they?"

"Are they? Even ours?"

She laughed. "It's not my fault you surrounded them with all the trappings and safety nets of upper-middle-class life. You're the big rich architect, darling. If it was down to me, we'd be living in squalor up north." She slipped into her old, Yorkshire accent for the last bit and was surprised at how alien the pronunciation now sounded coming out of her mouth. But that was a good thing.

"*Upper*-middle-class? I'm not sure about that, your ladyship," Laurie said. "But regardless. I think you'd do all right for yourself. You're a tough cookie. Even if you won't ever talk to me about your life *up north*." His attempt at the accent was even worse than hers.

"Come on, Laur. You know I don't like to go there," she said. "It's in the past and best left there. And like I've told you a million times, there's nothing really to tell. I had a shitty childhood – got bullied a bit, and then my parents died within two years of each other when I was in my late teens. After that, I moved to London and met you. The rest is history, as they say."

"But being bullied, then losing two parents at a young age, that's got to affect a person. It might help you if you talk about it more."

"Do you think I need help?"

He sighed, realising he'd once more entered a dead-end street. "No, I don't. I didn't mean that, but . . . Never mind." He narrowed his eyes at his laptop screen. "Shit, it's almost nine. I need to get going."

He stood and snaked his arm around her shoulders, pulling her close and kissing her on the top of her head. It was sort of nice, but sort of annoying. She shoved him away. "I've got to do the rounds myself. I didn't realise the time either. Is Andrew still asleep?"

Laurie nodded, but he was back staring at the laptop. "Yeah. I'll get the twins dressed before I leave."

"Thank you."

Nadia walked over to the door and picked up the large bag of fresh towels that she'd left there the previous evening. Slinging the heavy load up onto her shoulder, she turned and smiled at her husband.

"Are you going to be at the office all day?"

"I shouldn't think so." He looked up from the screen and his eyebrows twitched. "Any reason?"

"Not really. I just don't feel we've spent much time together recently. Maybe we could snuggle up and watch a film tonight, once the kids are asleep."

"Yes. I'd like that. I'll see you later. Have a good day."

"And you." She opened the door and left, giving her hips a bit of sass as she did for good measure. Laurie still professed she was the most beautiful woman he'd ever met, and she believed him in the main, but after fourteen years of marriage and three kids, it was important to give out a little spice when you could.

She walked alongside the horses' field, taking in the majestic fillies as they gambolled in the grass, and then down into the bottom paddock – or, rather, *Sunrise Meadow,* as the hand-painted sign stated – where the two large yurts were situated.

Nadia had the idea of Elite Glamping five years ago and within just a few months had set up the business and had her first guests booked in. Not bad going, really. Since then, the yurts had been continuously in use and the glamping business had fast taken over the stud farm as her primary source of income. Not that they needed the money – Laurie's architecture firm brought in more than enough – but she was her parents' daughter and it would have bothered her a great deal to think of herself as a kept woman. Despite her mother's traditional Bengali heritage, she'd gone to university and had become a staunch feminist and freethinker. She'd defied her own parents by marrying Nadia's non-Hindu father and would have hated to think of her daughter being subservient to anyone. But she would have been glad to find her married to a man who loved her and supported her. Because in the end, that was all that was important. Love. Support. Those two things had got Nadia through a lot of bad times over the last twenty years. A *lot* of bad times.

No one was in sight as she got up to yurt number one but that didn't stop her from holding her breath as she walked up the steps to the small decking area that spanned around the side of the yurt and provided enough space for a picnic table and an electric stove. Carefully, she removed one large and one small towel from the bag and placed them on the table. If Mr Jameson was still inside the yurt, he wasn't making any sound and she didn't want to risk disturbing him and getting caught up in another awkward conversation.

She tip-toed down the steps and hurried away, face scrunched up in case she heard his whiny voice calling after her.

Miss Morgan . . . one thing . . .

Thankfully, she reached yurt number two with no interference, but this time she was almost certain she could hear movement inside the large bell tent.

Were they . . .?

She listened, not daring to go up the steps as the Snowdons' muffled giggles drifted out from under the canvas. Nadia took two more fresh towels out of the bag and placed them gently on the bottom step before backing away. At least some people were having some fun around here.

Another job completed. She hoisted the bag up on her shoulder and headed back up to the house. She'd only been walking for a few seconds when she heard a terrible sound coming from the stables. It sounded like the screech of a demon, almost human but not quite. She stopped in her tracks, but her heart felt like it was continuing on its trajectory, trying to burst through her chest. The sickening screeching noise was now accompanied by a loud banging and thumping sound and then a flurry of grunts and neighs.

It was Tudor. He was in trouble.

Chapter 5

Nadia dropped the bag and ran up to the stables as fast as her legs would carry her. As she passed by the paddock, she glanced over and met Buttercup's gaze. Her dark eyes were open wider than usual and she was pacing up and down in the way a caged animal in a zoo might do.

"Don't worry, girl," she called over. "He's all right."

Please let him be all right!

She got up to the main block and entered the stables via the doorway that faced the house. Tudor's stall was over on the opposite side, in the corner. It was the largest stall in the building and as she got over there, she saw him charging around the space, barging into the walls and flicking his head around like he was possessed.

"Tudor, darling. Calm down." She held her hands up as she approached, but her gentle manner did nothing to assuage his disposition.

She'd never seen him like this before.

What was going on?

The old stud could be rather grumpy if he was too hot or hungry, but he was also friendly and lackadaisical most of the time, especially with her. They were friends. She still rode him occasionally. But now he looked at her like he hated her. Like she'd done this to him. He lurched around, banging his flank into the wall and making more noise. In the stable next to him, Heath was watching on, seemingly unmoved by what was happening to his father. Either that or he was terrified. Nadia's first instinct was to get into the stable with Tudor to try to calm him down, but thankfully reason kicked in and she stopped herself before she did so. It was a bad idea getting into a stable with a fifteen-hundred-pound stallion at the best of times. When he was acting this erratic, it could be the last thing she ever did. One kick from those hind legs and it could be all over. Instead, she climbed up onto the bottom rung of the metal gate and leaned over so he had a better view of her. He was still snorting and grunting like he was in a lot of pain, but he had stopped pacing so much.

"What is it?" she asked, holding her hand out, giving him the option to come over for a scratch. Tudor liked it when you scratched behind his ears, but today, he was having none of it. He stared at her and bared his teeth as if taken over by madness.

Nadia puffed out her cheeks. It was awful seeing the poor thing like this.

What's wrong, Tudes?

"It looks like something's spooked him."

Startled, she twisted around to see Mr Jameson standing a few feet away. He was wearing red chinos tucked into black wellington boots and a fawn hunting vest over a navy-coloured turtleneck sweater. The way he was standing, with his arms behind his back and his pointy nose in the air, reminded Nadia of the character of Mole from her childhood copy of *The Wind In The Willows.*

"Mr Jameson," she said. "You shouldn't be in here."

He stared at her and stuck out his round belly, taking the Mole impression to new extremes. "I was passing by on my way out for a walk when I heard the hullabaloo. I'd say something has spooked him."

"Yes, thank you. You already said that." She climbed down from the fence and took a step closer to Mr Jameson. "Did you see anything?"

"Like what?"

"I don't know. A stray dog, maybe?"

Mr Jameson screwed up his nose. "I'm afraid I didn't see anything," he said. "I was over in the field on the other side of the house, entranced by what I thought was a willow tit, when I heard the screams. I came over to investigate. You beat me to it."

"I see. Thank you for your concern." She turned back to Tudor and as he tilted his head to one side, she mirrored him, sticking her bottom lip out the way she did with the twins when they were having a grump. "What is it, my sweet old man?"

"It wasn't, by the way," Mr Jameson muttered.

She turned back to look at him. "Pardon me?"

"A willow tit. It wasn't one. I thought it was, but I was mistaken."

"Ah. Right."

"It was just a coal tit, unfortunately. They look similar, but are two a penny around here."

She closed her eyes. "Well, Mr Jameson, thank you for your help, but I need to get on. And like I say, you really shouldn't be here. Or up in the back field, come to that. If you wouldn't mind sticking to Sunrise Meadow and the connecting tracks, that would be great—"

"Ah, look there. I imagine that was why the poor bugger has got so upset."

She opened her eyes to see Mr Jameson pointing into Tudor's stall, and as she followed the direction of his finger she let out a gasp.

"Oh, Tudor. No. How did that happen?"

The large black stallion had turned away from them and she could see there was a deep gash about three inches long above his gaskin on the left-hand side. Against his shiny black coat, the bright red welt appeared more grotesque than it normally would. Poor Tudor. But is it a cut or a tear? Or even a bite?

Nadia brought her hand up to her mouth as the large stallion turned around to face her. He seemed calmer now and wasn't stamping or snorting as much, but there was something in his eyes she hadn't seen before. They were wild and full of vigour as if the injury had awakened in him a deeper level of instinct. If he'd leapt over the side of the stall and galloped away down the track, she wouldn't have been surprised. He looked desperate and angry and riddled with mute puzzlement. The injury had spooked him all right.

Holding eye contact, she took a step forward, raising her hands as she did. They'd trained Tudor well, and he did as he was told most of the time, but creatures like him could never be completely tame. Some people were the same. You could give them a fine home, and provide them with food and luscious surroundings. But after experiencing the evils of the world up close, you were never truly content. You just pretended you were.

"You need to get the vet to have a look at that." Mr Jameson had shuffled up alongside her and his words made her jump again.

"Yes. Thank you. Of course I'm going to speak to the vet," she said, stepping to one side to put some distance between them. "I'm going to ring him right away."

"It looks like someone's had a go at him with a knife if you ask me."

But no one is asking you, Mr Jameson!

"Let's see what the vet says." She smiled and waited for the old man to leave, but he didn't seem to get the message. "And I do have to get on with things," she added, gesturing at the open doorway behind him. "If you wouldn't mind vacating the area, that would be very helpful."

Mr Jameson nodded sagely and wagged his finger at her. "You know you need to be careful, Miss Morgan."

"It's *Mrs* Morgan. And what do you mean?" She was losing her patience fast.

"I mean what I say. You need to be careful. If you take a lot on as you have done, things can slide. You can miss things. You wouldn't want to get messy. That's when accidents happen." He sniffed and rolled his shoulders back. "Anyway, point taken. I'll be going on my walk. Good day."

He turned around and sauntered out of the stable block. Nadia walked over to the door and watched as he walked down the track before disappearing around the side of the big oak tree next to the gate.

"What the hell was all that about?" she whispered to herself.

An icy shiver ran down her body, dimpling the skin on the backs of her arms.

That's when accidents happen . . .

Was it just her being paranoid, or did that sound sinister? Was he trying to warn her? Scare her? Or, more likely, was he just a weird old man with dubious social skills? She shook the thoughts away as Tudor whinnied at her.

"Don't worry, Tudes," she told him. "We'll get you patched up and on the mend in no time."

She gave him a lacklustre wave of her hand and then hurried back to the house to make the call.

Chapter 6

The twins were colouring in at the table and Andrew was watching TV on the couch when Nadia burst into the main living space a few minutes later. She kissed Edward and Emily on their little heads and walked over to the lounge area. The picture on the television screen showed a gaggle of bronzed, good-looking people with overly white teeth and not much on in the way of clothes. If she'd had time to consider it properly, she'd be asking her thirteen-year-old son why he was watching such trash – and perhaps even stopping him from doing so – as it was all she could think about was calling the vet and finding out what had happened to her prized stallion (prized in her eyes at least, to the sperm-buying world, not so much). She marched across the room, casting her gaze around and searching for the house phone or her iPhone. Any phone.

Where were all the blasted phones?

"What are you doing?" Andrew grumbled, as she walked over to the couch and began lifting cushions. "Mum! Move, I can't see."

"Have you seen the phone?"

"Which phone? The house phone is on the table."

She shot her head up to peer across the room. True enough, there was the house phone laying in the middle of the dining table in front of Emily. She'd looked there just now, she was certain. Hurrying over to it, she scooped it up and dialled seven, the number she'd pre-programmed for the vet.

Dr Ralph Simmons had been a semi-regular visitor to the stables ever since the stud farm had opened. He was good at his job, even if Nadia wasn't a massive fan of the man. He was surly and brusque and despite her being half a foot taller than him, had a knack of looking down his nose at her. In the same way that Mr Jameson did, come to think of it. She narrowed her eyes as she thought of the odd little man and his weird comments from earlier. What had she ever done to him but be an excellent host and show interest whilst he waffled on about bearded tits?

She gasped as a thought hit her.

What if it was Mr Jameson who'd hurt Tudor?

She had no idea why he'd want to. But he could have got into the stable without her seeing and hid before she got there. Only to reappear as if he'd just . . .

No! Stop that!

You're being paranoid again. It doesn't help.

She straightened up and swallowed down her panic as the dial tone chirped in her ear. The phone rang twice before being picked up by Angela, Dr Simmons' receptionist, who Nadia had always got on well with.

"Hi, it's Nadia Morgan, down at Camborne Stables. I was hoping Dr Simmons might pay us a visit this afternoon. It's our stallion, Tudor. He's hurt and needs stitches and maybe some antibiotic shots. I can't tell whether it's a bite or if something has attacked him, but he was frantic a few minutes ago, jumping around like a mad thing. I'm hoping Dr Simmons can calm him down and find out what's happened." She was speaking ten to the dozen and had to gulp back a mouthful of air once she was done.

"Oh, dear," Angela said, jumping in before Nadia could continue. "The poor old thing. That sounds awful. But I'm afraid Dr Simmons is over in Bodmin presently, delivering a calf. Is the horse still in distress?"

Nadia glanced at a space on the far wall, which, if the wall wasn't there, would give her a direct eye-line to the stables. "I managed to calm him a little." She pulled out a chair from under the table and sat. "I don't know what happened. I've never seen him that way. He was pacing and snorting and lurching around like he didn't know what to do with himself. That's why I can't help but think it's an animal that has hurt him. A stray dog perhaps."

"Okay, well don't worry, Nadia. The second Dr Simmons gets back to the surgery, I'll have him ring you. Is that okay?"

"Thank you, Angela, I really appreciate it."

She hung up and clutched the phone with both hands, staring at it like it might offer an explanation. She was trembling, but her mind had gone completely blank. What the hell was happening to her? Was she losing her grip? Was it stress? Or something worse?

"Is Tudor poorly, Mummy?" Emily asked, looking up from her colouring book.

"Oh. No, baby. He's fine." She smiled, feeling a frisson of nervous energy in her stomach. "I LOVE the colour of that dinosaur!"

"It's a rainbow dinosaur."

"I know! I can see!"

Still clutching the phone, she got up and shuffled over to the lounge area, slumping into the armchair beside the couch where Andrew was reclining.

She sat and watched her firstborn for at least five minutes before he finally glanced over at her. When he did, all she got was a sneer.

"What's wrong with you?"

"Oh, you do know I exist, then?" He met her question with a tut and an eye roll. It was a standard teenage response, really, but today she couldn't take it. "Other people live in this house, you know, Andrew? Did you hear me on the phone just then? Or maybe all the commotion down at the stables?"

He shrugged. "You told Emily it was fine. What's going on?"

She looked over at the twins. They were both engrossed in their work. "Tudor's been attacked," she whispered. "He's got a big open wound on his leg." She glared at her son and when he didn't respond, she waved her hand angrily at the television screen. "What *are* you watching, Andrew? In fact, give me the remote. Give it to me!" She stood up and grabbed it off the coffee table in front of him, pointing at the screen and switching the television off as she retook her seat.

"Hey! I was watching that. It's funny."

"It's far too grown up for you. Anyway, don't you have any homework you should be doing?"

Andrew sat up and crossed his arms. "It's Saturday afternoon!"

"All right, well, why don't you see if Simon or Toby want to do something? I'll drive you to one of their houses if you want me to. It's too nice to be stuck indoors."

"Simon and Toby are probably getting ready for the party."

It was Nadia's turn to tut. "I see. Is that what this is all about? You're sulking because I won't let you go to the party. I've told you, Andrew, you're too young to be mixing with older kids and with no adults present."

"You just want me to be a good little boy and to do as you say."

"Yes. That is what I want," she told him. "Can I also add that I'd like it if you smiled at me once in a while as well?"

He shook his head. "Whatever."

The ungrateful little . . . He didn't even know how lucky he was. So far, he'd had an idyllic childhood full of joy and laughter and had wanted for nothing. The ungrateful brat. She could hear her own parents in her head and what they would have said in her position.

Don't you realise how much we gave up for you?

Don't let us down, darling.

Don't let us down . . .

"There'll be time for parties when you're older."

"But Mum, everyone thinks I'm a weirdo as it is. I'm the only brown kid in my class. I'm fat. I wear glasses. I won't get invited to any more parties at this rate."

"You're not fat!" Nadia snapped, leaning forward, shifting instantly into the role of protective mother. "And don't say brown. Who thinks you're a weirdo?"

Andrew shrugged. "I don't know. Everyone. They call me Asian Computer Man."

"Who does? Who calls you that, Andrew? Have you told your teachers?"

"It's fine, Mum. It's just jokes."

"Is it? Because names like that can hurt a person, Andrew. They eat away at your self-worth. If these people are being cruel, then you need to tell someone. Me and your dad, first. Then your teachers. Do you want me to come into school and speak to them?"

"God! No!" Andrew cried. "Don't you dare. Everyone takes the piss out of each other. It's what happens. They think I'm a nerd because I'm good at coding and stuff. Don't worry, I'll have the last laugh when I'm a brilliant programmer and making millions."

Nadia chewed on the inside of her lip. Her heart was pounding and her hands were both clenched into fists. She released them and flattened her palms on the tops of her thighs. She was projecting. She knew that.

"It won't be forever, darling," she said. "I promise. No one finds being a teenager easy. But you're a good boy. Dad and I are very proud of you."

Andrew didn't look at her, but his silence made her think the comment had landed. That's all she could do, keep on bombarding her kids with love and reassurance in the hope they'd be confident enough to make the right decisions when the time came.

"It'll probably be a lame party, anyway," he mumbled.

"Yeah. And maybe we can ask Dad if he'll drive and pick up a takeaway pizza later."

"Pizza? Really?"

Having takeout was a rare treat for the Morgan family on account of the fact they were out in the sticks and no food establishments would deliver this far.

"We'll ask him when he gets home. Once the vet has been."

"Cool. I hope Tudor's okay."

Nadia smiled. "Me too."

It was horrible seeing her baby so glum, but she wasn't backing down. She'd said no to the party, and that was the end of it. And she was right. There'd be plenty of time for parties when Andrew was older.

She was about to say more when she heard a phone ringing. She stared at the house phone on the chair arm beside her, but the screen was dull and the keys weren't lit. Another wave of confusion washed over her before she saw Andrew in her peripheral vision waving at her.

"It's your iPhone, Mum," he said, talking to her like she was stupid. "It's over on the island."

She looked up. "Oh? Yes." She got off the couch and hurried over to it. Dr Simmons had both her numbers and must be calling her back on this line. But as she picked it up, she saw the caller ID displayed a phone number rather than the word 'Vet' like normal. Perhaps Angela had got a message to Simmons while he was out on call.

"Hello, Nadia Morgan," she said, on answering.

The person on the other end was silent for a second. "It's me," a woman's voice replied. Nadia knew straight away who it was, and the realisation sent a prickle of nervous energy down her arms. "I'm sorry to call you on your personal line," the voice continued. "I know we said we wouldn't. But it's urgent. Are you able to talk?"

"One second," Nadia whispered, edging past Andrew, who had switched the television back on and was watching one of those Japanese cartoons he liked. She pushed into her bedroom and shut the door behind her before going to the bed and sitting on the end. Once settled, she brought the phone back to her ear.

“Okay, I can talk now,” she said. “What do you want?”

Chapter 7

Despite them not speaking for over five years, Nadia had recognised Diane's voice in an instant. She still sounded the same as she always had. She still did that thing of overly attacking her consonants and lengthening the vowels in certain words – garage and plaster, for instance – that clashed with her broad Bradford accent.

"Are you at home?" she asked.

Nadia made eye contact with her reflection in the mirror that stood on the bureau at the end of the bed. "Yes. I am."

"Shit, love, I'm sorry. I shouldn't have called. I should have texted you first, at least. That's my bad. I need to speak with you, though. It's important."

The reflection staring back at Nadia looked pensive and pale. But that was understandable. Talking to Diane brought up a lot of emotions and memories. Too many to deal with all at once.

"What is it?" Her voice came out hoarse and croaky. She swallowed. "What's going on?"

The line went silent for a second. "Did you know she'd been released?"

"Stacey?" She frowned into the mirror. Of course she meant Stacey. Who else would she mean? "Yes. I think so. When was it?"

"End of last year. After twenty-one years inside. It was her birthday yesterday. She was thirty-eight. Makes you think."

Nadia ran her tongue around her mouth. Of course. The twenty-sixth of May. Stacey's birthday. She knew that. Was that why she'd been so discombobulated these last few days?

"When did you last hear from her?" Diane asked.

"God. Never. Not since the trial. She wrote to me once, but it was nasty and I didn't engage with it too much. Back then I was . . . You know . . . And I just wanted to put it all behind me."

"Yes. That's a good thing. You weren't supposed to have any contact with each other."

Nadia caught her reflection once more. The woman in the mirror looked tired but had a supercilious smirk on her face that she didn't appreciate. She dropped her expression.

"No contact, hey?"

A hissing sound came over the line. The sound of Diane sucking air through her teeth. "Yes well, I knew we were pushing our luck, but I made a professional decision back then and I stick by it. You needed help. And I wanted to help you. Jesus, there you were, a seventeen-year-old girl whose parents had both died while she was inside. My heart broke for you. Especially after everything. You didn't deserve what happened to you, kiddo."

Nadia sniffed. It surprised her how calm she felt. In fact, she felt numb. She wondered if it was a self-defence mechanism. Like with Stacey's birthday, maybe her subconscious was working in the background, taking everything on board, and would have her drive off the cliff into Hell's Mouth in a few years. She hoped not.

"Anyway, I didn't call to talk about my misdemeanours as a social worker," Diane said. "We might have a problem."

"Oh? What's that?"

"They released Stacey under licence. Meaning she's supposed to check in with her supervising officer every two weeks. Only she's missed her last four appointments. No one knows where she is."

"I see," Nadia said. "That is a worry. Sorry, Diane, how do you know all this?"

She sighed. "I know the officer in question. She's an old friend of mine. Yes, I know, we shouldn't be discussing cases and we're all as bad as each other. But it's because we actually give two shits about the poor kids whose lives we're entrusted with. Even after they centralised all the safeguarding and duty of care structures, things still get lost in the system and people don't get notified. Mary – Stacey's supervising officer – thought it was in everyone's best interests if she informed me of the news. Especially after what happened . . ."

Nadia straightened her back. "What happened?"

"She came to see me. Stacey, I mean. About this time last year. It was only a day or two after she was released. I've no idea how she got my address, but there you go. Probably from Mary." She laughed but stopped herself. "I invited her into the house, mainly because I didn't know what else to do with her standing there on my doorstep. She didn't look any different. Her hair is still that same dark red colour, thick and wiry. She still has that same intense stare. I always thought she put it on to look tough . . ."

"Diane!" Nadia cut in. Her old Youth Justice Worker often went off at tangents for no reason. "What happened?"

"She wanted to know where you were." Her voice dropped an octave and all the joviality faded from her tone. "She said she wanted to get in touch with you. To talk to you. I didn't tell her anything, of course, and never would. I said I'd not had anything to do with you since your release from the secure training centre. But I'm not sure she believed me."

Nadia ran her tongue across her top teeth. She was shaking. "Why are you telling me all this?"

Diane sighed a pointed sort of sigh like she was trying to prepare her for the worst. "At the end of last year, I had a break-in at the house. I was away visiting my sister, so I didn't find out until a few days later. They took my laptop and some old files. At the time, I put it down to local drug addicts seeing an opportunity and taking it. But since Stacey went missing, it's been playing on my mind . . . I'm sorry, kiddo."

A heavy shiver shook Nadia's body and ran down her arms. Now she felt silly for being calm a few moments earlier. The woman looking back at her from the mirror looked timid and fragile. Her thick black wavy hair, usually Nadia's best feature, appeared lank and lifeless.

"So, whoever took the laptop has my details?" When Diane didn't respond, she took that as a yes. "Diane! No!"

"I'd saved all my contacts' details on the hard drive. Plus, scanned notes of all my cases. I thought I was being thorough, keeping a digital and a hard copy. Belts and braces and all that. It was all password protected, but I'm told that doesn't mean much if you're determined enough. I can see now that was a mistake, storing everything in one place."

"Did they take anything else?" Nadia asked.

"No. But that doesn't mean they were only—"

"Do you think I'm in danger?" Her mind raced to Tudor and the missing Marge. Were they a part of this? Was this Stacey coming to get her revenge?

Diane cleared her throat. "I didn't say that. Which is why I didn't call straight away. I didn't want to worry you unjustly. And we don't even know where she is. She could be in South America for all we know, living the life of Riley. I'm sorry, Nadia. I shouldn't have called. The police know she's missing and have people looking for her. The probation service is involved as well. It's probably nothing, but . . . you know . . . she did kill someone."

"Two people."

"Yes. Two people." There was another long pause. "I just thought you should know. But I'm sure there's nothing at all for you to worry about. Do you hear me?"

Nadia nodded at her reflection. "Yes. I hear you." But her mind was already swimming with ideas and notions. None of them were helpful. "Listen, Diane. I've got to go. Thanks for the call. I'll speak to you – well – whenever. Take care."

"God bless, kiddo."

She hung up and stared at her phone until the screen faded to black. A part of her had always worried this day was going to come, but that hadn't prepared her for the reality of the situation. More troubling thoughts hit her, memories of that day. The third of August two thousand and one. Another date that was forever etched into her soul.

She stood up and walked back into the lounge. Andrew was still lolling on the couch, dead eyes staring at the television screen. As she shuffled past and slumped into the armchair, he raised his head.

"Are you okay?"

She nodded, but didn't look directly at him. "Yes, I'm fine."

"Who was on the phone?"

"Just an old friend. No one important."

"Okay, it's just you look like you've had bad news. You've gone really pale."

She shook herself. "Have I?" She sat up and planted on a smile. "I'm fine, darling, don't worry. I'm worried about Tudor, that's all."

She'd once vowed to herself that she'd never lie to her children. Not about the important things, at least. One day, she even hoped to find the words to tell them the story of her life. The true story. Yet she was still waiting for the right moment to tell her husband that one, even after sixteen years.

But she wasn't lying to Andrew. She was worried about Tudor. The problem was now she was worried about so many other things as well.

THEN . . .

6 September 2000

The first day at a new school is always hard. But when you're new to the area as well, it can be the scariest thing in the world. Despite her mum and dad both inundating her with positive messages and words of encouragement, she still felt the nip of trepidation as she stared up at the school gates for the first time. Beck Hill Comprehensive School was a sprawling complex of low-level prefab buildings joined onto a large three-storey red brick sports hall by a covered walkway. They had built it in the late sixties but it didn't appear to have had even a sniff of paint since then.

Normally she would walk the twenty-five-minute journey to and from school, but this morning, it being her first day, her dad had driven her to the gates. He and her mum were now both twisted around in the front seats, staring at her.

"Make sure you listen to your teachers and do everything they say," her mum said, sounding more Bengali than she'd ever done. "You are a very clever girl, but you are easily distracted. You need to pay attention, yes? Don't be messing around."

"I won't," she mumbled. Sitting on her own in the middle of the bench seat in the back of her dad's BMW, she felt very small. She wasn't ready for this. Clutched in her lap was her new leather satchel, complete with a new pencil case and calculator inside. Wrapped around her neck was a thick scarf in the school colours, burgundy and green.

"Can I go now?" she asked.

She didn't really want to go. She wanted to stay here, where it was warm and safe. But that wasn't viable, so the next option was to get it over with as soon as possible. Like ripping off a sticking plaster.

"You'll be fine, my darling," her dad added, perhaps picking up on her trepidation

"Yeah. I know." She looked up at his round face and then out the window at the sea of kids milling past the car on their way into school. They all seemed a lot more grown up and meaner looking than at her last school.

"Everyone's in the same boat here," he said, reaching over and grabbing her hand in his. "Don't forget that. Some kids talk a good talk but they're all as nervous as you are – starting a new term and in a new form and the like. Just keep your head down and do the work and you'll be fine. And if anyone says anything nasty to ya, you give them a good smack around the head."

"Gerry!" her mum cried out. "Please don't be telling her stupid things like that."

"She knows I'm only joking, don't ya love?" But the way he winked at her told her he wasn't joking. Not that she'd ever have the nerve to do anything of the sort. She was a quiet girl and small for her size. Add to that the fact she'd been the only mixed-race child at her last school and it went some way in explaining how out of place and uneasy she felt.

"I've got to go," she said, grabbing the door release handle and pulling it towards her. As the door clicked open, a draft of cool air entered the car, whipping its icy shards around her bare legs. She leaned forward and pulled her socks up as far as they went, and even as a nervous twelve-year-old, she got the metaphor. She might have looked young for her age, but she was clever, and smart with it, even if her being streetwise was the result of the many books and television programme she consumed, rather than real-world experience.

"Do you want me to pick you up tonight?" her dad asked as she climbed out and turned back to peer into the car.

Yes, she wanted him to pick her up! She wanted that more than anything else. But she'd already noticed a few kids looking her up and down disdainfully as she'd got out of the car.

"No. It's okay, dad. Thanks. I'll walk home. I need to, don't I? You won't be here every night."

"Okay love. Good decision. Have a good day."

"Work hard," her mum shouted as she slammed the door shut.

She turned and stared up at the school, wishing for her dad to drive away. But she knew he wouldn't until she was out of sight. She straightened her back. The first step was hers to take. She grabbed the strap of her satchel and walked through the school gates.

* * *

The rest of the day went by in a flash. She was in Mrs Ramsey's class, a young woman with thin blonde hair and a kind face who was fresh out of teacher training college. In the morning she had the class do the usual getting-to-know-you games. They sat around in a circle, clapping the syllables of their names to learn what each other was called. They got into pairs and had to tell their partners two facts about themselves, which then had to be relayed to the rest of the class by the said partner. It all felt uncomfortable and awkward, but it was the same for everyone and after a while, she began to settle into her new environment. She was surprised, also, to see that there were so many Asian kids in her class – and in the school in general. At her last school, over in Pudsey, her year group had been predominantly white with just her, a boy called Ali, and a Chinese girl called Ming the only ethnic contingents. But here in Bradford, the mix was incredible. There were kids whose parents were from Pakistan and India, as well as other Bengalese kids like her. There were Sikhs and Muslims and Hindus and a lot of Irish Catholics. There were even a few children from the Middle East, whose families had moved to the UK when the Gulf War started. It felt good to be surrounded by such a rich palette of skin tones and cultures. For the first time, she wondered if she might fit in somewhere.

But unfortunately, that idea was short-lived . . .

It was whilst walking home that evening that she first met the girl who would make her life a misery. Zoe Evans. She'd already seen her in the corridor that morning and had heard her name whispered in hushed tones, pointed out as someone to avoid. She was in the same year as her but seemed much older than everyone else. But that was the thing about twelve-to-thirteen-year-olds. They could look like children or young adults depending on where they were at in terms of puberty. Zoe already had breasts and long legs and was almost a foot taller than most of the other girls. Most of the boys, too. She had long, mousy brown hair that she scraped back into a high ponytail, and she wore lipstick and mascara – a big no-no at Beck Hill. Someone said that even the teachers feared her, so they didn't say anything.

"Oi, you! Wait there!"

The words reverberated down the street and, even though there were about seven other kids all walking in the same direction, she knew they were aimed at her.

"Oi! I said wait!"

She stopped and turned around, gripping onto the strap of her satchel for dear life. "Hi," she mumbled.

Zoe Evans marched up to her and prodded her finger into the middle of her chest. "You're new around here, aren't you?"

She nodded. "Yes." Her voice had no breath behind it, and the word was barely audible.

"You're a mongrel, is that right?"

"Sorry?"

Zoe scoffed and looked around at the two girls flanking her. A white girl with red hair and an Asian girl called Farah who was in her class and had incredibly long black hair.

"Look at this one," Zoe said. "She doesn't even know what I'm talking about, do you? You're a mongrel, love. A half-caste. Neither one thing or the other."

"Because I'm mixed-race?"

Zoe slapped her on the chest. "There we go. She gets it." Her face dropped into a grim scowl. "Fucking half-caste bitch.

Do you think you're better than us because your dad drives a BMW?"

"No. Course not. I never said anything. I don't even know you."

"No. You don't," Zoe hissed. "But you will do. You'll know me soon enough don't worry about that. You smelly mongrel bitch. Fucking half-caste." She spoke with a broad Bradford accent, and the way she attacked the curse words made them sound even more violent than normal. "Where you even from, anyway?"

"Pudsey."

Zoe smirked. "Don't be fucking clever, bitch. Where are you from originally? Why do you look like this?"

"My mum's family is from Bangladesh, but she was born in this country the same as me," she stammered. "My dad's Irish, but he moved to England when he was two. He's from Manchester."

Mum.

Dad.

Where were they now? Why couldn't they be here? Why had she refused her dad's offer of a lift? She needed them. She needed them so much.

Zoe's smirk turned into a sneer. "Well, watch yourself, mongrel. Posh bitch. Cos I'll be watching you." She held up her hand in front of her face, and flicked at the air. "Go on then, run off home. We're not keeping you."

They stared at each other for a moment before Zoe lurched forward, making her jump. This caused the three girls to break out into peals of bitter laughter. Hoisting her satchel up on her shoulder, she turned around and set off, walking as fast as she could. Her body was shaking, and she felt like she was going to be sick.

Why was this happening? She wasn't that different, was she? She was only a few shades lighter than Farah. Why was she being singled out by this horrible girl?

As she walked on, the group of children around her grew fewer as they peeled away to return to their respective houses. By the time she got to the end of her road, she thought she was the only one left, but as she crossed over to the other side of the street, she heard something ping off the lamppost in front of her, and a second later something hit her on the back of the neck. It was small and hard and felt like a piece of gravel. Instinctively, she glanced back over her shoulder and, as she did, her heart sank. Zoe was still there. She'd hung back ten metres but was matching her pace step for step. It was as if she was stalking her, and the thought of that caused another shiver to ripple down her back. As their eyes met, Zoe grinned and held up a handful of gravel to show her.

"Keep walking, bitch," she said and chucked another piece of gravel. "I've got plenty of ammo."

It missed and flew past into the garden to her right, but that only seemed to anger Zoe. She began flinging the gravel harder and faster. The sharp pebbles caught her on her bare arms and legs. One piece hit her on the ear.

"Please," she wailed over her shoulder. "I'm sorry if I've upset you. I didn't mean to. Please stop."

She quickened her pace. Her house was at the very end of the long suburban street. It would take her another five minutes to reach it. Five minutes of hell. She tensed and bore the pain as what must have been a handful of gravel ploughed into her back. But that had to be the end of it now. She put her head down and walked faster. Behind her, she could hear Zoe running to catch up.

“Oi, wait, I want to talk to you.”

She didn’t stop. Another thirty seconds and her house would be in sight. If she just kept going, she’d make it. Zoe couldn’t hurt her so close to home. Could she?

“I said wait!”

She lurched back as Zoe yanked at her satchel. The leather strap moved up her chest and snagged around her neck. Before she knew what had happened, Zoe was in front of her.

“You’re a real little princess, aren’t you? The dirty mongrel princess. Is that what we should call you?”

She looked down at her feet. “I just want to go home. I don’t know why you’re doing this. I’ve not done anything to you. I—”

She shut up as Zoe slammed her hand into her neck and squeezed at her throat. “You just want to go home, do you? To your weird half-caste house with your weird posh parents. You make me sick.”

“Please,” she hissed, pawing at the hand around her neck. “That really hurts.”

“Hey! Leave her alone!”

It was a new voice. One she hadn’t heard before. Both she and Zoe looked over to the other side of the street, to where an older girl was standing on the pavement. She spoke with a broad accent and her voice was deeper than most girls their age. She was broad, but not fat, and her reddish-brown hair was up in two plaits on either side of her head.

"Piss off," Zoe told her. "We're just messing, aren't we? We're mates."

"Is that right? Cos I saw you lobbing a load of stones at her just now. I don't think I'd like it if me mates did that to me." She walked over to them. She was the same height as Zoe and looked to be a couple of years older.

As she got nearer, Zoe released her grip on Tahani's neck. "I wasn't doing anything."

"Good," the new girl said, looking Zoe up and down. "I've seen you before. Where do you live?"

Zoe stuck her chin out. "Delph Hill way."

"Yeah? Well, this is my street. So, why don't you sod off back to Delph Hill and we can all chill? Yeah? *Yeah?!*"

Zoe didn't move at first, but then she shook her head and walked away. "Whatever, bitches." She snorted back noisily and spat a mound of green phlegm onto the pavement.

The two girls watched her walk away, then looked at each other.

"You all right?" the older girl asked.

"Yes. I don't even know why she was doing that. I've not done anything to her."

"Some people don't need much excuse, do they? You've just moved here, haven't you?"

"Yes, about a month ago."

"That's right, I saw the van. What's your name?"

She swallowed. "It's Tahani."

"Tahani, ey?" She closed one eye and tilted her head to one side. "Cool name. Well, pleased to meet you, Tahani. I'm Stacey."

Chapter 8

Dr Simmons hunkered down next to Tudor, stroking him gently on his flank as he examined the wound.

"What do you think caused it?" Nadia said. It was the second time she'd asked and, like the first time, the question was met with a grunt but no proper answer. Instead, Dr Simmons stared at the laceration with a concerned expression squashing his rotund features.

He'd called on the house phone whilst Nadia was making the children some sandwiches for lunch and said he'd call in on his way back to the surgery. He'd arrived thirty minutes ago, but so far, he'd done nothing and said nothing of any help. She was losing her patience with him. She'd always suspected Simmons had a problem with her for some reason. Either that or he was one of those vets who were better around animals than people. But that would imply he had a kind, empathetic manner with the animals in his charge and she'd never seen evidence of that, either.

"When did this happen?" he asked, prodding two fingers at the skin next to the wound.

Nadia held onto Tudor's bridle, stroking his nose to calm him as he stamped and snorted. "This morning. There was a real commotion in the stables. All the horses were making a racket and when I ran up from the bottom field, I noticed he was bleeding. I was worried that a stray dog might have got in. Or a fox . . ."

"Have you seen any stray dogs around?"

"No."

"It is in a strange position to be an animal attack," he said, still looking into the wound rather than at her. "Hmm."

"What is it?" She lay her cheek on Tudor's nose, rubbing at his neck. "It's okay Tude. You're going to be okay. What is it, doctor?"

"Unfortunately, the tissue on either side of the wound is now necrotic, so I'm going to have difficulty closing the wound."

"What does that mean?" she asked. "Will he be okay?"

"Oh, yes, he'll be okay. It is not a deep wound. I can dress it, and as long as we keep the area moist and clean, it should heal on its own within a week."

Nadia smiled into the horse's big brown eyes.

Why the hell didn't he say that in the first place, hey Tudor?

"Do you have everything with you that you need?" she asked.

Dr Simmons lowered his head and regarded her over the top of his black-framed glasses. "It is just a saline solution and some dressings. And a tetanus shot. I have everything in the car, yes." His tone was impatient, bordering on patronising. She wished for a moment Tudor would rear up and kick the cocky so-and-so through the stable wall.

She swallowed her frustration. "Is there anything I can do to help? Do you need me to hold him while you work?"

"It is best if you wait over there. Or in the house even," he said. "I can call you when I'm done."

"Oh, I see." She let go of Tudor and patted his nose gently. "I'll wait over there if that's all right. Just in case."

Dr Simmons breathed noisily down his nose, rather like a horse might do. "Fine. I'm going to my car. I'll be back in a moment."

She watched him shuffle away and then turned to Tudor, rubbing her palm along the short hair on the bridge of his nose. "Don't worry, my big brave horse," she whispered. "The man is going to make you all better. I'm sorry you got hurt. I won't let that happen to you again. Silly Mummy for letting it happen."

Out of nowhere, an image flashed in her mind. Of that day by the creek. She and Stacey standing side by side, staring into the water . . .

Nope.

Stay in the present!

She screwed her eyes up to try to crush the image. What was the point of going over it all again? She'd spent years wondering 'what if' and it never got her anywhere. The past was the past. It was supposed to stay where it was. That was the vow she made to herself when she left Bradford behind and moved to London all those years ago.

There is no use going over things you can't change, she told herself. *It only upsets you and ruins your chances of happiness. And look around, Nadia. The present is great. You've got a beautiful home, beautiful kids, and a loving husband. You owe it to your parents and yourself to enjoy this life you've created.*

She'd had a terrible childhood, and tragic things had happened. But she was a different person today. Quite literally. She'd ceased being Tahani Carroll the moment she set foot in London and until recently, she'd barely given that young girl another thought. She missed her mum and dad, of course she did, but whenever she considered them, it was always from a place of who she was now, rather than who she'd been when they were alive.

It was over twenty years ago now that they'd died. Even though it was her mum who had the long illness, it was her dad who died first. She believed he'd died of a broken heart – after what she'd put him through – and her mum did little to help dissuade her from that idea. When the cancer finally claimed her, a year later, it was almost a relief. Almost. But it didn't stop her from blaming herself for their deaths. If things had been different. If she'd been different. If Stacey and Zoe hadn't been in her life, then maybe they'd still be alive. But how they'd fit into her present-day set-up, she had no idea. So, maybe it was best this way. Even if, on days like today, she missed them terribly.

Come on, Nadia. Chin up.

She rolled her head around her shoulders and coughed to clear her throat. Nadia Morgan was happy and proud of who she'd become. She'd had to go through some major psychological contortions regarding her ego and sense of self to get to this point, but regardless, she was here to stay. The human mind was both strange and incredible. The human spirit even more so. Not that she believed in God anymore. But she still felt there was more to life than just the surface-level stuff. You could call it spirit, you could even call it a survival mechanism, but it was there, and it was driving her. It was what had got her through the bullying and torment when she was younger, and then those years in the remand centre. It was still working for her, and whatever it was, she was glad of its presence. It was a powerful thing. But it had to be, to allow her to feel safe and content in a world where such horrible things could happen.

"I'm just going to be over there," she told Tudor on hearing a car door slam shut. "Dr Simmons is going to make you all better."

She slapped her old stallion gently on the shoulder and backed out of his stall, maintaining eye contact with the majestic beast and pointing over to a pile of straw bales in front of Daisy's stall, showing him where she would wait. Hoisting herself up onto the top bale, she found her legs didn't reach the ground. She wondered about going back to the house, to distract herself with some cleaning, but Andrew had agreed to look after the twins, and she wasn't going to pass up an opportunity for him to pull his weight a little. A moment later, Dr Simmons returned with a leather bag and as he walked past, the way he looked at her made her feel like a silly child.

"Let me know if you need anything," she called over, but he ignored her.

She watched him as he pulled on a pair of disposable plastic gloves before a large fly buzzed around her head and she waved it away, breaking her concentration. Maybe it was for the best that she wasn't involved. Tudor was her baby, and she hated to see him in pain. She chewed on her lip as he snorted and whinnied, and Dr Simmons shushed him down. She was a bad person. This should never have happened. And then there was Marge. Where was the poor cat? Out of nowhere, terrible thoughts invaded her consciousness. Was Tudor's injury an accident, or was something more sinister afoot at Camborne Stables? And if that was the case, could it be *her*? The thought that somehow Stacey was behind this made Nadia's stomach churn.

"Mrs Morgan. Do you have a minute?"

She looked up to see Simmons peering at her over the top of the stall.

"Coming." She pushed herself off the hay bale and hurried over to him. "What is it?"

He moved over to the side of the stall and pointed to one of the wooden planks that made up the stable wall. Nadia squinted to get a better look at what he was showing her, and then let out a yelp. "Oh, shoot. Really?"

It was a nail, sticking out of the wood about half an inch. The end was mangled and rusty. A quick assessment of its height, relative to Tudor's wound, made her feel sick. How the hell had she not noticed it?

"This seems to be the likely culprit," Dr Simmons said, flicking the end of his finger on the nail. "It's quite sharp. I imagine he brushed against it and it tore the flesh. It's easily done. I suppose." The way he said the last two words, he made it sound like it was her fault. Probably because it was.

"I can't believe I didn't see it," she said, shaking her head. "I'm in this stall twice a day, every day. You'd have thought it would have been obvious."

"Mmm," came the reply. "Do you have pliers, Mrs Morgan?"

"Yes, I think so." She glanced around, her eyes falling on Laurie's large metal toolbox that was sitting on top of the bench against the internal wall. Rushing over there, she pulled the concertinaed compartments up and out to reveal a plethora of metal tools and boxes of screws. "Here we are."

The pliers were old and rusty but they still worked. She carried them over to the doctor, who grabbed them out of her hand and went to work pulling out the nail.

"Thank you," she said. "You're going above and beyond doing that."

Dr Simmons shrugged and handed her the pliers followed by the bent, rusty nail. "He'll need a tetanus shot, but luckily, I have some."

"Great," Nadia said, holding up the nail. "Thank you so much."

She returned the pliers to the toolbox and threw the nail in the wastebin before walking back to her bale. She sat and waited as Dr Simmons administered the shot. Once done, he gave Tudor a brief stroke on his long nose and exited the stall.

"He'll need a second dose in four weeks," he said, pulling off his gloves and handing them to her to dispose of. "I'll get Angela to call and book it in for you."

"Yes, of course. And I'm so sorry. I don't know how that happened. I'll make sure I check his environment more thoroughly in the future."

"Yes," Dr Simmons said. "He'll be fine now, anyway."

He bid her farewell, and she watched as he waddled back to his car and turned it around before driving away.

When he was out of sight, she let out a long breath, which seemed to deflate her entire body. But it felt good. She didn't realise how tense she'd been.

A nail. A blasted nail. Not a vicious stray. Not some dark, vindictive character from her past. A nail. She shook her head in dismay. What a fool she'd been, allowing her imagination to run riot like that. She walked over to Tudor's stall and watched him. He seemed content enough and, satisfied all was well, she said her goodbyes and headed back up to the house. She'd expected Laurie to be home by now, but he must be caught up at work. As she got up to the top of the drive, she heard Emily and Edward shouting from inside the house. They were probably hungry. Looking at her watch, she saw it was almost five. Despite feeling exhausted, it was time to make dinner. And a large glass of wine wouldn't go amiss either.

Chapter 9

"Mummy! Mummy!" Edward's voice echoed down the hallway.

"In here." Nadia straightened her back and returned to the bubbling pot of tomato and basil soup on the stove. She'd been standing over it for the last half hour, but rather than focusing on making dinner, she'd been daydreaming. Her thoughts had transported her back to Bradford. Back to her old street. Back to the creek on that fateful day . . .

Snapping her attention back to the present, she saw dusk had arrived. The sky was a pale pink colour above a wash of greys and petrol blues.

Daydreaming. It was a strange term for what she'd been doing. *A day-nightmare* more like. She looked at her watch. It was a few minutes after six. Laurie still wasn't back yet. That was strange.

Edward burst into the kitchen, closely followed by his sister. Tears were streaming down his face and as he ran into Nadia, he wrapped both arms around her leg.

"What is it?" Peeling him off her, she knelt so she could look him in the eyes. "What's happened, darling? Tell Mummy."

He tried to speak, but the poor thing couldn't get his words out through the tears. Nadia looked at Emily for an answer.

"It's Marge," was all she said.

The words hung heavy in the air. "Where is she?" Nadia asked, getting to her feet.

Emily sniffed and pointed to the front door. "Down the side of the stables. Near the main gate."

"And is she . . .?"

Emily nodded and stuck her bottom lip out in such a cute way that Nadia wanted to squeeze her tight and never let her go. The twins were bright for their age and they knew enough about life to know that things died. Yet seeing it up close for the first time was a hard lesson.

Nadia stood and looked over at the lounge. Andrew was still in position on the couch but was now playing on his Nintendo Switch. "Andrew, love," she called over. "Can you watch the twins for a moment while I pop down to the stables?"

He groaned dramatically, perhaps still annoyed that she'd had to renege on her offer of takeaway pizza. But that was Laurie's fault, not hers. Why did she always take the brunt of his annoyance?

"Andrew!"

"Yes. All right." He looked over. "Come and sit on the couch. I'll put something on TV."

Good enough. Nadia knelt again and beckoned her youngest children to her. "Okay, you two, I know this is horrible. But please try not to think about it. Whatever you saw, it's not Marge. Not anymore. She's somewhere else. Do you understand?"

The twins sniffed and nodded in unison. "I'm going to go check. You go sit with Andrew and watch some cartoons. It'll be dinner soon. And maybe we can have ice cream for afters. Would you like that?"

Another nod and even the hint of a smile from Emily.

She stood and guided them over to the couch. "I'll be back soon, Andrew," she said. "You've not heard from Dad, have you?"

"Nope." He didn't look up from his game. "Where is he?"

"Work. I think. He should be home any minute." Her mind was trying to spin off into dark places, but she pulled it back. "Keep the twins here, okay?"

"Uh-huh."

She grabbed her jacket from off the back of one of the stools and headed for the front door, stepping into her wellington boots on her way out.

The air was cool and pleasant on her flushed cheeks as she made her way down to the stables. Near to the front gate, Emily had said. That meant whatever they'd seen would be on the right-hand side, near to the manure heap and Laurie's workshop.

The lights inside of the stables came on as she got closer, illuminating the area in stark white light. She saw the body straight away. It was next to the corner of the stable in the long grass. From this angle, she couldn't quite make out what it was, but as she hurried down the slope, an impromptu gasp of horror escaped her.

"Oh, gosh!" She put her hand up to cover her mouth as she stepped closer. She knew it was Marge from the colour of her fur, but that was about all she had to go on. The animal's head looked as if someone had put it through a wood chipper and the poor thing's body was flayed open like it was in a vivisection lab.

"Marge," she whispered. "What happened?"

The cat's rib cage was crushed and her insides ripped out. As Nadia's mind raced once more to scary places, she heard a car engine and, looking up, she saw Laurie's green Range Rover trundling through the gates. As he trundled past her, he looked out the side window and frowned as if to say, what are you doing? But he must have seen the look on her face because he pulled up and was out the door and over to her in a few strides.

"Nads. What is it?"

The care and concern in his voice hit raw emotion, and she burst into tears. "It's Marge," she wailed. But it was so much more.

He grabbed her and pulled her to his chest. He smelled good, and she wrapped her arms around him the way Edward had done to her a few minutes earlier, holding onto him as if her life depended on it.

"Oh, dear," Laurie said, lifting his head off her shoulder to examine the remains of the family cat. "It looks like a fox got her."

Nadia twisted around and stared at the mess of fur and blood. "A fox? Really. Cats can usually handle themselves against foxes."

"Yes, if they're fit and healthy. Marge was old. She can't have had much fight left in her."

"I don't know, Laurie. Would a fox do something like that? The way she's all splayed out . . ."

He put his arm around her shoulders. "What else could it be? Other than a stray dog maybe, but I've not seen any around. Poor old Marge." He squeezed the top of her arm.

"Why don't you get inside and I'll sort her out? Do the kids know?"

She shuddered. "The twins found her. They're distraught."

"Bugger," he muttered. "But they're young. They'll get over it. How about we have a proper burial for her in the morning? Make a thing of it. It'll be good for them."

"Will it?"

"You know what I mean. Character building." He laughed, bitterly. "Sorry. I don't even know what I'm talking about. But we'll make it nice. They can say goodbye to Marge properly, make a card or something."

Nadia smiled and the connected emotions went some way in buoying her mood. "Fair enough. Come on inside. Dinner's nearly ready."

They wandered up to the house, Laurie with his arm around her still. It felt good. She felt safe. But she always had done with Laurie. That was one reason she'd fallen in love with him so quickly and why she still loved him with all her heart. He had the confidence and self-assuredness that came from having a good background and never having to worry about his safety. No one bullied him at school. His parents were still alive and together. Money had never been an issue. But he was kind, too, and he loved her and still did cute romantic things, like putting rose petals in her bath and buying her gifts out of the blue, even after all these years.

She knew he wanted her to share her past with him and at times like this, when she felt so protected and close to him, she might have risked telling him everything. *Almost* everything. At the start of their relationship, he'd been more curious and had asked her often about her life before him. What was school like for her? Who were her friends? What did her parents do? It was sweet of him, and she'd come close a few times but always pulled back. It was better this way. Better for him, for their relationship. Better for her.

Instead, she'd played down her past, telling him her life before London was dull and unremarkable and – if he got too pushy – that she wasn't ready to talk about her parents' deaths. She'd reassured him he had nothing to worry about, only that she'd rather leave her past where it was. No doubt it was weird for him – to love someone yet not know about a massive part of their life – but, as she told him, it would be a plus for most men. There were no in-laws to have to deal with, no exes still in the frame, nothing for him to get hung up about. After a while, he'd accepted her wishes and hadn't brought it up in years but on days like this . . . It would be nice to offload some of her concerns.

"What are we having?" he asked, as they got to the front door. "For dinner, I mean?"

"Soup and garlic bread, is that okay? I was going to text you to pick up a pizza, but with everything going on I forgot. Sorry. I know soup is a bit rubbish after you've been working all day and . . ."

"Hey," he said, placing his hand on her arm. "Soup sounds great. Come on, let's get inside. I'm starving."

Chapter 10

True to his word, Laurie got up early the next day and dug a grave for Marge whilst Nadia and the children slept. He'd chosen a nice plot underneath a large azalea bush in the front garden. The twins were still upset. Andrew too, surprisingly. But Nadia hoped, given time, the memories would fade and they wouldn't be overly traumatised by what they'd seen. But then, memories didn't always fade. The bad ones especially seemed to linger forever. You could try to kid yourself that they didn't matter so much anymore, that you were a different person and that the past no longer affected you. But then something happened, like the phone call from Diane, and it threw you right back to that time.

Laurie must have picked up that she was feeling a little delicate because he told her to stay in bed while he took the kids outside to conduct a rudimentary service for Marge. The kids wouldn't mind, he said. But the second they all left the house fell quiet and it only made her more antsy. Instead, she got up and made a fresh pot of coffee before cracking open her old laptop and opening a new browser window. For a long minute she stared at the screen and the blinking cursor in the search box.

Did she really want to do this?

Did she have the required mental energy?

She reached up and placed her hand on the top of the laptop, ready to shut it again, but something stopped her. Instead, she took a deep breath and typed *Stacey Wilson* into the search bar.

She sipped on her coffee as the search engine flashed up its bounty. The top few results were social media pages of people with the same name, but as she scrolled down through the results, she came across an archived news story from the Bradford Echo, dated the twenty-second of November two-thousand-and-one. Three days after the trial. With the rim of her coffee mug resting on her bottom lip, she clicked on the article and leaned back as it flashed up on the screen.

Shock as local girl, 16, sentenced to just 10 years for the murder of her friend

Just ten years. It was long enough. Especially as Stacey had been sixteen when it happened, which meant she spent the last eight of those years at Foston Hall in Derbyshire. A real adult prison. Full of real adult prisoners. Rather than rehabilitating her, prison had had the opposite effect on young Stacey. The way Diane had relayed it to Nadia, she'd fallen in with a bad crowd and ended up killing a fellow inmate by stabbing a sharpened biro into their neck. She got another ten years for the attack with no chance of parole. Twenty years in prison. And now she was missing, presumed . . .? What?

On the run?

Out for revenge?

Nadia closed her eyes, remembering the last thing Stacey had ever said to her. They'd been good friends, but on that day, as they'd crossed paths in the stark grey corridor, Stacey had glared at her with genuine hatred in her eyes.

"I'm going to get you," she'd hissed. "Just you wait."

Nadia clicked off the page. There was no point getting herself worked up for nothing. Yes, it was horrible that Marge had died in such a brutal fashion. But it had to be a fox. As Laurie said, there was no other explanation. The same with Tudor. She'd almost let her mind run away with her regarding his injury and look at what happened there. Nothing more sinister than an old nail caused his wound.

Voices drifted in from the hallway, closely followed by a draft of cool air as Laurie and the kids returned. She closed the laptop and slipped off the stool before heading over to the pantry to gather things together for breakfast. That was enough raking up the past. She had her family around her; she was safe; she was happy; she was alive. There was a lot to be thankful for, and she owed it to herself to remember that. No more silliness.

* * *

After breakfast, Laurie headed into town to pick up a parcel and persuaded Andrew and Edward to go with him. Neither had wanted to initially, but the promise of a milkshake from McDonald's on the way back had swung it for them. Nadia knew Laurie was only doing it to give her a little respite, and she loved him for that. He had tried to involve Emily in the expedition as well, but not being as big a fan of the golden arches as her brothers, she'd opted to stay at home and watch the film *Brave* for the tenth time that month.

Nadia was in the utility room folding sheets a while later when her daughter wandered in with a forlorn look on her face.

"What is it, darling?" she asked.

The small girl shrugged, and it was as if she had the weight of the world on her shoulders. "I don't know."

Nadia placed the sheet down and focused all her attention on her. "Are you sad about Marge?"

"Yes. But it's okay, isn't it? Because she's in Heaven and she's happy."

Nadia smiled. She and Laurie had agreed not to push the God or Heaven thing too much with the kids, but she understood why he might have gone there. When a small child is staring at you asking where their beloved pet is you'd say anything to take their pain away.

"Yes. I'm sure she's very happy wherever she is."

"What are you doing?" Emily asked.

"I'm doing the laundry for the guests. It's Sunday today, so we need to change their sheets." She carried on folding.

"That's not how Grandma does it," Emily told her.

"Really?" she replied, trying to keep her voice breezy. "How does Grandma do it?"

She got on with Laurie's parents, but his mum, Patricia, could be a bit of a stickler for certain things. The first time she and Derek had visited the new house after they'd moved in, Patricia had asked Nadia where she kept her dinner napkins.

The answer was nowhere because she didn't have any and didn't realise people still actually used them but that wasn't a good enough response it seemed. Another time, good old Patricia had brought her own fish knives, knowing Nadia was making sea bass and didn't have any of the special implements. But she meant well. Most of the time.

Emily sighed like someone much older than her six years. "She just does it differently. She crisscrosses the corners."

"Ah well, we've all got different ways of doing things," Nadia replied. "There's not always a right or wrong way."

The frown didn't leave Emily's face. "Most of my friends at school have two lots of grandparents. Josie Matthew has three lots and Toby says he has four grandmas, but I'm not sure if I believe him."

Oh, Em.

More raking up the past. Was the entire world conspiring to mess her head up? She'd read somewhere that when you began thinking a certain way, you noticed evidence for it everywhere. It was called the frequency illusion, or something. That was probably what was going on here. Because there had to be an innocent explanation. It was a nail, and it was a fox and this question arose because Emily was a typically curious six-year-old.

"You do have two sets of grandparents," she said. "Only my mummy and daddy are in heaven with Marge." She cringed internally as she spoke, but it was the best she could come up with on the spot. "They died before you were born. But they would have loved you very much, I'm sure."

"What were they like?"

"Well, my mummy – your grandma – her mummy and daddy were from another country originally. A place called Bangladesh, which is a hot country far away. They came to England just before your grandma was born. And your grandad was from Ireland but lived in England most of his life too. They were really kind and fun." She smiled to herself, seeing them in her mind's eye. "I loved them both."

"Why did they die?"

Nadia blinked the image away and laughed. There was nothing like a small child's bluntness.

"I'll tell you about it properly someday," she said. "When you're older."

"They must have been nice if they were your mummy and daddy because you're really nice."

Emily turned around and wandered back into the main space, leaving Nadia to catch her breath. Wow! That had hit her harder than she'd expected. She wiped her eyes with the side of her hand and chucked the remaining sheets back into the basket. She'd finish folding them later.

She left the utility room at the exact moment Laurie and the boys burst through the front door. "Hi Mum," Andrew said, rushing past her. "I'll be in my room."

He was gone before she could reply. Edward waddled over to her and held up his cup of milkshake. "Look what I got, Mummy. Guess what flavour?" He had chocolate all around his mouth, but she went with it.

"Oooh, was it strawberry?"

"No."

"Banana?"

"Nooooo!"

"I can't think of any other flavours."

He threw his head back. "It was chocolate, silly." With a laugh, he scurried away into the front room. She watched him go before wiping at her eyes once again.

"Are you all right?" Laurie asked, coming up to her. He grabbed her upper arm and squeezed it. "Have you been crying?"

She smiled through a shudder and sniffed. "No! Well . . . yes. But it's nothing. Just Emily being sweet. Don't worry, it's just hormones. You know . . . that time of the month."

"Ah. Enough said." He let go of her arm. "Do you want anything?"

She shook her head. "No. Thank you. I've got everything I need."

"Okay." He held up a bag for life with a bundle of cardboard tubes sticking out of it. "The blueprints arrived, so I'll just take them up to the office. Then how about we have a nice cup of coffee and some cake? I stopped at Tesco Metro on the way back too and got a carrot cake. That one you like."

It was all she could do to keep herself from bursting into tears. "I don't deserve you," she said.

"I know that," he replied, smiling, so his eyes crinkled at the corners. "But you'll do for me."

He winked and went through into the kitchen, leaving her standing alone, not sure what to do with herself. Maybe it was time to talk to her husband about the past. Would he judge her for it? Would it change anything? After all these years, it would certainly be an enormous shock for him, but would that be all it was?

She sucked in a deep breath and held it in her lungs. No. She couldn't tell him. They'd come too far down this road together. It could destroy them. Long ago, she'd vowed to keep her past a secret from her husband, and that's how it should stay. If she was to nullify the effects of this stupid frequency illusion, then she had to stop thinking about what happened.

So, stop bleeding well thinking about it!

She straightened her back and stuck her chest out. This was it. A new start. Forget about Stacey Wilson and Zoe Evans and all that nonsense. What happened was in the past and she was living in the present. That was all that mattered. She put on a big smile and went to join her family.

Chapter 11

Nadia was in Elenore's front room the next day when the grim realisation hit her. But up until that point, she'd been having a pleasant enough day. She'd woken early and gone for a five-kilometre run across the fields as far as Banon's farm and back again, returning before even Laurie had woken up. Even at 6 a.m. the sky was bright and clear and despite it being May, she felt summer in the air and the thought filled her with a renewed vigour and optimism. Once back home, she'd done the rounds, delivering fresh bedding for the yurts, before mucking out and feeding the horses. Tudor was pacing around his stall but looked better, and the dressing on his thigh didn't seem to bother him. She spent a few minutes stroking his mane and scratching him behind the ear, which had an even more positive effect on her mood.

Once she'd showered and dressed, the rest of the family was awake and she'd made them all a leisurely breakfast before completing the usual one-hour-round-trip school run in just fifty minutes. Yes. All was well with the world. Nadia Morgan was back in control. Just as she liked it.

Laurie had still been at home when she returned and despite him being a little preoccupied, she'd even coaxed him into sex. It was unheard of for them to do it in the morning, especially on a Monday morning, but their lack of intimacy had been playing on Nadia's mind and she worried if they didn't do it soon, they might grow apart forever. She'd been waiting for Laurie to instigate something, but she was a modern woman. Why should she put it all on him? Her dad always used to say if you take responsibility for your happiness, then you've only got yourself to blame if you're not. She sometimes felt it was a brutal assessment and ignored a lot of deep-rooted issues, but she got his point. So, she'd bitten the bullet and led her husband into the bedroom. It was brief but passionate and she enjoyed the closeness and the release it provided. If she was completely honest with herself, this was one of the main reasons she'd instigated the trip to the bedroom. She yearned to be out of her head for a little while. To be lost in the moment. It had done the trick.

She'd laid in bed for a while after Laurie had gone into work, staring at the ceiling and laughing to herself at how silly she'd been. In the warm glow of the morning, laying in her super king-size bed with fresh linen that smelt of roses, she felt a million miles away from the pain of her past.

She was a different person today.

"Would you like a cookie?" Elenore called through from the kitchen. "I have shortbread or chocolate chip?"

"Not for me, thank you," Nadia called back, tapping her stomach. "I'm trying to be good this week."

"Oh?" Elenore said, entering the room with two cups of steaming tea. "Are you doing something special?" She placed the cups down on the coffee table in front of Nadia and took a seat beside her on the couch.

"Nothing like that," she replied. "I just want to be good to myself. In every way. I was reading an article recently about how what you eat can affect your moods."

Elenore stuck out her bottom lip and shrugged in that way only French people can pull off. "I'll take your word for it."

Nadia laughed, and Elenore did, too. "I know I sound like a hippy earth mother," Nadia said. "It's just, I've just been all over the place recently. I'm trying to do whatever I can to keep myself sane and calm. It's not easy."

"Not easy with two businesses to run and three children," Elenore added, raising her eyebrows. "I don't know how you do it."

"Or why, huh?"

"Now, Nadia, I never said this. I have a lot of respect for you and what you do."

Nadia picked up her drink and held it in her lap. "Did you never want kids, yourself?"

Elenore's eyes flashed. Just for a second. But it was enough to make Nadia's heart sink. "Oh, shoot. I didn't mean to . . . I'm so sorry. What was I thinking? Elenore, please forgive my insensitivity. I wasn't—"

"No, no. Don't be silly." She waved her away. "It is not like that. The truth is, I never wanted children. Neither did Yanis. But I never expected to be alone at forty-five either. Life, huh? It never goes the way you planned it." She looked away.

Nadia's shoulders sank. "I'm such a blithering idiot sometimes."

"Please. It is fine." Elenore turned back with a wide smile on her face. "I miss him, that's all. *C'est la vie.*"

"I bet you do."

The air fell silent between them, but it didn't feel that awkward to Nadia. It was nice. There was a lot to be said for sitting in witness to another person without feeling like you had to punctuate every second with talk.

"That reminds me actually, I must go to London in a few days to see my solicitor."

Nadia sipped at the tea. It was red hot. "Didn't you have to see him a few weeks back? There must be a lot to sort out."

Elenore grimaced slightly. "Yes. I did. And there is. Forms to sign and hoops to jump through. But soon everything will be in my name. It is but formalities, though, I am assured. However, it will be another overnight trip, maybe a couple of nights. Will you watch the house for me again, please?"

"Of course, but you don't have to worry about anyone breaking in. It just doesn't happen around here miles from anywhere. You know, I don't think we've locked our doors the whole time we've lived here."

This was true. They hadn't. But as she heard herself saying those words, a feeling of unease rumbled in her soul. Because maybe she should start locking the doors. Just to be on the safe side. Until she knew for certain.

"Thank you," Elenore said. "It was this way too back home in France. Peaceful. Safe."

She looked away again, and a deep sadness appeared to wash away her usual bright demeanour. Nadia bit her lip. Idiot. She was still hurting. But of course she was.

"I'm so sorry," she said. "I've come around for a chat and ended up upsetting you. I didn't mean to bring up the past."

"It is fine. Don't worry." She looked back with a smile. "It is nice for me to think about Yanis. We weren't together for as long as I would have hoped, but the time we did share was very special. I see you have the same with Laurie, no?"

Gosh. That was a question and a half.

"Me and Laurie?" Nadia said. "I suppose so. He's a good father, a good husband." She almost said a good provider but stopped herself in time. That was the sort of thing her mum would have said.

Elenore was still looking at her as if she wanted her to continue.

"We have our ups and downs," she told her. "Like any couple."

"But you love him?"

"Oh, yes. Very much. I'd be lost without him."

Elenore closed her eyes with a smile. "That is sweet. Good for you, Nadia."

"Thanks." She felt her cheeks burning and took a big gulp of tea to try to reset herself. It was still hot and burnt as it travelled down her throat, but it had the desired effect. She tossed her hair back over her shoulders. "Have you got any plans for the money?" she asked.

It might have been a bold question, but for Nadia, someone who didn't have much money growing up, the idea of asking made sense. To her, money was a good thing, something to be proud of. The perfect tool for doing things that made you happy. Why not acknowledge that and be grateful for what you had, rather than squirrelling it away and being coy about your riches like most people? Besides, Elenore was French. She probably appreciated bold questions.

"Not yet," came the reply. "But I hope to travel a little more. I shall sell this house and spend a few years in different countries. I have always wanted to see the Far East."

"Oh wow. Excellent," Nadia exclaimed. "I'll miss you, though. If you go. It feels like only yesterday you were moving in."

Elenore reached forward and tapped Nadia on the knee. "I know. It has been great getting to know you. You have been so welcoming to me."

This time, the abrupt silence that descended felt awkward. Elenore removed her hand from Nadia's knee and the two women stared at each other. Nadia swallowed and leaned back.

"Have you got any other plans for when you're up in London?" she asked. "Are you going to do any sightseeing?"

"Probably not. I have visited many times and seen most of the big attractions before. I like London, but it is full of people and chaos." She laughed and Nadia did too, perhaps a little too heartily. She coughed to cover it and sipped at her tea as Elenore went on. "I'm hoping to meet up with an old friend of mine. A Swedish girl called Lisa. We first met when we were young girls of eighteen and attended Eurocamp together. We kept in touch, but for one reason or another we haven't got together since. She is a buyer for a fashion house in London and is always away on trips. But this time, our calendars are in alignment. It will be good to see her again after all this time."

"Yes, I bet it will. Wow! That's a long time to have not seen someone."

"I know. We have arranged to meet in Covent Garden, in front of the Opera House. But I worry I could go up to the wrong person. I don't know if I will recognise her. The last time I saw her, I was twenty-five. Almost twenty years ago. People change a lot in that time."

"Yes," Nadia said and laughed, before stopping herself. She placed her drink down on the coffee table as a shiver of nervous energy shot through her. "People do change a lot in that time."

The realisation hit her like a kick in the stomach.

"Nadia? Are you okay?" Elenore leaned forward, a concerned look on her face. "What is wrong? You look like you have seen a ghost."

Nadia got to her feet. "Yes. No. I mean . . . Sorry, Elenore. I just remembered there's something I need to do." She was heading for the door as she spoke. "Thank you for the tea, and I'll make sure I watch the place for you while you're away." At the door, she stopped and smiled back at her friend. "Sorry about this. I don't mean to be rude. But I must go."

She turned and headed through the kitchen and out of the front door. As the warm Cornish air hit her face, she sucked in a deep breath to try to steady herself. It didn't help. With her head down, she hurried up the lane towards her house.

You look like you've seen a ghost . . .

The words echoed in her head as she marched past the stables. She hadn't seen a ghost, but she'd sensed something even worse.

Chapter 12

The house was empty as Nadia burst through into the living space and cast her eyes around the room. There it was, at the end of the island where she'd left it yesterday evening, her old laptop. She made a beeline for it, switching it on before she'd even sat down. As the old machine whirred into life, she clambered up onto one of the bar stools and sat in front of it.

"Come on, hurry up," she whispered at the screen.

She drew in another deep breath, trying to stay calm. For the first time in as long as she could remember she wished for noise, the bleep of Andrew's computer game, the shrill shrieks of the twins as they raced around pretending to be characters from Paw Patrol or PJ Masks. The house was too quiet. Twisting around, she peered through the triple-glazed glass windows at the fields beyond. The horses were down in the main paddock, but there wasn't another human in sight.

The computer screen flashed up with the login window and she hunched over the worn keys to tap in her details. Hitting return, she leaned back, telling herself to stay calm. She knew she tended to make mountains out of molehills and create monsters from shadows. But she'd also experienced more horror and tragedy than most people ever would. When you'd seen monsters for real, it was harder to dismiss them so readily.

The desktop screen flashed up and, not waiting for it to settle, she clicked on the internet icon, cursing the stupid egg timer as it loaded. Elenore's words were still reverberating in her head as she waited.

Why hadn't she realised this earlier?

The last time she'd seen Stacey Wilson, Nadia had been thirteen years old and Stacey herself just sixteen. That was twenty-one years ago. People changed a lot in twenty-one years. Especially if they've made a concerted effort to step away from who they once were. Or if they'd spent most of that time in prison.

When Diane had called with news about Stacey, Nadia had been so caught up with the thoughts of the past she hadn't considered the ramifications of what it meant to come face to face with her old friend after all these years. Back then, she was a thick-set girl with reddish-brown hair and perpetual bruises on her legs. She had no clue what she looked like now as a thirty-eight-year-old. She could be anyone.

Anyone.

And the thought of that terrified her.

Nadia wasn't the most computer-literate person in the world, but she could use search engines and knew about search history. She clicked open the articles she'd been reading the previous day, eyes scanning the pages for a photo. But a part of her already knew it would be pointless. Most of the articles didn't even mention names, just vague details of the case. As she read them again, grim nausea gripped her, and she had to run to the sink. Gripping the sides of the porcelain, she dry-heaved into the bowl, not bringing anything up. The room swirled around her and she held onto the side of the sink for dear life, gulping back a lungful of air.

Don't pass out.

Keep it together.

She closed her eyes, but doing that, she could see Stacey standing in front of her. Her face was twisted in anger. The way she'd stared at her in the courtroom corridor.

I'm going to get you . . . Just you wait.

Then it was Zoe Evans' face she could see on that day down at the creek. She saw the anger in her eyes turn to shock and then terror. And then . . .

Nadia raised her head from the sink and stared out of the window, watching as a small bird looped the loop above the hedgerow at the foot of the garden. It was enough to snap her back to the present, but her heart was still pounding.

Don't do this.

It's not helpful.

None of it is.

She twisted on the cold tap and stuck her head under it, lapping at the water with her tongue like a feral cat, desperate for sustenance. As she finished, she realised that was an apt metaphor for how she felt sometimes. A feral cat playing at being domesticated.

Once satisfied she wouldn't be reacquainted with the English muffin she'd eaten for breakfast, she returned to her laptop. At the bottom of the old Bradford Echo article were links to other articles on the same site. One of them was the story of the *Evil Child Killer* who'd got another ten years in prison for killing a fellow inmate in Foston Hall. It turned out they had moved Stacey to Bronzefield in Surrey after that. The high-security women's prison had only just opened when she arrived, and for a time she was one of the most high-profile inmates.

Surrey. It was a long way from Bradford. It was a long way from Cornwall too, but it felt closer somehow with both places being down in the South. A shiver ran up the back of Nadia's head.

If only she could see a current photo of Stacey as she was now, it would put her mind at ease. Diane had said on the phone she hadn't changed much. The same thick wiry hair, she'd said. But people could cut their hair, they could dye it, they could straighten it. It meant nothing. The start of a headache throbbed at her temples and she screwed her face up to keep focused as she considered everyone she knew who was of a similar age.

Would she recognise her if she saw her? Had she seen her?

Was she here in Cornwall?

Was the thing that she'd worried about for the last fifteen-plus years finally coming true?

For a long time, she'd become obsessed with the idea that Stacey would come looking for her, but as time had passed, other aspects of life had taken hold and she'd let the fears drop away. She had Laurie and the kids to take her mind off things. Then there was the stud farm and the glamping site, more distractions that she'd created for herself so she didn't have to face the terror of her past or the dread of her imagined future. Because if she never got off the hamster wheel, everything would be all right. She could race to the finish line without being caught.

That was her hope, at least. But as she'd found out all those years ago, hope didn't get you very far in the cold light of the truth.

She closed the laptop and placed both hands on the lid. The plastic was hot on her skin.

"Stay calm," she muttered to herself. "No point letting your imagination run away with you."

She looked around as an idea hit her. Where was her phone? Why did she keep misplacing it?

Feeling once more like she was going crazy, she slipped off the stool and did a full circuit of the vast room before returning to the kitchen island and seeing it lying next to the laptop. Cursing herself, she picked it up and swiped open the screen. Diane's number was still at the top of her recent call list and before she could talk herself out of it, she tapped on the number. Despite the growing tightness in her chest, she was too far down the rabbit hole to pull herself back. Tudor's injury. Marge's grisly death. The dark figure Elenore had seen on the track. There was too much weird stuff going on for it all to be a coincidence. Something wasn't right, and she needed to know what was going on before it was too late.

Chapter 13

Diane picked up after two rings. "I wondered if you might call," she said. The fact she didn't even say hello made Nadia even more uneasy.

"Can you talk?" she asked, glancing around the room. The house was as empty as it had been all day, but the act of looking caused a wave of nervousness to ripple through her.

"Yes, of course," Diane said. "I take it this is about you and Stacey?"

"What else?"

She walked across the room and through into her bedroom, where she sat on the bed, cross-legged, with her back against the headboard. It was a small thing – and silly; she knew – but she felt safer here with the external wall behind her and the rest of the house spanning out in front. If her old friend was lurking somewhere about to attack, at least she'd see her coming. What she'd do about it after that was another matter.

She returned her attention to the call. "Has Stacey changed her name?" she asked.

Diane made a sound like Tudor when he was eating, blowing air down her nostrils. "Yes. But I can't tell you her new name. I'm sorry, I have to draw the line somewhere."

Nadia had been expecting this response, but she wasn't letting her old social worker off the hook that easily. "It's just . . . I don't know what she looks like these days or even what her name is. And the more I think about that, the more anxious I get. What if she's here, in Cornwall? What if I've already met her?"

She hadn't planned on what she was going to say and as she heard the words coming out of her mouth, the implications hit home.

Whoa.

What *if* she'd already met her?

"Do you remember what she said to me in the corridor after the verdict?" Nadia asked. "You were there. Do you remember?"

"I do. But people say a lot of things when they're scared and angry. She was only young back then she—"

"She was old enough to go to prison, Diane. Real prison. That must have been awful for her. Especially once she knew what sort of sentence I'd got."

"It was fair. You did your time too, don't forget that."

"Six years to her ten and only four of them served inside. Yes, it was hard, but it wasn't a real prison, was it? Stacey spent ten years in a top security prison, surrounded by murderers. That's got to alter a person hugely. And I can't imagine it doing so for the better."

"Prison affects people in different ways."

"When she turned up on your doorstep, how did you feel? Were you happy to see her?"

Diane sighed. "Point taken. But I don't know what you want me to tell you."

"I want you to tell me I'm being stupid, that I've nothing to worry about. Only you can't, can you? Because no one knows where Stacey is. I'm worried she's here, Diane. I'm worried she's playing nasty games with me, trying to get back at me. And yes, as I say that out loud, it sounds ridiculous – but I don't know what she looks like or sounds like or what she's calling herself these days. I could be in real danger and I've no way of knowing."

She caught herself and stopped. Her voice had risen a couple of octaves. Closing her eyes, she drew in a sharp breath and exhaled just as sharply. The mirror on her dressing table presented an image of a tired-looking woman with frizzy hair and wild eyes. She looked like her mum. Or, rather, the way her mum had looked at the trial. Like she'd seen and heard too much and didn't know how to go back to being the person she'd been before. But that was the same for everyone involved in that trial. It didn't last long, but its implications were far-reaching.

A new image flashed across Nadia's memory. Zoe's mum and her auntie in the gallery, crying. Her mum had shouted something at Stacey as the events of that day had been read out. That one day, a sunny afternoon in August, when all their lives changed forever.

"Is there anyone, in particular, you're worried about?" Diane asked.

"What do you mean?" She sat upright and flattened her hair with her other hand. "I don't know who I'm supposed to be worried about, that's the point."

"I understand. But I'm trying to help."

"Well for starters, there's both Melissa and Elenore, my neighbours. They're about the right age, give or take."

"Okay, and thinking about the two of them, could either of them be Stacey?"

"I don't know. I don't think so."

"Right. Anyone else?"

"I've got a guest staying with us, in one of our yurts. But she's got a family with her."

Diane didn't respond. Giving her the silent treatment perhaps, or letting her conclude herself that she was overthinking this. "Do you think I'm being paranoid?"

"It's good to stay on your guard," Diane said. "Especially until we know where Stacey is. I can tell you that there is a small-scale manhunt in progress and the police are confident they're going to find her."

Nadia nodded at her reflection. The fact that Diane seemed calm, bordering on blase, about Stacey's disappearance was oddly reassuring. Yet some aspects of the last few days still troubled her.

"Do you think I should call the police?" she asked.

"And tell them what?"

She was ready to bring up Tudor's injury and Marge's demise, but at the last second she stopped herself. Diane was a good friend, but she didn't suffer fools, and Nadia was aware she sounded rather obsessive and chaotic.

"I don't know. That I've concerns about my safety. Did you speak to the police after the break-in?"

"I did. But it was the usual thing. *Don't hold your breath about getting your stuff back. Here's a crime reference number for the insurance.*"

"Did you tell them you thought it was Stacey who broke in?"

"No. Because I don't know it was. I'm sorry, kiddo. I'm regretting telling you. I've rattled you for no reason."

"Not necessarily. You said Stacey was looking for me that first time she came to see you. Do you remember her being the sort of person who'd let things go? Cos I don't."

For some reason, she'd fallen back into speaking with her old Bradford accent, perhaps picking it up from her old social worker. But why? She hadn't spoken like that in so long. It had been a conscious decision by her to lose the accent, and a good one. The less she acted like the person she'd been, the better.

She coughed and felt a sharp pain in her right shoulder where she'd been holding it tense. She sat up from the wall and rolled both her shoulders back.

"Please, Diane," she said, slipping back into the newsreader accent she'd perfected over the years. "I appreciate what you're saying. I just want to put my mind at rest."

Diane made another soft snorting sound. "I know you do. But we're on dangerous ground even having this conversation and being in contact with each other for the last twenty-odd years. But I've always liked you. You're like the daughter I never had."

Nadia smiled down the phone. Although she wasn't sure whether the statement was true. Their relationship had been friendly and supportive over the years, but she'd never felt a great deal of love from Diane. But then, people expressed love in different ways.

"I might be able to find a current photograph of Stacey," Diane said, speaking as though someone was listening to their conversation. "I can't promise anything, but I'll see what I can do."

"That would be helpful."

"But I can't promise anything."

"I understand."

"Okay, kiddo. I've got to go, but I'll let you know what I find out. In the meantime, please try not to obsess about all this. I'm sure Stacey is probably on a bender somewhere and will turn up with her tail between her legs soon enough."

"Yes." Her smile broadened, but with it came tears. She wiped them away as she climbed off the bed. "Thank you."

"I'll speak to you soon."

Nadia hung up and threw the phone on the bed before walking over and standing in front of her bedroom window. The world outside looked luscious and inviting. Down in the bottom paddock, Daisy, her oldest mare, was cantering up and down whilst her younger sisters Dandelion and Buttercup were grazing contentedly near the fence. Above them, a flock of starlings flew across a cloudless blue sky.

Being in such a beautiful part of the country on such a glorious afternoon, it was difficult to imagine evil existing anywhere in the world. Once more, she reminded herself how blessed she'd been to have found Laurie and created this new life for herself. Many years ago, she'd vowed to herself that she would never let her past ruin her present. Since then, she'd done everything she could to forget about who she was and what had happened.

She still had that power.

She turned from the window and went back through into the lounge. The clock on the wall said it was almost three. She'd have to set off for the kids in ten minutes. But that was good. Anything that took her out of her paranoid thoughts was good. She went back into the bedroom and through into the en suite bathroom, undressing on the way to the walk-in shower and stepping inside the glass cubicle. As the hot water cascaded over her body, she felt the pressure and the pain of the past few days washing away. She even chuckled to herself. Was Stacey Wilson a genuine threat to her and her family? Possibly. Was it likely she'd broken into Diane's house to get Nadia's address? Not very. The teenage Stacey was hot-headed and impulsive, and she doubted she'd changed much. She wasn't the conniving type. Not at all.

She let out another chuckle as a rush of endorphins lifted her spirits. She was being paranoid. That was all. What happened to Tudor and Marge was horrible but they were isolated incidents. There was no reason for her to tie them to Stacey or her past or anything else.

Placing her head under the water, she closed her eyes and told herself she wouldn't let these silly thoughts plague her for a moment longer. Her time had been served, and now she was living the life she deserved. Nothing – her silly paranoia included – would destroy what she'd built for herself here. She owed it to herself to be happy, but she owed it to the memory of her mum and dad just as much.

She twisted off the water and grabbed a towel off the rack. It was time to put all this behind her once and for all. The past was the past, and that's where it could damn well stay.

THEN . . .

4 March 2001

"Go on, Tahani, inhale it back. Oh, my god you're not even doing it right." Stacey laughed as she coughed out a large plume of smoke. It hurt her chest and burned her throat. Why did anyone find smoking pleasurable?

"Ugh, that's horrible." She passed the cigarette to Stacey. "I don't want it. It tastes like dirt."

"Fair enough," Stacey said with a shrug. "It's 'cos you're not doing it properly, that's all. Once you get the hang of it, it can be a real buzz." She took a long drag and closed her eyes. She held the smoke in her lungs for a moment before blowing it down her nose.

"You look like a dragon," Tahani said.

Stacey opened her eyes and grinned. "Does it look cool?"

"Pretty cool, yeah." She tilted her head to one side to take in her friend. "Aren't you worried about your mum finding out you smoke? She might smell it on your clothes."

"She knows I smoke."

"Really? My parents would kill me if they found out."

Stacey sniffed and set off walking. "She smokes, so what is she going to say to me? She doesn't care, anyway. Too busy with her new boyfriend, *Danny*."

Tahani was inexperienced for her age, but even she could pick up on the contempt in the older girl's voice. "Don't you like him?"

"No, he's a creep. I keep catching him staring at me. Dirty old fucker."

Tahani didn't know what to say to that, so she said nothing. As they passed by Woolworths, Stacey finished her cigarette and flicked it at the window, sending a tiny explosion of sparks raining down onto the pavement.

A frisson of nerves shivered up Tahani's spine as she glanced around to see if anyone was looking at them, but no one was. She knew her mum and dad didn't like her hanging around with Stacey Wilson and if it got back to them she'd been seen with her – and smoking as well – they'd ground her for the rest of the summer, no question.

Being an only child, Tahani often felt cramped and constrained, but she knew her mum and dad loved her and only had her best interests at heart. Ever since Stacey had appeared on the scene, they'd tried to steer their daughter away from her influence. Gently at first, but as the weeks and months went on, they'd become more vocal in their distaste for their friendship. What they didn't seem to understand was that Tahani felt safe with Stacey. It wasn't only that she was a few years older. She was tough, as well. If only she went to Beck Hill, rather than St James's on the other side of town, things could be so different.

The bullying had got worse in the last few months. Zoe had turned the whole year against her. Most of the other kids called her mongrel, or worse, but it wasn't just the name calling. She'd be walking to a lesson and suddenly get a sharp pain in her upper arm where Zoe had sneaked up and given her a 'dead arm.' Another time she opened her lunch box to find it full of dirt and worms and as she looked up, she saw most of her class watching her with malicious grins on their faces. She'd never felt so alone.

Why her?

What had she done wrong?

She didn't tell her teachers in case it made things worse, and likewise with her parents. The only person she could confide in was Stacey. But her usual response was that she should hit back.

"I'm telling ya," she'd say in her broad Bradford accent. "People like her, you only have smack 'em once and really mean it, and they won't hassle you anymore."

But it was easy for her to say. She was strong and confident and didn't care what anyone thought of her. Tahani often wished she was more like Stacey. She daydreamed most days about being strong enough to stand up to Zoe. But when it came down to it, she took the punches and the name-calling and did nothing to stop them, like the little mouse she was.

It was really dragging her down.

"Ah shit," Stacey spat as they got to Bridge Street, where they could catch the bus home. "I was supposed to pick up some medicine for my mum. Shit! Shit, shit, shit!"

She spun around and then turned back as if trying to work out what to do.

"Is it important?" Tahani asked.

"Yeah. It is." She didn't blink. "I'm going to have to go back. I can't go home without it."

"But the bus is here, look."

"You catch it," Stacey said, backing away. "I'll get the next one. I'll see you later."

"But—"

"I've got to go."

Before Tahani could respond, or even offer to come with her, she'd run off. She watched her race down the side of the interchange and disappear around the corner. Tahani had not seen her friend look so worried before and wondered if she should go after her. But it was almost four and her mum and dad were expecting her home soon. She got on the bus and paid the driver before heading upstairs without really thinking about it. She was the first person to board, and she took a seat halfway back, settling into her seat as more people got on. Two girls her age came up the stairs and sat at the front and then a group of lads who she recognised from school but who were a few years below her. One of them smirked on noticing her and she braced herself for a comment, but it never came. As the bus shuddered into life and pulled away from the stop, she leaned the side of her head against the window. It was a fifteen-minute car journey back home from town, but the bus took over double that time due to all the stops it made along the way. She sat back in her seat and looked out of the window as the bus trundled through the outskirts of the city, picking up more passengers as it stopped in Little Horton and alongside St Luke's hospital. It had been a long day and, as was usually the case, the drone of the engine lulled Tahani into a daze, but at the next stop the noise of young people boarding the bus captured her attention.

She heard laughter and shouting. And a voice she recognised. She tensed, wide awake at once.

No. Please, no.

Why did this keep happening?

Footsteps clattered up the stairs and three girls appeared on the top level. Zoe saw her straight away, a wide grin spreading across her face. Behind her were the two girls who'd been with her that first day, who Tahani now knew were called Bethany Stanfield and Farah Meer.

"Look who we have here, girls," Zoe sneered. "It's our little mate. How are you doing *Tahooni*? Been to town, have ya?"

She nodded but didn't make eye contact. Whether this was a good move on her part or not, she wasn't sure, but she couldn't bring herself to look up. Her entire body was shaking.

"You look scared, love," Zoe said, swaggering past and sitting in a free seat on the other side of the aisle a few rows back. "You don't need to look so worried. Everything's cool. We're all mates, aren't we?"

Tahani turned back to the window, searching desperately for something to distract herself as the bus set off again.

"Where's your ugly girlfriend, mongrel?" Zoe called out. "She not here looking after you today?"

She turned around, catching the eye of the woman sitting behind her. She had a concerned expression on her face but looked away almost immediately. Everyone on the bus was staring forward, either too absorbed in their own world or in that same engine-induced stupor she'd found herself in before the worst possible thing had happened.

"What are you looking at, dickhead?" Farah asked, and the three girls all burst out laughing. "Turn around yeah, we don't need you staring at us, weirdo."

Tahani did as she was told. What else could she do? There were three of them, and she had no comeback. She felt dumb and numb and like a little girl. All she could do was stare out the window and count the seconds until it was her stop. They were almost there. Out of the window the rows of houses had turned into the recreation ground. She could see the row of shops – Divine Cuts, Ladbrokes and the Happy Shopper – which were set back from the road and indicated it was time to get off.

Without looking back at the giggling trio, she leapt up from her seat and swung herself into the aisle using the vertical handrail. At the top of the stairs, she pressed the button and heard the bell ding, to inform the bus driver that someone was getting off. With her breath stuck in her throat, she hurried down the steps, past the driver's cab and jumped out onto the pavement.

"Thank you," she called out to the driver, the politeness drummed into her by her mum and dad still innate despite being terrified.

She hit the ground running and headed straight for the snicket – the narrow pathway that ran down the side of the shops and led to the estate where her road was. It being summer, lush green trees hung over the top of the lane, making it darker and gloomier than usual, but she put her head down and hurried on. It would take her a few minutes to get to the end of the snicket before it opened out onto Merridown Street. After that, it would be another minute before she reached her own street and safety. She was going to be okay. She'd survived. She was—

"Oi. Where you are going in such a rush?"

No!

It felt like her heart had stopped. Zoe had got off the bus after her. Why? This wasn't her stop. She lived miles away. It was stupid. Pointless.

Tahani carried on walking, not looking around despite the calls and insults drifting down the snicket behind her. A rock about the size of her fist smashed into the wall to her left and rolled a few metres in front of her. She glared at it as she scurried past. If it had been on target, it could have knocked her out. Killed her, even. Was that it? Were they here to kill her? Was that what was about to happen?

"Mongrel! Mongo girl! Where are you going? We only want to talk to you."

She stopped. She didn't know what else to do. Her heart was thumping in her chest and she was visibly shaking. Turning around, she saw Zoe and Farah striding towards her. Zoe had a malicious grin on her face as she got closer.

"Who are you running away from?" she asked. When Tahani shrugged, she shoved her in the shoulder. "Hey! I'm talking to you."

"I'm going home," she mumbled. "I need to go home. My mum will have my dinner ready."

"Oh, will Mummy have dinner ready for you?" Zoe mocked. "Oh, right. We don't want to keep you, do we, Farah? You best get going then."

She eyed the two girls. She had no idea what it was about her they hated so much. They called her mongrel – like most of the other children did at Beck Hill thanks to Zoe's influence – but to hate someone just because their mum and dad weren't from the same place seemed ridiculous.

"Your dad not picking you up?" Farah asked. "In his Beamer?"

And why did they keep bringing up her dad's car? The way they were talking, they seemed to imply it meant her family was rich. But that wasn't true. Far from it. Tahani knew nothing about cars. All she knew was that her dad's car was red, and the radio didn't work very well. But she'd seen Farah's dad's car, and it looked nicer than theirs. It was definitely bigger.

It was Farah she stared up at now. "You're the same as me," she whispered. "Why are you doing this?"

"What do you mean? What are we doing?" Zoe butted in. "We're not doing anything, are we Far? And she's not the same as you, mongrel. Is she? She's cool. Not a goodie, goodie weirdo."

She shoved her again, and Tahani stumbled backwards. A burst of energy bloomed in her belly, but rather than it being helpful, it quickly morphed into less brusque emotions. She sniffed back tears as Zoe and Farah loomed over her.

"You think you're better than us, don't you? Swotting away in class. Getting good grades. You want to be a professor, do ya? Or a doctor? Is that it?"

She shook her head and looked at her feet. All she wanted was to be safe at home with her mum and dad.

"Go on then," Zoe said. "Fuck off. We're not keeping you." She gestured for her to move with a flick of her hand like she had done on that first day.

But it was a trap, Tahani knew it.

She studied Zoe for a second longer, before turning and shuffling away down the snicket. She'd only journeyed a few steps when she felt a hand grab her hair and then a pain in the back of her knees. She cried out as the world twisted on its access. Her vision distorted in a swish of colour as the ground rushed up to meet her. She landed on her side with a thud and the impact knocked all the air out of her. She gasped for breath, trying to stabilise herself. Rolling onto her back, she tried to push herself upright but Zoe leapt on top of her. With her knees pressing against Tahani's ribs, she straddled her torso. Leaning over, she grabbed her throat, digging her fingernails into her skin. Tahani struggled and cried for help, but the words came out muffled. Zoe's hand tightened around her throat as she fought for air, arms flailing by her sides.

She heard Stacey's voice in her head.

You only have to smack 'em once and really mean it . . .

She had to try. Otherwise, she was dead. Lifting her arm over her head, she punched out with all her strength, hitting Zoe on the side of the head. The impact sent a shock wave of pain into her wrist but did little to dislodge her attacker. It just made her squeeze harder.

Zoe scoffed nastily. "You hitting back are you, mongo? You want a fight, do you?"

Tahani wriggled her hips in an attempt to get free, glaring up at Farah as she did. Their eyes met, but the other girl looked away. The look on her face was halfway between relish and relief.

"Fucking loser," Zoe snarled. She released Tahani's neck, leaving her gasping for air, but as she was gulping back a large breath, Zoe's fingers clamped around her jaw and squeezed her mouth open.

Again, she tried to shout for help, but her words had even less energy behind them than before.

Zoe snorted up her nose and hacked up noisily, making a horrible sound with her throat. Still gripping Tahani's jaw, she leaned over and spat a large ball of green phlegm into her open mouth. The slimy wad hit the back of Tahani's throat and she recoiled in disgust and shock, spluttering out a painful cough as she fought against the choking invader. Zoe shoved her hand over her mouth and pressed down hard.

"Swallow it, ya smelly mongrel," she hissed. "That's a present for ya."

Tahani's eyes bulged as she tried to shake her off, but she knew it was pointless. Zoe was grinning manically at her, nodding for her to do as she instructed. As her last ounce of resolve and dignity faded away, Tahani swallowed down the thick phlegm.

"Oh my God, she's actually done it!" Zoe cried, looking over her shoulder at Farah. Then back to Tahani. "Open your mouth, mongo, let us see."

She did as she was told. Because what was the point in doing anything else now? The bullies had won. They were stronger and scarier than her. She had nothing left to give.

"Stinking mongrel," Zoe said, climbing off her, pushing Tahani's head down into the hard concrete path as she did. One last insult. "You stay there, okay? Stay lying there until we've gone. Do you understand?"

Tahani nodded and let out a whimper.

"What a loser," Farah said. "You're a disgrace, Tahani, you know that? And your mum's a disgrace as well. You tell her that from me."

Tahani stared up at a tree hanging over the path. It was a sycamore and through its wide leaves, she could see the sky was turning from blue to grey. She wanted to be at home with her mum and dad. Anywhere but here. She'd never felt so alone and disgusting and scared.

Was this what life was going to be like now?

Was this her fate?

As Zoe and Farah sauntered off, laughing devilishly to themselves, tears formed in her eyes and escaped down the side of her head into her hair. She felt sick and stupid and unsure of what she was supposed to do now. She waited for what she thought was enough time for Zoe and Farah to be out of sight and then clambered to her feet. As dusk descended, she wiped her face, brushed herself down and set off home. Her mum would have dinner ready and would be furious with her for being late. But she already knew she couldn't tell her what had happened. Ever. To do that would only make things worse.

Chapter 14

Tudor was back to his usual grumpy self the next morning as Nadia led the mares past his stall and down into the paddock so she could muck out their stalls.

"How are you feeling?" she asked him as she walked back into the stables. "Is that nasty cut healing?" She leaned over the fence to examine the dressing. There was a tiny spot of rust-coloured blood in the centre where it had seeped through the gauze, but apart from that, it looked good. Dr Simmons was coming back tomorrow afternoon to check on him and would change the dressing. Tudor turned to her, regarding her with his big brown eyes.

"A silly nail, hey?" she said. "I'm so sorry. I won't let anything hurt you again. Come here." She held her hand up, and he stepped forward, butting her hand with the front of his nose. "Good boy, that's my good boy." She gave him a stroke before stepping off the bottom rung of the fence. "I'll leave you to it," she told him. "I've got to clean your girlfriends' stalls."

She grabbed the fork and wire brush from where they were leaning against the wall and placed them on top of the battered old wheelbarrow before wheeling the tools into Daisy's stall. The smell of ammonia tickled the inside of her nose, but she didn't mind the smell. These days she was used to it. It was part of her world. As she shovelled piles of wet straw and manure into the barrow, she smiled to herself as a memory came to her. Her dad would always do this thing when they went on long car journeys, pretending he enjoyed the horrible smells coming off farmer's fields. As a young girl, she'd pull faces and make disgusted noises at the putrid odours drifting into the car from outside, but he'd sniff back dramatically, grinning widely and exclaiming how wonderful he found the stench. When she was really young, it shocked her how pleasing he found the rotten smells, but as the years went on, she realised he didn't like them at all and was just having fun with her. That didn't stop them from going through the same routine whenever they passed a smelly field or sewage works, of course. The charade even carried on into her teenage years, right until that summer. After that, she didn't go on car journeys with her dad ever again.

It took her thirty minutes to muck out all three stalls, including trips to the manure pile, and once done, she felt the same bristle of endorphins and sense of satisfaction as she always did. She was a slim woman, but stronger than she looked these days. Who needed the gym when she had this as a workout every morning? Which was useful seeing as the nearest gym was a forty-five-minute drive away.

Once done in the stables she headed into the house, and after showering and dressing for the day she laid out breakfast for everyone – cereals and croissants today, she wasn't in the mood for anything else – and put on a pot of coffee. While it brewed, she filled a basket with some fresh eggs, more croissants and a selection of tiny pots of jam. Placing the basket over the crook of her arm, she carried it down to Sunrise Meadows. It was still relatively early, especially for people on their holidays, and there was no sign of life at either of the yurts. She arrived at Mr Jameson's first and walked up the few steps to the decking area and left the breakfast items on the table under a tea towel. Breakfast wasn't included in the price, but she liked to offer a few complimentary items, as a surprise, halfway through her guest's stay. It was the little things that counted if you wanted good reviews.

As she headed over to yurt number two, Mrs Snowdon poked her head out and smiled into the sunshine already making itself known over the hillside. Nadia waved as she stepped out on the decking and stretched her arms above her head, but she didn't see her. She was wearing white shorts and a lemon vest top. When she'd first arrived, Nadia had thought her hair was brown, but now, in the morning light, she saw it had a definite reddish tone to it. In fact, it was the same colour as . . .

"Oh, hello," she called out as she stretched her head to one side, noticing Nadia. "What a lovely morning. And such an amazing view."

Nadia smiled and nodded. "Isn't it? We're very lucky." As she reached the bottom of the steps, she squinted up at the woman. She guessed her age as being about thirty-five, the same as her. But it was feasible she was a few years older than that. Thirty-eight, for instance.

"Do you and your husband have plans for today?"

"Oh, he's not my husband," she replied. "Sorry, did you think . . .?"

Nadia shook her head. "No, I'm sorry. For some reason I had it in my head that you were married. Mr and Mrs Snowdon."

The woman threw up her eyebrows. "No, I'm still a Bradley. For now, at least! I'm Louise, by the way. Sorry, I didn't catch your name. Darren did all the checking in and stuff, didn't he?" She glanced inside the yurt and dropped into a stage whisper. "He's a bit useless."

Nadia smiled. "No problem. My name's Nadia. It's nice to meet you, Louise."

"*Nadia?* What a lovely name."

The two women stood there smiling at each as the conversation suddenly dried up. Nadia studied Louise's face as much as she could without making it obvious. She had a square face with a wide jaw leading down to a small chin. Her nose was slightly bigger than average, but she was attractive and had a pleasant smile. Did women who'd been in prison for twenty years have such white teeth?

"How long have you and Darren been together?" She asked the question before engaging her brain and, as Louise's eyes widened, she immediately regretted it. "Gosh, I'm so sorry," she spluttered. "I don't know why I said that. I'm not usually this nosey!"

"It's fine," Louise said. "It's six years this year. Too long to have still not popped the question, hey?"

"Oh! I don't know! That's great!"

What?!

What the hell did that mean?

Stop this Nadia, stop it now.

And why did she feel so relieved? Just because she'd said they'd been together six years, didn't mean it was true. If this person was Stacey, hell-bent on vengeance, she wasn't going to tell her.

Me and Darren? Only a few months. I met him online and asked him to help me destroy your life.

Nadia screwed up her face to reset her thinking. When she opened her eyes, Louise was staring at her with a confused expression wrinkling her brow. "Is everything okay?"

"Yes. Fine." She held up the basket. "I brought you some eggs and pastries."

"Aww, thank you. That's lovely."

There was certainly something about Louise that seemed familiar, but as Nadia stepped up onto the decking beside her, she felt no unease in her presence. She took that as a good sign. Lots of people had reddish brown hair, probably hundreds of thousands of them in the UK alone. Nadia placed the eggs and croissants on the table along with three pots of jam, two strawberry and one apricot.

"Where are you from originally?" Louise asked.

Nadia stiffened. "Sorry?" Louise's tone was friendly, but that question had a lot of dark energy behind it.

"I mean, you're not from Cornwall, are you? I picked up a bit of a twang just now. Yorkshire, perhaps?"

Her shoulders relaxed, and she laughed. "Really? Can you tell? Darn it. I thought I'd lost my accent years ago."

"Oh, really?" Louise smiled at her. It was sweet, bordering on condescending. "I'm from up that way too, originally."

"How funny. You can't tell." She was putting on a good front, but she felt prickly heat across her chest. Her heart was beating faster than she'd have liked. "Whereabouts?"

Louise narrowed her eyes as she looked at her. "Just outside of Bradford. Do you know the area?"

Nadia swallowed. "Sort of. I'm from Pudsey, originally. Near Leeds?"

"Ah yes, like the bear. Children in Need."

"That's right." The two women stared at each other as another awkward silence fell between them. This time, however, Nadia felt a distinct unease. Looking around, she backed away and down the steps onto the wet grass. "Well, I'd better get on with my chores. Leave you to enjoy the day."

Louise squeezed her shoulders up around her ears. "Yes. We shall. You have a good day, too."

Nadia nodded and walked away up the field, through the middle of the two yurts. Once she was out of sight of Louise, she quickened her pace, not stopping until she was safely inside the house. She closed the front door and rested her back against it, panting loudly as her chest rose and fell.

What was that?

Here in the sanctuary of her cool hallway, away from the outside world, she let out an involuntary laugh. She sounded hysterical, but she couldn't stop herself. It felt like she was releasing a surplus of pent-up emotions, memories, and feelings that she didn't even know she'd been carrying around with her.

She closed her eyes. "You silly idiot," she whispered to herself. "Louise is not Stacey Wilson. She can't be."

This wasn't her trying to convince herself. It was the truth. For a start, despite having the same hair colour, she looked nothing like her. Stacey had a small, bulbous nose and a mouth that was turned down, even when her face was relaxed. Resting bitch face, they called it these days. But Stacey's had been more like a resting monster face. Louise was gracious and genteel, whilst Stacey, at least as a sixteen-year-old, was rough and abrasive. It was unlikely that twenty years in prison had refined those aspects of her personality.

Nevertheless, Nadia had a problem. Even though she was adamant that the link between her guest and her old friend was purely the result of an unhelpful imagination, she was shaking with nerves as she went through into the kitchen to find Laurie and the kids eating breakfast. She couldn't live her life like this.

"What's wrong?" Laurie asked as she moved over to the kitchen island and placed the empty basket down.

"What do you mean?"

He lent back and his thick eyebrows knitted together over his slender nose. "You look terrible. Did you not sleep well?"

"Great. Thank you very much," she snapped. "I'm sorry that I'm not the radiant goddess you were expecting." She went to storm past him, heading for her bedroom, but Laurie put his arm out to halt her.

"Nadia. Stop. Please." When she did, he sighed. "I'm sorry, darling. That came out wrong. I'm worried about you, that's all. You look stressed out."

She stared out the window, then at the bedroom, looking anywhere but into her husband's concerned face. That's because I am stressed out she wanted to yell.

"I'm fine," she said, but her voice didn't sound like it belonged to her. "I'm just tired. I need an early night tonight."

Laurie looked at his watch. "Why don't you go back to bed now? I can do the school run. I should have enough time."

She plucked up the courage to look at him. Mercifully, she didn't burst into tears as she stared into his kind blue eyes. She lifted her hand and rested it on the side of his face. With his tanned skin and chiselled jawline, he was still a very good-looking man. She didn't deserve him.

"Thank you, but I'll do it," she said. "I need to go into Bodmin for a few things, so it makes sense for me to take them."

"Aww. Let Dad take us," Andrew said, looking up from a bowl of soggy mush that was once Weetabix. "He drives faster than you. It's way more fun."

"Don't be an oaf," Laurie told him. "Your mum can drive just as fast as me. I was in the car with her when she was learning. Some of those corners . . . I had my heart in my mouth."

Nadia didn't respond. She didn't have the energy, and she worried any sort of release, even laughter, would bring tears. Instead, she patted Laurie on the shoulder and headed for her bedroom. She'd love for him to take the kids to school, but she needed to do it. Right now, all distractions were welcome.

Chapter 15

Five minutes into the school run, however, Nadia was regretting her decision. Distractions were indeed welcome but today the twins were playing up more than usual and their constant screams and cries of *Mummy he/she did X* only added to her dark mood. Beside her, in the passenger seat, Andrew sulked out of the window. He hadn't said a word since they set off, but that wasn't unusual and she'd long since stopped trying to get any conversation out of him, especially in the mornings. He was thirteen and regardless of how surly and cocky he might be at home, she got the impression he was struggling to find his way. She knew how he felt.

Stopping at a red light, she turned to look at him properly. When was the last time she'd seen him smile? Christmas? Perhaps there'd been the hint of one when he'd opened his Nintendo Switch, but she couldn't remember.

"Mummy!" Emily shrieked from the back seat. "Edward is pulling faces at me."

She glanced in the rear-view mirror. Her youngest son was sitting in his car seat facing forward with a blank expression, but she could tell by his over-the-top stiffness that Emily was likely telling the truth.

"Edward, don't pull faces at your sister, please. It's not nice. She doesn't like it."

"I wasn't doing."

"He was!"

"I wasn't! Mummy, she's lying. I was—"

"Stop it! Both of you!" She twisted around in her seat, waving a sharp finger between the two of them. "I'm having a dreadful week and the last thing I need is you two messing around. So, play nice or shut up. Do you hear me!?"

The twins practically jumped out of their car seats. Edward snorted and Emily made a soft whimpering sound. Nadia hardly ever shouted at her kids, but she was at the end of her rope. She sat back in her seat and shoved the stick into first as the lights turned green.

"Look, I'm sorry for shouting," she said, keeping the tone of her voice low and under control. "Mummy's just a little stressed at the moment."

Next to her, Andrew grunted. "Why are you stressed?"

"Lots of reasons," she replied, indicating left and joining the southbound A30. She shot him a smile, which she hoped was reassuring. "But don't worry about me, darling. Everything's fine."

"I'm not worried," he said. "I was just wondering, that's all."

"Yes, well, thank you for that," she said, pressing her foot down on the accelerator and leaning over to turn the radio up. "It's nice to know my son gives a damn about me."

No one really spoke for the rest of the journey except for the odd whine from Emily about Edward's face pulling, which Nadia ignored. The DJ filled in the gaps, playing a mixture of hits old and new, but Nadia wasn't listening. Regardless of how firm she'd been in her resolve earlier, she'd drifted into the flights of fancy that had occupied her thoughts for the last few days. Not that there was anything fanciful about her thoughts. Flights of fear would be more fitting.

She was finding it difficult to consider everything that had happened recently from a balanced viewpoint. She'd lived in Cornwall, in that same house, for more than half her adult life and apart from a couple of events – a broken fence when she forgot to put the handbrake on the car; the previous Farmer Baron's heart attack whilst walking his dog a few years back – nothing had happened of any note. That's how she liked it. Peaceful. Calm. Safe. The fact they'd never felt the need to lock their doors said everything you needed to know about their world. Yet in the past week, there'd been Tudor's injury and Marge's brutal death. She'd been telling herself it was only sheer bad luck that these distressing events had happened in such proximity, but what if it wasn't? Stacey Wilson, a convicted murderer with a history of violence – who had stated in front of three witnesses that she was going to *get* her one day – was out of prison and her whereabouts were currently unknown. If you added that fact to the mix, could she still say she was just being paranoid? And what about the dark figure Elenore had seen on the track?

"Mum! Calm down."

She'd been tapping the steering wheel in time with a song on the radio but was now slamming the heel of her palm into the leather with far too much force. Andrew was staring at her like she was crazy.

"Sorry," she said with a grin. "Must have been getting a bit too into that tune."

"It wasn't that fast." Andrew shook his head and went back to sulking out the window.

This was happening far too often. She was acting weird and people were starting to notice. She was going to make herself ill if she didn't watch herself.

Since making a new life for herself as Nadia Kelly – and then Nadia Morgan after marrying Laurie – she'd tried to approach life from a serene standpoint. The new persona had provided her free rein to create herself as a better, more rounded individual. And that's just what she'd done. Nadia Morgan was an excellent mother and a perfect wife. She worked hard and didn't sweat the small stuff. She was good-natured, friendly and a lover of life. A part of her knew that this conscious decision to leave her past behind – to rewrite who she was – could equally be viewed as her sticking her head in the sand. But she'd always brushed those ideas away whenever they bubbled up. She was happy. She had a good life. Why would she spend another second dwelling on the traumatic events of her past? Besides, those things had happened to Tahani Carroll. That wasn't who she was.

That person was dead.

She dropped Andrew off at the high school and then doubled back on herself to drop the twins at their primary school a mile outside of Bodmin. All was forgotten between Edward and Emily as Nadia helped them out of the car and watched them walk across the playground like miniature partners in crime. It made her heart swell to see her children so happy and content, attending a good school. But some days – days like today when she would rather be in bed with the covers pulled up over her head – it felt like a long drive there and back.

She and Laurie had considered five schools in the area when Andrew was first gearing up to begin his journey in education. Fletchers Bridge Primary, the one the twins now attended, was the furthest away from their house but it also had the best Ofsted reports and Nadia had picked up good vibes at the open day. Besides, everything was far away when you lived in the middle of nowhere. But it was worth it for the views and the space and the sense of privacy. At least, it had been. Before being out in the open with hardly anyone else around and the nearest police station thirty miles away suddenly became a point of concern.

She turned up the radio as she joined the A30 towards Bodmin. The DJ was playing an old Elton John track and she sang along, glad to not be thinking about Stacey Wilson and Zoe Evans for a few minutes. Indeed, she was so focused on losing herself in the music that she drove right up to a police roadblock before a traffic officer stepped in front of the car and waved her to stop. Slamming on the brakes she pulled up in time and wound down the window as the police officer walked over to the car.

"Is it an accident?" Nadia asked. "Is the road closed?"

The police officer was a woman. She had white-blonde hair tied back in a low ponytail. She gave Nadia a half-smile, half-grimace as she rested her forearm on the car roof and leaned down to make eye contact.

"There are some climate protesters up ahead, I'm afraid. A few of them have chained themselves to the bridge." She gestured with her chin at the footbridge that spanned across the road a few hundred metres in front of them.

"Oh," Nadia replied. "What do I do?"

The officer raised her head and pointed to the slip road over to the left. "You'll have to get off here. Where are you heading?"

"Bodmin. I'm just going to do a bit of shopping."

"Are you a local, then?"

"I live up by Hawk Well. We have stables up there." The officer nodded and stood upright. "It's going to add twenty-five minutes to your journey, but nothing we can do, I'm afraid. If you head for Millpool, you'll be able to enter Bodmin that way."

"Righto. Yes. Thank you," Nadia said. "A blasted nuisance, aren't they?"

The officer clicked her teeth. "You said it. They're the first ones we've had down here. They're protesting about the overuse of Range Rovers and other big cars in the area. Gas-guzzlers, they call them. Which is stupid because we don't use the term gas in this country, do we?"

She laughed, but Nadia didn't. Laurie drove a Range Rover.

"I'd best get going then," she said. But the police officer was already walking away from the car, flagging down a dark grey 4x4, coming up behind her.

Nadia shoved the car into first gear and pulled away, veering over to the slip road and shifting into second and then third as she left the A30 and drove up a slight incline to meet a roundabout. Once there, she leaned over and scrambled in her bag for her phone, shoving it into the cradle on her dashboard and opening the maps app. After typing Bodmin into the search window, it told her it would take nineteen minutes to get there. Not too bad, all things considered. She turned up the radio and set off for the town.

Chapter 16

Considering it was mid-week and not even past eleven, Bodmin was full of people. After living out in the countryside for so long busy places made Nadia uneasy at the best of times, but today, with everything that had happened recently - and all the dark, confusing thoughts swirling around in her head - she found it downright unpleasant.

On the corner of Fore Street and Market Street, she huddled into the recess of an unused doorway to catch her breath. In front of her, people milled about, using the pavements and streets to get to where they were going, walking with purpose and alacrity. Everyone seemed angry. Deep frowns creased their foreheads as they weaved around each other and bustled for space.

It was too much.

She couldn't do it.

She needed space.

She needed the green fields of home.

Reaching into the inner pocket of her handbag, she pulled out a scrap of paper on which she'd written a list of items she needed to purchase. New dressings for Tudor were top of the list. Although Dr Simmons had visited and replaced the original dressing, she didn't think it would hurt to give her cherished stallion fresh dressings every day until he healed. She also had to get some vegetables to go with the chicken she was making for dinner and Laurie had asked her to pick him up a pack of socks. All easy enough tasks, but with all these people around, it felt like she was swimming underwater.

Come on, Nadia, pull yourself together.

What did she think was going to happen? Stacey wasn't lurking somewhere in the crowds, ready to attack her. Things like that didn't happen outside of Hollywood movies or BBC dramas. She was a normal woman, with a normal life, going about her normal business.

And so what if Stacey had gone missing? She was an ex-con. That's what happened sometimes. Often, probably. Even as a teenager, she was reckless and impulsive. These days she'd have been diagnosed with ADHD or similar, but back then she was simply labelled a problem child. It didn't excuse what happened, of course. Nothing did. But it explained why she might break her licence and fail to attend supervision meetings.

Feeling calmer after giving herself this stern talking to, Nadia ventured out from the safety of the recess and headed for Horse and Hound Supplies, situated halfway down Market Street. The shop was empty as she entered and after a couple of laps of the aisles, to further calm herself in the relative quiet, she went up to the counter and bought a pack of veterinary-approved dressings and a box of feed supplements for good measure.

As she left the shop, she felt rain in the air and as it was almost lunchtime decided she'd grab a bite to eat before getting the rest of the things on her list. She knew of a nice coffee shop nearby that sold amazing pasties. As if in agreement, her stomach rumbled as she hurried through the crowds and dipped down the next street. The coffee shop was at the far end, but she could smell the wonderful aromas of baked goods and real coffee before she even got there. But as she pushed open the door and stepped inside, her heart sank. The place was already full of people.

She glanced around, trying to ignore the frisson of nervous energy that was now ruining her mood. It wasn't a problem; she told herself. If there was nowhere to sit, she'd go somewhere else. There were other cafes, and other sandwich bars. She was about to leave when an old man and woman who'd been sitting at a table in the far corner got to their feet. Without waiting, she hurried over there.

"Excuse me, are you going?" she asked as she got closer.

The old woman looked her up and down and sniffed. "Yes. We are."

"Great, thank you. It's busy today." She smiled at the couple, choosing to ignore their apparent contempt. Whether this was because of her tenacity in claiming their table, or the colour of her skin, she didn't care. Cornwall wasn't as multi-cultural as Bradford or Leeds and, whilst the odd sneer still hurt, the way she saw it, it was their problem, not hers.

The old couple shuffled away without further comment and she settled down with her back to the corner. It was a good table. She could see the whole of the café from this position, and no one could sneak up behind her. She picked up the bi-fold laminated menu and perused its offerings. On the walk here she'd made her mind up that she'd have a classic Cornish pasty, but it was always fun to read the menu. She was scanning the drinks list, wondering whether to have a latte or a tea when she glanced up.

Oh . . . No . . .

It felt like time had stopped. The room zoomed into sharp focus and her heart did a backflip as she saw a woman sitting alone at a table on the other side of the room. She had wiry, reddish-brown hair tied up in a high ponytail and a perpetual sneer that could be described as the epitome of 'resting bitch face'.

Resting monster face.

She was looking straight at Nadia and as their eyes met; she didn't glance away. She just kept staring at her without blinking.

Nadia swallowed down a yelp and raised the menu in front of her face as if hiding was even an option.

It was Stacey.

It had to be.

She had the same hair, the same facial expression, and the same glimmer of evil in her eyes. Nadia peered over the menu. She was still staring her way but seemed to be looking through her.

What was she doing?

Nadia's heart was beating so fast that she worried she was about to have a heart attack. Maybe that would be best. It would solve a lot of problems.

Would it be quick?

Would it hurt?

She glanced around her at the other people in the café. None of them was taking the slightest bit of notice of her. Some were engaged in conversation with their tablemates, others were hunched over their plates of food, biting down greedily into crumbly pastry or flaky sausage rolls. She glanced back at the woman. At Stacey. She hadn't moved. She looked like a waxwork. An evil, tormenting waxwork.

"Hello, there. Sorry for the wait. What can I get you?"

Nadia jumped at the voice beside her. Looking up, she saw a curly-haired woman holding a small notepad and a pencil in readiness. She smiled and nodded at the menu in Nadia's hand. "Have you decided?"

Nadia swallowed. She knew she was supposed to respond, but words felt foreign to her. She stared at the woman. "I . . . Sorry . . . No." She pushed away from the table and got to her feet. "I've got to go. Sorry."

She shuffled around the side of the table as the waitress muttered something that she didn't catch. The exit was about three metres in front of her. Stacey was sitting two metres away. The way the tables were laid out, she had to go past her table to get to the door. Time stopped once more, and she felt herself drifting forward. Her limbs didn't feel like they belonged to her and an intense shiver of dizziness distorted her awareness. Then she was at Stacey's table, looking down at her.

"Why are you doing this? Why can't you leave me alone?"

Her words came out fast and frantic, but she couldn't slow down. She had to say her piece. She had to nip this in the bud before it went any further. She couldn't feel her face, but it didn't matter.

The woman sat back and pulled a face as Nadia went on.

"You can't do this. It's not fair. I'm not the same person I was. I've got a new life. I've got children and a husband. I'm happy. Please. Leave me alone. I'm sorry about what happened to you, but that wasn't my fault. And the trial . . . That was them, not me. I swear to you. They said I should . . . I never would have—"

"Excuse me. What are you talking about?"

"What?" Stacey's voice caught Nadia by her surprise. "What did you say?"

"What are you saying? Who are you?" Her voice was deep and harsh sounding and she spoke with an accent. It could have been German or Austrian. Somewhere around there. As Nadia was flapping her mouth, trying to find her words, a man appeared and addressed the woman in an unfamiliar language. They exchanged a few more words and the woman – who was clearly not Stacey – gesticulated at Nadia.

"I think you may have the wrong person," the man told her. He was tall with blond hair and wore round spectacles. "We only arrived in Cornwall yesterday. We are from Switzerland. We are on holiday here."

Nadia swallowed, turning from the man to the woman and back again. What the hell was she doing, approaching strangers in cafes, accusing them of stalking her? Up close now, she could see the woman looked nothing like Stacey. She had brown eyes, whereas Stacey's were green. What was she doing? These were the actions of a mad woman.

"I'm so sorry," she gasped, holding up her hands. "I don't know what came over me." She hurried to the door and pushed through to the outside, gulping in the cool air and holding onto the side of the doorframe to steady herself.

She wiped a tear from her cheek. This was no way to live. Cornwall was supposed to be a fresh start. A new life. A new identity. After her mum and dad died, after she'd been released, she'd promised herself she'd make a proper go of life, to never think of the events of that summer ever again. But the memories were erupting all around her, coming so fast she couldn't ignore them. They were making her act like a crazy person.

But maybe she was a crazy person.

Maybe she had been all along.

She looked over her shoulder as a wave of crushing despair washed over her. Tudor's dressings were still on the floor by the table. But she couldn't go back in there now. She couldn't do anything. Stepping away from the doorway, she pushed through the crowds and headed back to her car. She needed to get away from here. She needed a lie down in a dark room. She needed a drink.

THEN . . .

26 May 2001

Tahani rubbed at her face. She couldn't believe what she was hearing. This was so unfair. They were being so unreasonable.

She was sitting on one side of the kitchen table with her mum sitting opposite. Standing beside her mum with one hand on the edge of the table was her dad. She looked up at him and smiled meekly, hoping he was just going along with her mum's wishes and that she might sway him. But as he caught her gaze, he replied with a thin-lipped smile, like he always did in these situations.

Sorry, darling. It's up to your mum.

"But it's Stacey's birthday today. I said I'd go around and see her. I've made her a card."

"No, Tahani," her mum said. "I've made my decision, and you must accept this. That girl is bad news. Your father and I don't want you hanging around with her anymore." She crossed her arms as if that were final.

"But she's my best friend. She's my . . . friend."

She was about to say she was her only friend but stopped herself in time. Even now, with her parents acting so unfairly, she didn't want to worry them. If they knew what was going on at school, with Zoe Evans and the other girls, they'd kick up such a fuss it would make everything a hundred times worse. Also, despite the fact they were trying to keep it from her – talking in hushed tones in their bedroom when they thought she was asleep – she knew her mum was ill. She didn't know the full details, but even now, as stern-faced as she was, she looked tired. Her dark brown eyes didn't have the same sparkle they usually did.

"That girl is no friend of yours. She's nothing but trouble," her mum went on. "Isn't that right, Gerry?"

Her dad cleared his throat. "Seems that way, darling. We both think it's best if you make some friends your own age. There are loads of girls at school I'm sure would love to be your friend. You're clever, funny, kind."

She snorted. Clever, funny and kind got you nowhere at Beck Hill. Not when those traits could easily be reframed as swotty, weird, and weak. Add to this, the fact she didn't fit in with the white or the Asian kids and she felt as alone and troubled as she always had done. Stacey was her only friend. She understood her. She might not have had the same problems as Tahani, but she knew what it felt like to be an outcast and alone. Her dad wasn't around and her mum was too busy with her new boyfriend. Stacey had told Tahani she didn't expect a birthday card from either of them.

It had been two months since Zoe and Farah had jumped her and Zoe spat in her mouth, and she still felt the shame of that day in the pit of her stomach. It was like she'd eaten something heavy and uncomfortable and she couldn't seem to get rid of it no matter what she did. She hadn't even told Stacey what had happened. She was too embarrassed and sickened by it. She'd just laid there and let it happen. Stacey would never have done that. She'd have fought back. She'd have made Zoe pay.

"Please, mum," she tried again. "Can I just go over and see her for ten minutes? I need to give her the card I've made."

Her dad sighed and looked at her mum, but she just narrowed her eyes at Tahani. "I've said no and I promise you, this is for your own good. You saw what she did to that poor boy? He was in the hospital for two days with a severe concussion. He had to have scans. They were worried he might have a bleed on his brain."

Tahani placed her hands on the table in front of her and stared at them. What could she say to that? Her mum was talking about Brett Hughes, a boy from her school. He'd been playing football down at the far end of their street where the garages were, kicking the ball at the side of one of them and volleying it as it bounced back. Tahani and Stacey had been watching him do it, but then Stacey decided she wanted to have a go and Brett had said no. The result of that was Stacey grabbing an unopened can of Coke from Brett's rucksack and chucking it at the young boy's head. Unfortunately, she'd been an excellent shot and the blunt object had hit him above his ear and knocked him out. The rumours were that he had to have five stitches and his head shaved, but no one had seen him since. It was a big thing. Most of the street had come out to see what had happened. Then, a few hours later, the police turned up at Stacey's house. Brett's parents had called them and wanted her charged with assault. They took her to the station and everything. Tahani and her mum had watched through their front window as they put her in a police car and drove her away.

"It was an accident," she told her mum, even though she knew it was useless. "She didn't mean to hit him."

"He could have died!"

"From a Coke can?"

"It can happen," her mum yelled. "And don't answer back. Do you see? This is what happens when you spend time with people like Stacey Wilson. You disrespect your parents."

"But I'm not . . ." she whimpered. "I'm not disrespecting you, honest. I just want to give her my card."

Her dad closed his eyes as if he was in pain. "Your mum has said no, Tahani. Let's leave it there, please. We don't want to fall out over this, do we?" He moved over and stood behind her mum, placing his hands gently on her shoulders. "Can you apologise to your mum, please?"

He lowered his chin and gave Tahani a hard stare. She hated it when he did that. She frowned but found herself saying sorry. Her mum regarded her for a moment longer and then uncrossed her arms.

"We only want the best for you, darling," she said. "You're a good girl. You're our good girl. You're going to be a doctor one day, aren't you?"

"Mum," she mumbled. "I don't know . . ."

"She's going to make us proud, whatever she does," her dad added. "We know you will."

Her mum reached up with one hand and took her dad's hand off her shoulder and held it. "We do," she said. "But let us not talk about this girl again. It is wearing me out. Now, excuse me, I need to go to the bathroom." She got to her feet and Tahani noticed she had to hold on to her dad to steady herself. She watched as she wandered to the doorway and disappeared into the hallway.

"Is mum alright?" she asked her dad once she'd heard the bathroom door close.

He cleared his throat. "Yes. She's fine. Don't worry, darling. I know everything seems a bit rubbish now, but it'll pick up. It always does. I promise." He gave her a big grin before sauntering off into the lounge.

Tahani stayed where she was at the table. The room suddenly felt very still and airless. The clock on the wall next to the door ticked away, telling her it was a quarter past three in the afternoon.

It'll pick up. How did he know that?

She knew her mum and dad only wanted the best for her, but they didn't know what was going on. They didn't know the truth. Stacey Wilson was all she had. She was the only person she could rely on. And they were stopping them from being friends. It wasn't fair. She was terrified about how she would cope with Zoe and Farha and Bethany without Stacey in her corner. She loved her parents, but they didn't know everything.

She got up from the table and ran up the stairs to her bedroom, slamming the door as loudly as she could. Doing that would only make things worse – her mum hated doors slamming and hated it even more when she sulked – but she needed them to know how upset she was. How angry she was with them for not letting her see her friend. She felt like a prisoner in her own life. They were old and stupid and they didn't understand what she was going through. Her dad even said to her once that her school days would be the best days of her life. What a stupid thing to say. If that was true, what was the point of even living? Right now, she was in hell and they didn't care. No one did.

Chapter 17

Nadia pulled her car up to an abrupt stop. She was on the track between her neighbour's houses, on the section that opened out wide so two cars could pass, but she didn't know how she'd got there. She switched off the engine and yanked on the handbrake. Her last memory was rushing back to the car after approaching that poor woman in the coffee shop. She must have conducted the entire journey back from Bodmin with her awareness all in her head, focusing on the catastrophising thoughts swirling around in her imagination. She'd not dared look away in case one of those ideas grew teeth and legs.

She tilted the rear-view mirror towards her and examined herself in the strip of reflective glass. Her skin looked pale and had a greenish tinge to it, but that was probably as much to do with the fact she'd not applied make-up this morning. The digital clock on her dashboard read 14:05. She would have to set off to pick the children up in an hour, but needed to slow her heart rate before she even thought about driving anywhere else.

Getting out of the car, she stumbled over to Elenore's house and walked down the path. At the front door, she reached up and banged the knocker on the wood as hard as she could. The sun reflected off the front windows, making it hard to see into the room beyond, but as her gaze drifted over to the driveway, she saw Elenore's car wasn't there.

Please be in.

She had no plan of what she was going to say to her friend – or why she'd stopped here rather than driving the rest of the way to her own house – only that something had compelled her to stop. She knocked again. Waited. There was no sound from the other side of the door. No movement behind the curtains. Elenore wasn't home. Why wasn't she home? She needed to see her.

Glancing over her shoulder, she could see into the new extension of Tom and Melissa's house. The kitchen lights were on and she saw movement through the window. An elbow was sticking out over the sink and looked to be Melissa's. She'd do. She didn't want to go home just yet. As well as leaving Tudor's dressings behind, she'd forgotten to get the vegetables to have with the chicken. Laurie might have to get takeaway pizza tonight, instead, which wasn't a big issue. But without the distraction that cooking dinner provided, she feared her mind would take her to dangerous places.

She turned around and walked down Elenore's path towards Melissa's house. As she got closer, she saw it was indeed Melissa in the kitchen and the sight stirred something inside of her.

Of course.

That was why her subconscious had her stopping here rather than driving to her own house. She needed to know if Tom and Melissa had seen anything.

Melissa waved at her as she approached and the front door opened before she got up to it.

"Hey, Nadia," she said, her usual breezy self. "Lovely day, isn't it?"

"Yes. Lovely and warm." The anxiety tearing at her soul still didn't stop her ingrained politeness from taking over. She was still her parents' daughter. "How are you?"

"Good, thank you. Are you coming in?" She stepped back to allow Nadia to enter, but as she did, her warm expression dropped. She even frowned. "Is everything okay? You look troubled."

Nadia puffed out her cheeks. She couldn't even hide it. At least it saved her some time.

"I think so. It's just . . . Oh, I don't know. I'm a little worried about something, that's all. I wondered if you'd seen anything."

Melissa stepped around the back of her and shut the front door. "What is it?" she said, before adding, "Come through, I'll put the kettle on."

"Not for me. Thank you," Nadia said but followed her through into the kitchen. Melissa gestured for her to sit at the pine dining table in the centre of the room, and she did.

"What's going on?" she asked, sitting too, and resting her arms on the table.

Nadia sighed but decided to go for it. Things had gone too far to be worried about sounding like a paranoid oddball. "A few weird things have happened over the last few days, that's all. First, Marge, our cat, was mutilated. Then Tudor got injured quite badly. I know on their own both these incidents could be explained as bad luck. But I'm worried they're connected. And that perhaps someone hurt them on purpose."

Melissa's mouth was hanging open. "What? Why would anyone . . .?"

"I don't know," Nadia said. There were some aspects she wanted to keep to herself. Until she needed to, at least. "But Elenore told me she saw someone on the track one night last week. A dark figure, with their face covered up. They disappeared into the woods when she spotted them through the window. I don't want to scare you, but it's got me worried. I don't suppose you've seen anything?"

Melissa reached over the table and grabbed Nadia's hand. "You poor thing. Are you worried about the children?"

Nadia nodded. "Yes."

And she was. Of course she was. But them being hurt was only a part of it. If this was Stacey, then she was the one in the firing line. If she was worried for her children, it was that they might grow up without a mother, like she'd had to. But it was typical for Melissa to think of the children first. It was this time last year that she'd confided in Nadia that she and Tom were going to stop trying to have children. After their fourth miscarriage, she'd had enough heartbreak for her whole life, she'd said.

"But you haven't seen anything? Or anyone?"

Melissa shook her head. "No. We love it here because you don't see anyone. It's like a haven away from the world, isn't it? Our little slice of paradise."

It was also typical of Melissa to only see the good in life. Every so often, after her second or third glass of wine, she'd let her guard slip and the sadness she covered so well was revealed. But it was rare that happened. She was what you'd call an eternal optimist, and Nadia loved her for that.

"A haven. Yes. That's what I used to think as well," she replied. "But lately I don't know. I've got such a bad feeling in my stomach and I can't shake it. I don't know what to do."

"You poor thing. You look exhausted," Melissa said, still holding her hand. "I'll keep my eyes peeled for anything untoward, but I think maybe you just need to get some rest. You've got the horses and the glamping, not to mention looking after three kids and a household. It's got to take its toll."

Nadia shrugged it off. She had a point, but this wasn't the result of emotional burnout. She'd seen what she'd seen. She knew what she knew.

"If you want, Tom and I can have the kids for a night, to give you a break. You know we always love to have them."

"Thank you, you're a good friend. That's very sweet." And then at once, she had an idea. "You know, Melissa, if anything ever happens to me or Laurie . . . His parents are getting on a bit now and neither of us has siblings . . ."

No!

Stop this!

What the hell was she saying? Laurie would be furious if he knew she was discussing this without talking to him first. And he'd have every right to be.

"I know it's a bit weird to bring up . . ." she continued.

Shut up!

Shut up now!

Melissa was leaning forward with a strange look on her face. Nadia caught herself in time and sat back, pulling her hand into her lap.

"I'm sorry. I shouldn't have said that. I'm just very stressed right now and I think I'm letting my imagination get the better of me."

Melissa swallowed and nodded too fast, but then her face relaxed into a smile. "No problem. I understand."

The two women smiled at each other for what seemed like too long. Nadia's cheeks ached. She opened her mouth, hoping words would come to her, but none did.

"But the answer is yes," Melissa whispered in a mock-conspiring fashion. "We'd be honoured to do that for you. And the kids, of course. If it were ever to happen. God forbid! We love the twins – and Andrew. You've done such good work with all of them."

The mood had settled. Nadia smiled as the darkness in her mind began to clear. "Thank you. Sometimes I wonder."

"Oh, no. They're a credit to you and Laurie. They really are."

Nadia was about to thank her again when a noise outside grabbed her attention. It sounded like a car engine. Shooting a look through the window, she saw a flash of red as Elenore's car drove past.

"She's home," Nadia said, getting to her feet before realising she was leaving Melissa hanging somewhat. "Thank you for listening to me and being the voice of reason. And the other thing . . . We'll talk about that some other time if that's okay."

Meaning never again if she could help it. She already felt terrible. It had slipped out in a moment of panic and she'd give anything to take it back.

"No problem," Melissa said, standing as well. "I'll ask Tom if he's seen anything when he gets home from work. And I'll keep my eyes open and let you know."

"Great." She was walking towards the door as she spoke and opened it as she got there. "I'll see you soon."

Melissa raised her hand to wave as Nadia left her house, feeling like the worst person in the world. It was another anxious thought to add to the growing list of anxious thoughts. She shut the door behind her and hurried up the track to Elenore's house, catching her as she was walking down her path.

"Elenore, wait," she called out. "Can I have a word?"

She stopped and turned around. "Nadia?" As always, she exuded composure, so at odds with Nadia's blustering approach. She lifted her head. "What is going on?"

"It's nothing. Well, I hope not," she said, deciding to go straight to the point rather than dilly dally with small talk. "I just wanted to ask you about the person you saw on the track. When exactly was it?"

"Did I not say? It was last Sunday. The exact time I'm less certain of, perhaps around eleven or eleven-thirty."

"And you think it was a man?"

"Not necessarily. I didn't see their face."

"So, it could have been a woman?" She was being pushy, and Elenore seemed taken aback by her approach, but she couldn't stop. She had to know, and she had to know right now.

"Yes. Most definitely," Elenore said, swaying her head from side to side and looking off over Nadia's shoulder, presumably seeing what she saw that night in her imagination. "They had a hood up over their face so I couldn't tell their gender."

"Okay. Thank you." It had helped to know this, but presently she wasn't sure how. The old phrase, know thy enemy, popped into her head. "And you've not seen anything since?"

Elenore squinted at her. "*Non*. And I don't think we need to worry. As I told myself at the time, it was probably one of your guests relieving themselves."

"We have a toilet block."

"I know, but only one, yes? It does happen on occasion. I see people using the woods. Don't worry, it doesn't bother me."

"Yes. Sure. Sorry. I will put something in our welcome pack about it . . ."

Elenore chuckled to herself. "I am serious. It is not an issue. I only say it so you will not worry. The man – or woman – I saw on the track is easily explained and not a threat to any of us. *Oui*? You look exhausted, Nadia. I think maybe you need a nap."

That was two people who'd told her she looked exhausted within ten minutes. But she didn't feel exhausted. She felt wired and like she never wanted to sleep again until she felt safe. Until Stacey Wilson was back under her supervising officer's jurisdiction.

"You're right, I think I do," she told Elenore. But glancing at her watch, she realised even if she wanted to rest, she couldn't. "Shoot, I'm late," she said, backing away. "I'll see you soon."

She strode back to her car and clambered in. The driver's door was still hanging open. Slamming it shut, she pulled the seat belt across her chest and clicked it home. She had planned on having a shower, but there was barely time to splash cold water in her face before she had to set off to pick up the children. A mother's work was never over. She started the car engine and drove up past the stables towards her house.

Chapter 18

Nadia didn't look up as the front door went. She knew it was Laurie coming home, but if it was the demonic Stacey Wilson of her imagination, then so be it. Let her kill her. She was past caring. She heard the familiar sound of her husband placing his briefcase on top of the shoe rack and then hanging up his coat, but didn't move as the door to the main living space creaked open.

"Nadia? What are you doing in the dark?" The hallway bulb sent a sliver of light spearing across the floor and along the kitchen island in front of her. It landed on the bottle of wine, showing there was now only a quarter of it left. It was one of Laurie's good bottles too, a 2017 Napa Valley Cabernet.

He moved into the room and switched on the light. "What's going on?"

"Nothing. I was just thinking about things. I didn't realise it had got dark."

Raising the bulbous wineglass in front of her, she drank back the remnants before picking up the bottle and pouring out the last quarter. She still didn't look at her husband. She felt prickly and brittle and like she was going to snap.

"Where are the children?" Laurie asked.

"The twins are asleep. Andrew's in his room doing his homework."

He laughed. "Or playing on his Nintendo, most likely."

"Yeah, well, he's a kid. Let him have his fun." She sniffed and gulped back a big mouthful of wine without tasting it. "I haven't made dinner. Sorry. Andrew and the twins had beans on toast. There's some leftover lasagne in the freezer if you want to defrost it."

Laurie went to say something but thought better of it. Instead, he smiled. "No worries."

Her phone was on the island next to the now empty bottle of wine. She swiped at the screen to see the time was 20:08. "You're late," she said.

"I know. I had a late meeting with Michael Greene over in Wadebridge and it overran. He's signed the contract, though. That should keep us going well into next year."

"That's great." She forced a smile but couldn't sustain it.

"Are you sure everything is okay here?" He picked up the bottle of wine and she snapped her head up to watch him as he examined it. Apart from a raised eyebrow, he had no comment. "You seem . . . troubled. Anything you want to talk about?"

She sighed. God, how much did she want to offload? What a relief it would be if she could tell her husband what was going on. But she couldn't.

For one thing, she wouldn't know where to start. She felt as if she was losing her grip on reality. That poor woman in the café had looked terrified when she'd confronted her. But for those first few minutes, she'd genuinely believed it was Stacey.

Perhaps that was the wake-up call she needed. It was time to face her demons head-on. And that started with looking in the mirror.

"Nadia? What is it?"

Nadia.

Her mum's name. She'd chosen it for that reason, but she also liked the fact it meant 'filled with hope' in Bengali. Kelly, the surname she'd chosen after leaving the secure care centre, was her grandmother's maiden name on her dad's side and meant 'warrior'. Nadia Kelly. A warrior filled with hope. It was a good name she'd chosen. A link to her past but the good parts. The parts she still missed if she allowed herself. Her mum and dad had been taken from her too soon, but by dying, they'd allowed her to move on without . . . baggage.

Wow! As the thought formed, she shook her head. What a callous bitch she could be sometimes. But it was understandable. She'd had to toughen up and fast. Not only because of where she found herself after the trial but because of the guilt she felt. At times like this, when she was drunk enough to risk examining her soul, she had to admit her parents being *taken from her too soon* was a rather generous way of looking at the situation. That phrase implied she had nothing to do with their deaths and she knew full well her actions that summer had a massive impact on their declining health.

Until recently, she'd been very good at burying the guilt and shame deep inside of herself or disguising it as other things. If she called it anxiety and remedied it with hard work and activity, she could live a relatively normal life. You couldn't dwell on dark memories if you were too busy cleaning stables and cooking dinner for everyone.

"Nadia?"

She finished the wine and turned to her husband. Her amazing Laurie. The man she'd fallen in love with all those years ago and who she was still in love with three kids later. He tilted his head to take her in. With his blue eyes and well-defined, perfect features, he was as handsome as ever. But it wasn't his looks that had made her fall in love with him so fast and so completely.

They'd met by chance in Kings Cross station when her debit card hadn't been accepted by the ticket machine for the underground. It was her first time in London and she was nervous about being in such a big city. She felt like everyone was staring at her as if they knew who she was, what she'd done. But Laurie, with his calm voice and even calmer manner, had leaned over and asked her if she needed help. She'd fallen for him the second she looked up into his eyes, full of empathy and acceptance. And those were the reasons she still loved him so much after all this time. He was kind but forthright. Gentle, but firm when he needed to be – and when she needed him to be. Plus, he'd accepted her from the start and never even touched on the usual questions she'd get from men. Where are you from originally? Are your parents Indian?

He accepted her for who she was in the present moment. That's all he seemed to care about. Later, when they'd had the inevitable conversation about ex-lovers and the like, he'd even accepted her wishes to keep her past to herself. She'd reassured him he had nothing to worry about, of course. And he knew certain, vague aspects about her life, that her parents were dead, that she'd had an awful childhood, but after a while, he'd simply chosen to love the person she was with him.

And that was how it should be.

Nadia had often heard people say that, as humans, we were simply an amalgamation of our experiences and our memories, but she didn't buy that. It was too easy. Because how did you explain the fact that with Laurie, she felt safe and happy for the first time since becoming an adult? It was her present that formed who she was. Not her past.

But despite Laurie loving her almost unconditionally from the moment they got together, his parents were a little harder to win over. They asked her the obvious questions and never seemed satisfied with her answers about where she went to school and what her parents had done for a living. Over the years, however, they'd softened. Especially when they saw how happy she made their only son. Then, when Andrew was born, that was it. Done. She was a part of the family. And with that, she thought the past was well and truly behind her.

How stupid she'd been.

"Nadia?"

The look on Laurie's face as she stared into his striking blue eyes almost set her off. She'd never seen him look so concerned.

"Something's wrong. Tell me." He moved the wineglass and bottle away from her and pulled out a stool. Sitting down, he shifted around so he was facing her. "Nadia, tell me. Please."

She shook her head. "I can't. I'm sorry." She felt wretched and horrible for so many reasons, but making her husband paranoid and upset was the icing on the cake.

"Why can't you? Is it about what happened to you when you were younger? Is that it?" He exhaled pointedly as if trying to calm himself. "You know I respect the fact you don't want to tell me about it, Nadia, but when I see you like this . . . God knows, it used to drive me crazy when we first got together, that you had a whole past that I didn't know about. But I've let it go. Only now I sense something about what happened to you is making you sad, and I feel you've been sad for some time and it's getting worse. So, what happened to you? What did you do?"

She sat up and glared at him. "What did *I* do? Why do you think this is about something I did?"

Laurie pulled his lips back over his teeth. "Bad choice of words. I didn't mean it like that. I just want to help you, Nadia. I love you and I can see you're struggling with something and I think it'd be good for you to talk about it. I'll listen without prejudice, I swear. There is nothing you can tell me that would change how I feel about you. You're my wife, the mother of my children."

His words wilted her. Tears formed in her eyes, but she made no move to wipe them away. He was such a good man, such a good husband. Could she tell him? After all these years, could she tell him the truth about what had happened that day? In her mind, she could see Zoe Evans' body like it was yesterday. She looked so small and vulnerable lying there in the creek, the shallow water turning red from all the blood . . .

"Let's go away," she said. "On holiday. We haven't been abroad since the twins were little. We could go to that villa in Spain for a few weeks. Or a month, even better. We can afford it."

Laurie recoiled. "We can afford it financially, perhaps. But what about this new contract with Michael? What about the stables, the glamping site? Aren't you booked up until the end of September?"

He was right; she was. But, to her, this seemed the perfect solution. If they got out of England for a while, then with any luck Stacey would be found by the time they got back. She couldn't terrorise her if she was in another country.

"Please, darling. We can make it work. Can't you delay the build with Michael for a month? I can get Melissa or Elenore to watch the yurts, I can pay them. And as far as the horses are concerned, we can hire someone to look after them as well. Sarah from the farm did it that time when we went to your parent's house for Christmas."

"I don't know. It's a lot of upheavals," Laurie replied. He was tapping his wedding ring on the granite surface of the island. A sure-fire sign that he was stressed.

"Please Laur. I need to get away. I need a change of scenery. This place is getting to me."

"Tell me what's going on with you and I might feel more inclined to go along with it," he said. "Why won't you talk to me? Is it that bad?"

"Yes. It is. Please, Laurie, we talked about this forever when we first got together. I thought you'd accepted that I never want to bring up the past. It's a different lifetime ago. It happened to someone else. Not me. The person I was then isn't who I am now."

"Jesus, it sounds like you killed someone or something."

Her heart felt like it had stopped. An icy chill ran down her back. "Don't be stupid," she stammered when she could get her words out. "I didn't kill anyone."

"Then what? Jesus. I don't even know who your parents were. Or what they did."

"I've told you. My mum was from Bangladesh. She was called Nadia too. My dad was Irish. He was called Gerry."

"Yes. Go on . . ."

She looked away. "Stop it. Please."

She was about to say more when she heard a terrible noise coming up from the stables. She looked back with wide eyes at Laurie. He'd heard it as well.

"Tudor," she gasped.

She ran for the door with Laurie behind her. In the hallway, she stepped into her boots and was out of the front door in seconds, racing down the drive towards the stables. Outside, the noise was louder and even more horrific, a deathly grunting and groaning sound, like the poor horse was fighting to breathe.

As Nadia got into the stables, she saw Tudor thrashing around in his stall. He looked to be in a trance, his enormous eyes were wild and unblinking, and he kept smashing his head into the side of the stall.

"Tudor! What's wrong?" Up close now, she could see white foam coming out of his mouth. He let out a terrifying whinny that reverberated around the stables, unsettling the other horses, who began stamping their hooves.

Nadia held her hand out to him, but he was thrashing too much. He looked desperate and in pain. When he glared at her, she could see fear in his eyes.

"What are you doing?" Laurie yelled as she went to unlatch the stall gate. "He could kick you to death right now. Don't go in there!"

She let go of the latch. He was right. But she had to do something. She pressed her hands together over her mouth like she was praying and watched in horror as her majestic stallion stumbled forward and crashed to the ground. She spun around and grabbed Laurie by the shirt.

"We need to get Dr Simmons out here," she cried. "Now!"

Chapter 19

Nadia couldn't stop pacing. She must have walked from the far side of the stable block to the side closest to the house over a hundred times in the last fifty minutes. Each time she returned to where Laurie and Andrew were standing, they'd appeal for her to slow down, to wait with them. But she didn't want to. She needed to feel like she was doing something. If you stood still in this life, you allowed the darkness to catch up with you. It was best to keep moving. It was safer that way.

Her poor Tudor. Dr Simmons had arrived about the same time that Andrew had stumbled down from the house, and his initial theory was that Tudor had been poisoned. Poisoned. Her beautiful stallion. Seeing him so frenzied had broken her heart. But to see him lying on the floor of his stall, fighting to breathe, was more pain than she could bear. He was so powerful, so strong. How did this happen?

"Nadia, stop, please," Laurie whispered as she walked back over. "This isn't helping anything."

Andrew stared at her with quizzical eyes. At least he knew better than to get her to stop. Either that or he was too scared to speak to her. She got to the far side of the stable and, like before, turned around and marched away from them. She knotted her hands into fists and her nails dug into her palms. Her bottom lip was numb and swollen where she'd been chewing on it.

It had to be Stacey. There was no doubt in her mind. She was here somewhere. Nadia raised her head, squinting through the gloom into the shrubs and undergrowth that surrounded her home.

Was she watching her right now, gloating at what she was putting her through?

Her mum and dad had been right about her all along. She was bad news. A troubled child with no chance of redemption. If only she'd listened to them all those years ago. If she had, none of this would have ever happened. She wouldn't have been down by the creek that day. Instead, she'd have been up in her room doing homework or painting. Like the girl they wanted her to be. A good girl. The girl she should have been.

She got to the end of the stable block and spun around to see Dr Simmons walking towards Laurie, pulling off a pair of off-white latex gloves. There was news. She quickened her pace, reaching her husband and son at the same time as the vet.

"What is it?" she gasped. "Will he . . .? Is he . . .?" Dr Simmons looked at Laurie and then at her. He had a grave expression on his face, which made her feel like she was about to throw up. "Oh, God! Oh no!"

"I'm sorry, Mrs Morgan. There was nothing I could do for him in the end. He's at peace."

"What happened?" Laurie asked, reaching an arm around Nadia's shoulders and trying to pull her close. "Can you tell us?"

Nadia shrugged his arm away. "He was poisoned. Wasn't he?" She glared at her husband. "Do you get it now? I'm not being paranoid. Someone poisoned him."

"I never said you were being paranoid," he hissed through gritted teeth, before turning back to Dr Simmons. "Is it true, doctor? Was it something he ate?"

"Or something he was given?" Nadia muttered.

Dr Simmons glanced between the two of them. She felt like grabbing his fat face and forcing him to look at her. Only her. Tudor was her horse. He was her baby. Why couldn't this stupid oaf get it through his thick head?

"We'll need to conduct a full toxicology report," he said. "But it is looking that way. I found remnants around his mouth of what I believe was hemlock. The plant is extremely poisonous to horses and causes death by cardiac arrest and asphyxiation. Which is what I believe happened here."

"Hemlock," Laurie repeated, glancing around him. "We don't have any growing around here. If we did, I'd have chopped it all down a few weeks ago when I cut everything back."

Dr Simmons nodded. "I was looking for it myself just now in the vicinity. But you are correct. I see none. And the remnants I found were crushed up as if they had been prepared before ingestion. Which does point to third-party involvement." He looked at Nadia and smiled cheerlessly before looking at the ground. "It is strange. But we should wait for the full toxicology report and autopsy before we jump to conclusions."

Nadia turned away and burst into tears. She couldn't believe it. Her Tudor. Her powerful stallion. Dead.

"Darling, come here," Laurie cooed, placing an arm around her. "Please don't cry."

With her eyes closed, she could hear Andrew shuffling and sensed Laurie nodding his head, probably telling him it was okay to go back to the house. She glanced up to see him walking away. Poor Andrew, he didn't need to see his mum like this.

"What will happen to him now?" she asked, looking past Dr Simmons into the stables. "To his body."

The vet coughed to clear his throat. "I can make arrangements for the carcass to be picked up. There are three options available to you. Group cremation is the usual choice. You won't receive any ashes, but it is the cheapest option. Then there is individual cremation, which is how it sounds and where you will get the ashes back. The third option, if the toxicology report comes back as I expect and there are no unnatural toxins found in his system, is that the hunt kennels over in Helston would dispose of the carcass."

Carcass.

Cremations.

It was too much for Nadia. She turned and buried her head in Laurie's chest. "We'll go for the individual cremation," he told Dr Simmons. "If you can arrange that for us, that would be great. Thank you."

"That is the costliest option, Mr Morgan."

A shudder of emotion rocked Nadia's body, and Laurie tightened his hold on her. "Money isn't an issue. We want the best for our Tudor."

"No problem. I need to make one last assessment for my files and then I will leave you in peace for tonight. I'll begin making the arrangements for his collection in the morning. And once again, Mrs Morgan – Mr Morgan – I am very sorry for your loss. When an animal such as Tudor dies, it is a terrible thing."

"Thank you," Laurie said and pressed his cheek against Nadia's head.

She pulled away from her husband's embrace to address the vet. "Thank you, doctor." She sniffed and wiped at her eyes with the heel of her hand. "I appreciate everything you've done for him."

Dr Simmons bowed his head before waddling away into the stables. Nadia turned back to Laurie.

"This wasn't an accident," she whispered. "I know it wasn't."

He frowned. "I agree that it's peculiar. But that doesn't mean the hemlock couldn't have made its way into his feed somehow. Perhaps we need to speak to our suppliers and see if—"

"No, Laurie! Someone did this. Someone poisoned him."

"But why?"

She pushed him away. "Because they want to get to me. They want to hurt me, Laurie. They want to destroy the things I care about."

"Who does? Who are you talking about, Nadia?"

She inhaled a deep breath, which provided her with enough resolve that she could continue. "Someone from my past. Someone who thinks I wronged her. It happened a long time ago, but she's only been out of prison for a year. She must have been planning her revenge all this time. You think Marge's death and Tudor's injury were accidents, but they weren't, Laurie. She did it."

"What are you talking about?" He grabbed her by the tops of her arms and stared into her eyes. "Darling, slow down. Tell me who you're talking about."

She gasped for air. She'd been speaking in a rapid staccato fashion, trying to get her words out before reason and fear could stop her. She closed her eyes to stop the intrusive thoughts on the cusp of her awareness from forming.

"I'll explain everything, darling. I promise. I know I sound cryptic and like a crazy person, but I'm not. And this can't go on any longer." She shook him off and began walking back to the house.

"Nadia!" Laurie caught up with her as she strode defiantly up the driveway. "What is going on? Where are you going?"

"To call the police," she said. "This has gone far enough. I have to speak to someone about what I know. Tudor and Marge did nothing wrong. But she's an evil person. She always was. My mum and dad were right about her. If I'd only listened to them . . ." She wiped at her eyes but didn't slow down. "She's here, Laurie. She's doing what she told me she would. And we have to stop her before she hurts anyone else."

THEN . . .

3 August 2001

It was the middle of the school summer holidays and Tahani was bored. Bored, bored, bored. Bored and frustrated. She'd completed the homework assignments set by her teachers in the first week and now – with her television time limited as always – she was stuck in the house with nothing to do.

Her mum and dad acted like it was her fault. "Go out and play with your friends," they'd say. "You don't want to be stuck in the house all holiday."

What they didn't realise was that she didn't have any friends. Not from school. The only friend she had was Stacey, and their ban on Tahani seeing her was still firmly in place.

The fact it had been raining for most of the holiday was hardly a consolation. The miserable grey skies only seemed to compound Tahani's sadness. She had a raincoat with a hood, she could have played with friends. Or, at least gone for a walk, to get some exercise and fresh air. But she couldn't even do that. Zoe Evans lived a twenty-minute walk away and the likelihood of running into her was low, but just the thought of doing so kept Tahani inside and afraid. She was thirteen and full of energy. This was no way to live.

Today the rain had stopped a few hours ago, and the skies were a wash of pale blue, dotted here and there with thick powder puffs of white cloud. Now and then, even the sun made an appearance from behind the clouds, as if mocking her or coaxing her outside.

"Why don't you go out, darling? It's a lovely day."

She turned from her bedroom window to see her mum standing in the doorway. She wrinkled up her nose. "Is everything okay with you?"

"Yes. Fine."

"Why are you inside on such a lovely day? Why not ring one of your friends and see if they want to do something? Or invite them over. You never bring anyone home. Are you embarrassed about me and your father?"

"No. Of course not." Tahani moved over to her bed, flopping down on top of it and staring at the ceiling. "But my friends from school all live across town. You won't let me off this street."

"That's not true. We just want you to let us know where you're going, so we don't worry."

"It doesn't matter anyway." Tahani sat up and pulled her legs up to her chest, wrapping her arms around the front of her calves. When she sensed her mum was still staring at her, she added, "All my friends are away on holiday."

Her mum didn't answer right away. Tahani held onto her legs, not looking at her. She felt stupid and shameful and angry but had no idea how to deal with any of those feelings.

"Fine," her mum said and sighed. "Well, I'm going to the shops. Do you want to come with me?"

"No."

"Are you sure?"

She buried her head into her knees. "I'm fine. Just leave me."

"Maybe when I get back, we can do something together?"

"Like what?"

"I don't know. We could do some baking? I can teach you how to make those parathas you like." It was her dad who was the affectionate one, but she knew her mum's stern and stiff manner was only because of her strict upbringing. And she was trying, Tahani knew that. This was her reaching out.

"Maybe," she said, offering the slightest of smiles as she looked at her.

"Great. I may be gone a few hours. Is that okay? I'm meeting Paula for a coffee as well."

"Fine."

Her mum nodded and backed out onto the landing. Tahani waited until she heard her descending the stairs before sliding off her bed and returning to the window. The world outside looked as inviting as ever. She remained there, staring out onto the street until she heard the front door open and then close again. Her mum walked down the path and looked both ways as she got to the street. She had that same scowl on her face that she always had. Even at the music recital at the start of the year, she'd had that same expression on her face. It had almost thrown Tahani off her clarinet rendition of Debussy's *Première Rhapsodie,* but she knew it was just how her mum was. She rarely showed emotions. But that didn't mean she didn't feel them. She was a good mum. She cared.

Although Tahani was sad and bored and the loneliest she'd ever felt, she knew her mum and dad were only keeping her from Stacey because they thought it was the best for her. They loved her and cared about her well-being, and she had to respect their wishes. The last thing she ever wanted to do was let them down. Doing that would be worse than anything Zoe would do to her. Well, almost anything.

She was about to go downstairs and watch some forbidden television when she noticed someone across the street. They were waving up at her window. As her awareness left her confusing teenage thoughts behind and focused outwards, she saw it was Stacey. She was standing in the snicket that ran between number ten and twelve on the opposite side of the street. Stacey's house was number sixteen and the fact she was a few feet back from the road made Tahani wonder if she'd been hiding there, waiting for her mum to leave. She was still waving and when Tahani raised her hand to wave back, Stacey beckoned her outside, gesturing frantically and pointing at the ground.

"No, I can't," Tahani mouthed at her. "I've got to stay in."

Stacey sneered and gestured for her to open the window.

"Are you coming out?" she called up once Tahani complied. She crossed over the road so she was standing at the end of their path.

"I'm not supposed to," Tahani told her. "My mum said . . ."

"She's gone out, hasn't she? Come on. It's so warm. Get yourself down here."

Tahani faltered. She wanted to. But if her parents found out, they'd be so angry and disappointed. "I don't know . . . What are you doing?"

"Going to the creek. Come on, it'll be fun."

The creek. She hadn't been since they moved here, but she'd heard other kids talking about it. It was where people went to smoke and drink the alcohol they'd stolen from their dads' drinks cabinets. She'd often wondered what it was like. She glanced over her shoulder. Her mum had said she'd be a few hours.

"Okay," she called down. "Wait for me."

* * *

The walk to the creek took them around twenty minutes, but it was so nice to be outside with the sun on her face. Tahani practically glided there. The suburban streets soon turned to vast green fields and the sandstone brick of the houses turned to endless dry stone walls as they marched on to their destination. As they swished through the long grass, sticking to the places where it had been trampled down by those who had gone before, she and Stacey talked about what they'd been doing since they last saw each other. Stacey was supposed to visit her dad, but the trip had fallen through, she said. She didn't seem too bothered by that, but it was hard to tell how she felt beneath her tough exterior. In turn, Tahani told her about school and how rubbish everyone was, even putting her mum and dad into that category, explaining how strict and unfair they'd been with her television viewing. She felt a twinge of something unpleasant in her stomach as she badmouthed them this way – something she'd never done or dreamed of doing – but, being with Stacey, she felt liberated and free and like she could say whatever she wanted without judgement. Either that or she was saying what she suspected the older girl wanted her to say. It was difficult to know sometimes.

Stacey didn't mention the fact that they hadn't hung out for the last three months - ever since her visit to the police station - but there was something about the way she acted that told Tahani she knew the reason.

"You know they never charged me for throwing the Coke can at that Hughes lad. No arrest. No caution even. It was a load of nonsense."

"Oh. Good," Tahani mumbled, unsure what else to say.

"He was fine after anyway, wasn't he? No bother." She chuckled and nudged Tahani. "He deserved it, though. The little shit. That's the thing, Hani, you've got to show these losers who's boss. Same with you and that miserable bitch. What's her name again?"

"Zoe," she said. "Zoe Evans."

"Zoe fucking Evans. I'm telling ya, Han. Next time she tries anything, you need to smack her in the face as hard as you can. Bust her stupid nose. You won't have any problems with her after that."

They got up to a stile that someone had built over the stone-wall and Stacey clambered over into the next field. This grass in this field was shorter than in the others and the land sloped down considerably. As Tahani stepped up onto the wooden plinth, she could see a row of tall trees and what looked like an old stone bridge.

"Nearly there," Stacey said, helping her down onto the other side. "The stream starts at the bottom of this field."

They trudged on without comment, Stacey leading the way and Tahani skipping along in her wake. Horse flies and midges fluttered into her face, but she brushed them away without fuss. She was just happy to be out in the fresh air, enriched with the buoyancy that being with Stacey always provided.

"It's so pretty down here," she said as they reached the bottom of the field and peered over the wall. On the other side, the terrain dropped into a flat basin about the size of a football pitch. The actual creek started from an underground source parallel to the field they were standing in. The water snaked around the basin in a shallow stream only a few feet wide before opening out under the stone bridge she'd seen from the upper field.

"Come on," Stacey called, setting off. "I was down here the other day and I saw loads of frogspawn. They might have hatched now. We can grab the tadpoles and pop their heads. It's well funny."

Tahani wasn't sure about that. It sounded cruel and not funny at all. But, regardless, she followed her friend down to the creek, leading with her right foot and steadying herself with her left as she skidded down onto the level ground. Once there, she froze.

Stacey spun around to glare at her. "What wrong?"

Tahani hadn't realised she'd made a sound, but an impulsive yelp of fear must have escaped her. Stacey was staring at her as if she'd just let out a blood-curdling scream.

"What is it?" she asked.

Tahani opened her mouth, but no words came. Instead, she pointed across to the other side of the basin, where a lone figure was sitting on a rock. As she backed away up the hillside, the figure lowered the can that they'd been drinking from and sat upright. It was Zoe Evans. She'd seen her at the same time. Getting to her feet, she chucked the can into the creek and walked over.

No . . .!

Why was this happening now? Today was about finding fun, a release from the grim reality of her life. All she wanted was a pleasant walk in the countryside. What the hell was Zoe doing here?

Stacey had seen her as well. "Hey, hey," she said, patting the air, meaning for Tahani to calm down. "You don't need to be scared of her. She's nothing. Look at the fucking state of her, anyway. Come back down and stand up to her."

Tahani's heart was beating so fast she could hardly concentrate, but she did as Stacey said, shuffling down to join her by the side of the creek. Her skin bristled with a thousand goosebumps. "Stacey, let's go," she whispered as Zoe jumped over part of the creek and headed over to them. "I don't want to stand up to her. I can't . . . I just want to go home . . ."

"No! Wait!"

Zoe was now a few metres away and up close, Tahani saw her face was scarlet and blotchy. Her eyes, too, were red, as if she had bad hay fever. Either that or she'd been crying. But why on Earth would she have been crying? This was Zoe Evans. She was tough and confident, one of the most popular girls in her year.

She jutted her chin out at Tahani. "What are you doing here, mongrel?" Her words came out a little slurred like she couldn't get her mouth around the middle consonants. Tahani hadn't mixed with any drunk people up to this point, but she recognised the signs from the television. “This is my place. My creek. You don’t get to come here.”

Tahani glanced at Stacey, but she wasn’t doing anything. She’d stepped to one side to allow Zoe a clear line of sight of her. But why? Stacey was supposed to be her protector. Her friend . . .

“I’m sorry. I didn’t know,” Tahani replied. “We’ll go.”

Zoe stepped towards her. She was now so close that Tahani could smell the alcohol on her breath. It was sour and sickly and made her feel nauseous.

“You’re a fucking dirty pig. Do you know that? You’re a fucking dirty half-caste bitch.” Spittle foamed at the corners of her mouth. Her eyes were wide and intense and Tahani had to look at her feet, unable to hold her gaze. “You think you’re better than me, don’t ya? Eh? You think cos your parents are rich, and you get good grades and play that big stupid recorder that you’re something special. But you’re not. You’re nothing but a dirty half-caste bitch. And you stink.”

Tahani didn’t look up. Her entire body was shaking with tension. She could sense Stacey watching the exchange. She could hear her voice in her head, telling her to hit back, to stand up to Zoe. But she couldn’t. She was too weak. She’d never hit anyone in her life.

Zoe stepped up and barged into her with her chest. Tahani stumbled back a step.

“Leave her alone, Zoe.”

Finally!

She drew her arms around herself, waiting for Stacey to step between them.

Nothing happened.

"Fuck off, Wilson," Zoe snarled back. "This has nothing to do with you. Why don't you piss off? It's between me and her."

She snatched at Tahani's t-shirt, grabbing a handful of her skin at the same time and making her cry out. "Please," she whined. "I'll go away. I didn't realise you were here."

"Yeah, well, I am. And it's too late."

She yanked at the shirt and Tahani stumbled into her, screwing up her face and bracing herself for the inevitable pain that was to come via Zoe's fist. Through the hair that had fallen over her face, she could see Stacey standing a few feet away. She was shaking her head as if she'd had enough, but whether she was annoyed with Zoe or dismayed at Tahani's pathetic attempt at standing up for herself, it was unclear. But Tahani needed her. She really needed her. Now more than ever before.

"Stacey," she whimpered. "Help me. Please."

Chapter 20

"But you don't know what name Stacey Wilson is going under now?"

The police officer – Officer Sara Bailey, she'd introduced herself as – gave Nadia an empathetic smile. But it was too forced, too over the top, to be anything other than a tactic from a police-client-liaison manual.

She shook her head in response to the officer's question. "No. I don't. I shouldn't even know about her missing her supervision appointments, but I'm still in contact with someone from that time. It was her who told me."

Officer Bailey glanced at her colleague, a male officer with thinning black hair. He'd introduced himself outside when the two police cars had arrived, but she couldn't remember his name. The look he and Officer Bailey exchanged gave nothing away, but through her current frame of mind, Nadia viewed them suspiciously.

"Do you think I'm crazy?" she asked.

"No, of course they don't," Laurie butted in, leaning over and placing his hand on her lower thigh. "They're just trying to understand all the details. We all are."

She stiffened. He didn't need to say that last part. It was a dig at her. But she let it go. There were bigger issues right now. She adjusted her position on the sofa, not brushing her husband's hand away, but not leaning into it either. Officer Bailey was sitting on their new regency-style high-backed armchair in dusky pink, the one Nadia loved but Laurie was uncertain about. She'd shunted the chair around so she was facing the couple, while her colleague stood behind her, peering into a notebook with a confused expression on his face.

"We just need to better understand the situation, Nadia," she said. "What reason has this person to poison your horse?"

Nadia blew out a long breath. How did she even start with Laurie sitting right next to her? The tension coming off him was palpable. It would be unfair for her to think he was enjoying this, but he still had questions and tonight he might get his answers.

She glanced out the window. There they still were, gawping up at the house. The Snowdons. Or, rather, Mr Snowdon and Ms Bradley. They'd been walking past the house on their way back to their yurt when the police had turned up. Louise had *oohed* and *aahed* as Laurie had explained to them about Tudor, giving her best, middle-class version of concern. But Nadia knew she was just being nosey. Now she was standing in the bottom field, squinting up at the house. She probably thought the toilet block concealed her from view, but from her position on the couch, Nadia could see her. Once again, she wondered about Louise, and this time she let the thoughts multiply rather than dismissing them as the notions of a paranoid fool.

Because why not? She was certain now Stacey was out there and until she was found, she could trust no one. Louise Bradley was the right age, she had the right colour hair, she even had the right face shape, sort of, if you accounted for ageing.

"Nadia?" Officer Bailey's voice snatched her from her thoughts. "Are you okay?"

She coughed. "Yes. Sorry. I've just got a lot on my mind right now. Can you repeat the question?"

"I was asking if you could relay to us why you believe Stacey Wilson is responsible for the death of your horse."

"And our cat." The words came out harsher sounding than she'd intended, and Laurie let out a humph of embarrassment as he nudged her side with his elbow.

"I know it's difficult, darling. And something you've pushed down inside for many years. But the police need to know what you know."

She nodded and stared into her open palms. This was it, then. She was going to go there. She inhaled a long breath and began. "It was twenty years ago, the summer of two-thousand-and-one when Stacey and I were involved in a terrible tragedy. A girl died. Down at the creek near where I used to live. In Bradford. There was a big court case. We both did time for it." She braced as she said the words, but Laurie didn't react, or at least, not audibly. She didn't dare look at him as she continued. "The girl was called Zoe Evans. They found Stacey guilty of murder and me of being an accessory. I'm sorry. I'm so sorry." She closed her eyes. She didn't know if she was talking to her husband or the police or even Zoe Evans. When she opened her eyes, she saw that everyone in the room was staring at her. Waiting. "I've not spoken, or even thought, about this for a long time," she went on. "I just wanted to put it all behind me. I was only thirteen, so I went to a secure training centre. But Stacey went to a proper prison. I think that's part of the reason she's so angry. The last thing she ever said to me was she was going to get me."

Office Bailey frowned. Her colleague scribbled in his notepad. "What happened, Nadia, down at the creek? Can you tell us?"

She closed her eyes and drew in a deep breath. They needed more. She had to make them see this was serious. Her entire family was in danger.

"You probably don't remember the case," she said. "It was over twenty years ago now. It was on the front page of a few of the papers when it happened, but it wasn't one of those stories that ran and ran. Nine Eleven had just happened, so that took precedence. I don't think anyone covered the outcome of the trial in too much detail. At least, I was told not." She exhaled, trying to control her breathing. Her hands were shaking more than she'd ever known them to. She was like someone from a silly cartoon who'd just seen a ghost.

Laurie cleared his throat and gave her leg a gentle squeeze. "It's okay, darling. Take your time."

Was that another dig at her? She didn't look at him. In front of her, Officer Bailey was leaning forward, regarding her with sympathetic eyes, urging her to go on. "We will search the database once back at the station, Nadia, but anything you can tell us now is very helpful. Our colleagues are down at the barn dusting for fingerprints, but as there was no visible sign of a break-in . . ." she trailed off.

It's a stable, not a barn, Nadia wanted to tell her, but she didn't. Instead, she looked at her hands. They were still shaking, and she clasped them together to stop them. She was suddenly aware of how quiet the house was. Andrew was in his room, probably listening at his door as you'd expect from any curious thirteen-year-old. Melissa had taken the twins down to her house to give them supper. She'd offered to put them to bed in their spare room as well, but Nadia had a sudden urge to collect them. They were her babies, and she wanted them close. It was safer that way. She couldn't trust people. No one.

But she needed to get rid of the police first. She raised her head and swallowed. "My name back then was Tahani Carroll," she said, and a ripple of nervous energy shot down her arms and legs. She looked at Laurie, pleading with him with her eyes not to hate her once this was over. He looked confused and angry, but at least he smiled as he met her gaze. She turned back to Officer Bailey. "My social worker advised I change my name when I got out of the secure care centre. I was there for four years. My parents both died whilst I was inside, so I was on my own at seventeen. I was scared, unsure of what I was going to do with my life. A brand-new start as a new person made sense. Diane, my worker, arranged the paperwork and a few weeks after my eighteenth birthday I became Nadia Kelly." She looked at Laurie. "And that's who I've been ever since. I'm sorry I never told you, but Tahani Carroll is somebody I wanted to leave behind. I don't want to think about that person, and what she was involved in, ever again."

Officer Bailey hit her with another empathetic smile, but there was now a sense of impatience behind her eyes. She wanted more. She wanted the full story.

"I was bullied a lot at school. I was small for my age and I guess more academic than a lot of the children in my year. They labelled me a swot and a teacher's pet. But there was one group of girls especially, led by Zoe Evans, who made my life a living hell. Zoe latched onto the fact that I was mixed race and that became her focus. There were lots of other Asian kids at that school, Pakistanis, Indians, and even some from Bangladesh, like my mum's family, but they were pure-bloods, and they stuck together. The Asian kids didn't accept me and neither did the white kids. Plus, they thought my dad was rich for some reason, which he really wasn't. He just cared about his family and worked hard to provide for us." She sniffed as a torrent of unexpected emotions washed over her. A tear ran down her cheek, but she made no move to wipe it away. It was penance. A sign of her secret inner world moving into the light. She went on. "Zoe Evans bullied me continuously for an entire year. In the end, I was suicidal and so full of shame I didn't know what to do. The school was no help. The teachers didn't seem to notice or didn't care. Beck Hill it was called." She nodded at the male officer, who hurriedly scribbled this down in his notepad.

"What happened between you and Zoe Evans?" Office Bailey asked.

Laurie gripped Nadia's hand. "She was horrible," she said, seeing Zoe's sneering face in her mind. "She turned the entire year against me. I was a pariah. But there was physical abuse as well. She'd throw rocks at me on my way home. One time, she beat me to the ground and spat in my mouth. I've not told anyone that before." Beside her, Laurie exhaled audibly down his nose, like he was trying to stay calm and he wanted her to know it. She ignored him and focused on Officer Bailey. "Stacey Wilson was my only friend. She was the only person who seemed to like me for me. She'd attended Beck Hill, but got expelled before I moved to the area and so went to a different school across the other side of town. They used to send a taxi for her, to make sure she'd attend. The council paid for it. I think. She was also a few years older than me, and tough. When we became friends, I felt like I'd found a guardian angel, or a bodyguard, as well as a friend. I felt safe and had someone who understood me a bit more. We were two outcasts together, I suppose. That's how we saw it. Stacey knew that Zoe Evans was bullying me and used to encourage me to stand up for myself. But I never did. I was too weak and scared." She exhaled consciously, similarly to how Laurie had done. It helped calm her, for what she knew was coming. "Then one day in August two thousand and one we were playing down by the creek. Stacey wanted to show me some frogspawn she'd found down there. But Zoe was there too. She was just sitting on her own, drinking a can of cider, I think. I remember she looked like she'd been crying. But I don't know why. She got angry when she saw me. Really angry. She came over and started on me like she always did, calling me names and pushing me about. Even with Stacey there, I was terrified. I thought she was going to hurt me." She paused, her mind racing as the events of that day ploughed through her memory. Even after all this time, she found it hard to make sense of it all. She saw Zoe's angry face. She saw Stacey standing behind her with her arms raised . . .

She shook her head to disperse the images forming in her mind and looked into Officer Bailey's eyes. The world turned into a tunnel, and she imagined it was just the two of them. Laurie was gone. He couldn't hear her. "The next thing I knew, Zoe was lying in the creek with blood pouring from her head," she whispered. "The water all around her was bright red."

"Shit," Laurie whispered. "And it was Stacey?"

Nadia nodded and placed her head on his shoulder. "It all happened so fast. It was horrible."

The male police officer cleared his throat. He sounded congested, but as Nadia looked up at him, she sensed he was losing patience.

"The police reports from the case can corroborate all this," he said. "And clearly it was a terrible time for all concerned. But this is a historic case that was completed and went to trial. What I'm finding hard to understand is why you think Stacey Wilson is now trying to hurt you. You were friends, no?"

"We were," Nadia said. "But she thinks I let her down."

"What do you mean?"

"Yes," Laurie said, leaning away from her slightly. "What do you mean? What did you do?"

There was that question again. Like he was accusing her of something. Did he not know her?

Did she not know him?

She sat upright and regarded each of them, Laurie and then the two officers. They were staring at her like she had the answers to life itself, but she'd already accepted they wouldn't like what she had to say.

"I broke the pact," she muttered. "We had a pact, me and Stacey. And I broke it. That's why she hates me. That's why she's tracked me down here. That's why she wants to make me pay."

THEN . . .

4 August 2001

Tahani was upstairs in her bedroom when the knock on the door came. It was the day after what had happened at the creek and she had hoped that she might get a few days of grace before the inevitable happened. But she knew it was coming. The knock was loud and abrupt, as if whoever was knocking meant business. She sat upright on her bed. The clock on her table told her it was a few minutes past nine. She'd only woken up a few minutes earlier. The knocking went again. Bang-bang-bang. In perfect time to her racing heartbeat.

It was the police. It had to be.

She slipped off her bed and tiptoed along the landing to the top of the stairs, ears alert to the sounds drifting up from downstairs. She heard her mum and dad in the hallway, whispering at each other. The bottom of the stairs faced the back of the house and you had to turn a corner to approach the front door, so she couldn't see who was there as the door opened and a draft of cool air shot up through the house. Her dad said something she couldn't make out. Then she heard unfamiliar voices, men's voices. There were two of them, one voice deeper than the other, but she couldn't pick out what anybody was saying. Her dad sounded confused. Her mum sounded outraged. She was probably telling the policemen that they had the wrong house, that her daughter would never be involved in anything remotely illegal.

But as she waited there, not daring to breathe, trying to pick out recognisable words in the conversation, she heard the door close and her mum's head appeared around the bottom of the stairs. As she looked up, Tahani stepped back, pressing herself against the wall of the landing.

"Tahani," her mum called up. "Can you come down here, please?"

Then her dad's voice. "Tahani! Down here! Now!"

She slid out from her hiding place and, gripping the handrail tight to allow for her jittery legs, made her way downstairs. Her mum and dad were standing shoulder to shoulder at the bottom of the stairs. Both stared at her as she got closer, looking for a sign of guilt, perhaps. Their eyes bulged out of their heads and their mouths turned down in a disappointed expression.

"The police are here," her mum hissed. "They want to talk to you."

She nodded but didn't know what to say. Her dad placed his hand on her shoulder and guided her down the hallway to the kitchen. There were two enormous men already sitting at the table. They were both wearing white shirts and ties and one of them had on a beige rain mac. She'd imagined them to be dressed in police uniforms – like the ones who had taken Stacey away – so the sight of them in plain clothes threw her even more. Were they the police? Or was this something else? Both men turned to look at her and a shiver ran down her arms and legs. She was still wearing her Powerpuff Girls pyjamas and crossed her arms over her chest as they looked her up and down. Her dad squeezed her shoulder gently, and they went into the kitchen together.

"Tahani, is it?" one of the men said in a broad Yorkshire accent. He looked to be the older of the two. He had short, grey hair and a round face. As he stood up from the table, he towered over both her mum and dad. His belly was enormous and hung over his trousers, causing the bottom of his shirt to bulge open, revealing a white vest beneath. "I'm DC Richards and this is my colleague, DC Stanhope. We're Detective Constables, investigating a serious crime that's taken place. Are you okay to sit down for me, please?"

He sat down and gestured at the chair opposite him. Tahani didn't move. She couldn't. Her legs didn't belong to her. It felt like she was floating a few feet above herself, watching the events unfurl but without being able to do anything to stop them. With her dad's hand still on her shoulder, he walked her over to the chair and pulled it out for her.

"Sit down, darling," he whispered. "It'll be okay."

She looked up at him, and he smiled, but she could see he was scared as well. She'd never seen her dad look that way and it sent another shiver of nervous energy shooting down her back.

"Do you know why we're here, Tahani?" DC Richards asked once she was settled.

She glanced at her mum and dad. They looked back at her with solemn faces and her mum nodded at her. *Tell them.*

Turning back to DC Richards, Tahani shrugged. "I don't know." Her voice was hoarse and quiet. She needed a drink of milk. Her stomach rumbled.

"Are you sure you aren't mistaken?" her mum added. "Tahani is a good girl. She has hardly left our house the whole of the holidays."

Neither of the officers responded. They didn't even look at her mum. DC Richards placed his hands on the table in front of him and clasped his hands together. "Do you know Zoe Evans, Tahani?"

She nodded slowly. DC Richards glanced at DC Stanhope next to him.

"When was the last time you saw Zoe?"

She shrugged. "Not sure."

"Well, I'm sorry to have to tell you this, but yesterday evening, Zoe Evans was found dead. Down by the creek." He paused and tapped his hands on the table. "Do you know what happened to her, Tahani?"

No.

This could not be happening.

She felt cold. Her throat hurt. She needed air. She looked at her parents. Their expressions hadn't changed since the last time she looked at them.

"Were you down at the creek yesterday afternoon at around two?" DC Richards asked.

Tahani didn't take her eyes off her mum. What did she say to that question? She'd got back home yesterday before her mum returned from the shops. She didn't know she'd left. She didn't know . . .

"Tahani?"

Her dad nodded at her. *Answer the question.*

Turning back to the policemen, she was met with grim stares. Any amicableness they'd displayed as she sat down was now gone. She swallowed. She'd never felt so alone in all her life.

"Were you down at the creek yesterday afternoon, Tahani?"

She nodded. "Yes." The word was barely audible because of her dry throat. "I was there."

"I see. And who were you with?"

She ran her tongue across the back of her top lip. Stacey's words echoed in her head. The pact. When she'd explained it yesterday, it all seemed so clear to her, so easy. But she hadn't countered on the harsh reality of being questioned by two surly policemen.

"Stacey Wilson," she croaked.

"Thank you, Tahani. I'm glad you told me that because someone has already identified you both as being there at that time."

"Who saw her?" her mum piped up and DC Richards visibly tensed.

"A neighbour of yours," he replied, shooting her a brief smile. "I won't divulge who at this stage, but they've gone on record to say that they saw Tahani and two other girls involved in an altercation. Now they were some distance away, on the top path, so couldn't see exactly what happened, but they said it looked heated. Was the third girl Zoe Evans, Tahani?"

She looked down at the table, focusing on a dark swirling knot in the wood. It looked like an angry face if you stared at it the right way.

"Tahani, we can do this here or at the station." It was DC Stanhope talking now. His accent was posher than DC Richards'.

It made him seem sterner, too. As she glanced up at him, he addressed her parents. "I'll be honest with you, Tahani will have to come with us anyway, but if she tells us what we need to know now, things will go a lot easier and smoother." He turned back to Tahani. "Your cooperation will be noted. Do you understand?"

She nodded and returned her attention to the angry knot.

"What happened, Tahani? What happened to Zoe Evans?"

"I don't know."

She could hear Stacey's voice in her head. She'd gone over the story with her three times as they'd trudged back home. Tahani couldn't really remember the journey, but she must have walked home because one minute she was staring down at Zoe, lying in the creek, and the next thing she knew she was on her bed with the covers pulled up over her head.

"You've told us you were there, Tahani. You and Zoe and Stacey were arguing. What happened next?"

She could hear Stacey in her head, telling her to keep quiet. Remember the pact. She glanced at DC Richards and DC Stanhope. Then at her mum and dad. Her poor parents. How could she do this to them? Their only daughter, mixed up in something like this.

If only she hadn't gone out with Stacey yesterday. They'd told her not to. They'd forbidden her to see her.

Why hadn't she gone to town with her mum instead?

Her dad cleared his throat. "Tahani, darling. If you know something, you need to tell the policemen about it. Tell them what happened. What did you do? What did Stacey Wilson do?"

Keep to the story, Hani, and we'll be fine.

It's the only way.

"What happened to Zoe, Tahani?" DC Richards asked.

We have to stick together. Do you understand?

This will be our pact.

She looked at her mum and dad. Tears were pouring down her face. She couldn't do it. She couldn't do it to them. They were her mum and dad.

"Okay," she told DC Richards. "I'll tell you what happened. I'll tell you everything."

Chapter 21

Officer Bailey and her colleague bade Nadia and Laurie farewell and said they'd contact them the minute they heard anything. They were going to contact West Yorkshire once back at their desks and see what they could share with them in relation to Stacey Wilson's disappearance.

Try not to worry, they told Nadia. But that was easier said than done. They didn't know Stacey.

She remained on the couch as Laurie walked the two officers to the front door. She heard them talking in the hallway, but couldn't hear what they were saying. In her paranoid state, she imagined them telling Laurie to keep a watch on her. They'd believed her story, but whether they believed Stacey was behind Tudor's death was another matter. A few times she'd caught the male officer looking at her like she was crazy.

Maybe she was. She was starting to feel that way.

She heard the front door close and then Laurie's footsteps walking back into the kitchen at the far end of the open-plan room. She didn't turn around to look at him but could picture the scene. Him at the far end of the island, standing with his hands pressed down on the granite worktop, shoulders hunched up around his ears. It was his default place to stand when stressed and considering his next move. She waited. When he didn't speak, she twisted around on the couch to discover she'd been right. His head was lowered and his long, sandy-blonde fringe hung over his face.

"Say something, then."

He shook his head and sighed. He didn't look up.

"Laurie?"

He shrugged. "Do we need to get the twins?"

"Fuck, Laurie! We need to talk." She hardly ever swore. Especially not the F-word. Even now, with all the stress and anxiety, she felt a twinge of guilt. She could almost hear her mum tutting in her head. "I'll ring Melissa and ask her if she'll put them to bed over there. She's already offered, so . . ." She inhaled to steady her nerves. "What do you think?"

"What do I think? Jesus Christ. I think that's rather a lot of information to take in at one go. You killed a girl."

"No! I didn't!" she cried. "Please don't think that, Laurie. I didn't say that. Stacey did it! Zoe was going to hurt me, and she hit her with a rock. She didn't mean to kill her, she was just trying to stop her."

Over the years Nadia had gone through many different emotions regarding Zoe Evans' death. For a long time, it was guilt and anger that were the overriding feelings whenever she thought of her. She was wracked with despair and spent many sleepless nights going over that day, wishing things had played out differently, imagining they had. But it was no way to live and there had come a point, not long after she met Laurie, when she'd made a new pact, with herself this time. If she was to have a normal life, she told herself, then she needed to put what happened behind her. It was horrible and tragic what happened to Zoe, but Tahani Carroll had paid the price for her involvement. It was down to Nadia to find a way to move forward.

They say you honour the dead by living a good life.

They also say living a good life is the best revenge.

Most of the time, it felt to Nadia as if that day at the creek had happened to someone else. Not her. And that was partly true. Now, when she thought of what transpired on that fateful day, it was as if she was remembering an old film rather than actual events.

Did they call that disassociation?

Or was it just self-preservation? She didn't know.

"But you were going to cover it up?" Laurie said, not leaving it alone.

Nadia sighed. "I was thirteen. I was terrified. I didn't know what to do. Stacey was older, tougher, and more streetwise. She told me what we should do, and I went with it. At first. But you heard what I just told Officer Bailey. I confessed in the end. I told the police everything. But that was just the start of my problems."

Laurie raised his head. His eyes were red and when he met her gaze, it was like he hated her. Her heart crumbled to dust at that moment. The same way it had done when her mum and dad first heard what happened. How could she put these people, who she loved and who loved her, through such torment?

"Stacey was standing up for me," she said. "And you've got to understand, Laurie. Zoe was horrible. She'd made my life an absolute misery for months. I was suicidal. She made me want to die."

"So, she deserved to die?"

"No, I'm not saying that! But . . . Oh, I don't know! Please, darling, don't hate me. I could never bear that. This is why I never told you what happened. I can't have you looking at me that way."

"What way?"

"Like you hate me." She wiped at her eyes with her hand. "Remember that I was a kid, Laurie. I was Andrew's age, but so much more inexperienced and scared and timid. Stacey was older. She said it'd be all alright if we stuck to her pact. If I told the police what she'd told me to say. But I couldn't do it. So I told them what had happened, about Stacey and the rock."

"That's something, at least." He pushed off the island and walked over to the couch. Nadia shuffled over so he could join her, but he made no move to sit. Instead, he stared out of the window, nibbling on his top lip.

"What do we do now?" she asked.

"We wait, I suppose. And see what the police come up with. If you're certain Stacey is the one responsible for Tudor being poisoned, then they'll find her. But doesn't it sound a little far-fetched? I mean, if she was so angry, why not confront you herself? Why play these sadistic games?"

"Because that's what she's like. We were only going to the creek that day because she wanted to kill tadpoles. She was angry at the world even then. I can only imagine what she's like after twenty years in prison."

"What if it's not Stacey?" Laurie asked.

She had more to say, but his question made her forget what it was. "What?"

"You just said it. You can only imagine. But what if there's another explanation?" She shot him a look. She'd been waiting for him to say something like this. But as their eyes met, he held his hands up. "Hear me out here, okay? I'm not saying I don't believe you. Tudor being poisoned, Marge's grizzly death, maybe they weren't accidents. Maybe someone is trying to get back at you for something that you did in the past. But what if it's not Stacey doing it?"

Nadia frowned. "Then who could it be?"

"What if it's someone who knew Zoe? A family member. Someone looking for vengeance. She died in August two thousand and one, you said, and she was the same age as you, thirteen? So, her parents are probably only in their sixties. Young and able enough to do something like this if they were so inclined."

Whoa!

She'd been so caught up in her obsessive thinking about Stacey, that she hadn't even considered other options. But if Laurie's theory was correct, how had they found her? It was Stacey who'd broken into Diane's office and . . .

Oh . . .

Now she thought about it Diane hadn't said it was definitely Stacey who'd broken in. Her mind spun, trying to remember the details of their conversation. No. Stacey had visited her. *Then* she had a break-in. It was only Diane's assumption it was

Stacey who'd stolen her laptop. Nadia put her head in her hands as confusing and conflicting thoughts swirled around in her head. She frowned, trying to grasp hold of one coherent thread. But she couldn't. She was exhausted. She was confused. She couldn't breathe . . .

Shit . . .

She really couldn't breathe.

Gasping for air, she glanced around her, arms flailing wildly. Laurie was next to her in a second and placed an arm around her.

"Hey, hey, come on now, I'm here. Deep breaths." He twisted around in his seat to face her and demonstrated sitting upright, sticking his chest out. "Everything is fine. You're not in danger. That's it. Find your breath."

She flailed around some more but finally drew in a lungful of air.

"Do you really think it could be Zoe's parents doing this?" Her voice sounded like a little girl's voice. It annoyed her because she wasn't weak. Not anymore. And she certainly couldn't afford to be right now.

"I don't know. It's just an idea that came to me."

Nadia went up into her head, running through everyone she knew who might fit the role.

"Oh my God!" she whispered. "Mr Jameson. I thought there was something weird about that guy. The way he looks at me. What if it's—"

"Now, now. Let's not get ahead of ourselves and start accusing our guests of murdering our pets just yet. I'm only throwing it out there as a possibility. Did you know this Zoe girl's parents at all?"

She shook her head. "No. She didn't live that close by. But Laurie, she was horrible, you know. Really, really horrible. I used to lie awake at night worrying that she was going to seriously hurt me. Other nights I'd cry myself to sleep after something she'd said to me or done to me at school. She turned the entire year against me. Called me awful, racist names. Do you know how hard it is to fit in at a new school and then to have that put on you as well?"

He didn't. She knew he didn't. Laurie had gone to a posh school in Kent, which was probably the whitest school in England if his old school photos were any indication. Laurie Morgan had wanted for nothing and never felt hardship or fear in his life. How could he understand?

But then he smiled, and she hated herself even more for thinking that way. It wasn't his fault he was born into that life. Just like it wasn't her fault, she was born into hers. And she'd been lucky, too. She'd had two parents who loved her and would do anything for her. Two more than Stacey ever had like that.

"It must have been terrible for you," he said. "I wish I'd been there. I'd have stuck up for you."

"Stacey stuck up for me. When she could. When she was around. That's why I still can't shake the idea that it's her who wants vengeance. We had a pact. But I was the one who told the police it was her who hit Zoe. It was because of me she went to prison. She said if we followed her story, it would be okay. And maybe it would have been. But I couldn't do it.

Not when I looked over at my mum and dad and saw the looks on their faces. So, I told them. I broke our pact. That's why she hates me."

Laurie pulled her to him, and she snuggled into his chest. "That's silly talk, Nadia. You did what you had to do. You told the truth about what happened. In the long run, that's all that matters." He rested his chin on the top of her head and, at that moment, she felt safe. Nothing else needed to be said. He'd protect her. Her wonderful husband. Her Laurie.

"I wonder if there's a way we could find out where this Zoe's parents are?" he mumbled, almost to himself. "Even if it's just to put our minds at ease."

Nadia puffed out a less contented sigh. How stupid was she to think they could leave this alone, even for a moment? "There might be a way . . ."

"Yes?" He raised his head and retrieved his arm from around her shoulders so he could look face her.

"There's someone who might know."

"Oh? Who?" But as he looked at her, he frowned, as if something had dawned on him. He sat back and snorted. "Wait a minute. You said something before, about knowing she'd missed her supervision appointments. How do you even know they released her from prison if she's changed her name? Didn't you tell the police you weren't allowed any contact with each other after the trial?"

Nadia shifted forward on the couch and rested her forearms on her knees. She'd been expecting the police to question this part of her story more, but they hadn't done. Probably because they thought she was a paranoid lunatic and had been humouring her the whole time that they were here.

But the frown hadn't left Laurie's brow. He was waiting for her to answer.

"The person who might know about Zoe's parents is a woman called Diane Chambers. She was my social worker and then supervising officer once they let me out on licence. My mum and dad had both died whilst I was inside, and she helped me get back on my feet once they released me. She found me a job and a flat and got me set up with a new bank account. She even helped me change my name. It was her idea. She said it would be good to have a fresh start and would mean the press would leave me alone."

Laurie was doing that thing with his hands that he often did when he was thinking, steepling his fingers together under his chin. "Makes sense," he said. "But that was whilst you were on licence. I don't think you're allowed to keep in touch afterwards. I certainly don't think you should discuss the case or the whereabouts of the other people involved."

Nadia leaned away from her husband. It felt like her heart had suddenly frozen over. His tone was harsh and cold. He reminded her of every nasty male teacher and lawyer she'd ever encountered.

"She was looking out for me. I didn't have anyone. At all," she said. "If it wasn't for Diane, I would never have moved to London, never have met you. She's been a damn good friend to me over the years. Like a mum to me."

"And yet I'm only hearing about her now? Jesus. You're not supposed to keep in touch, are you? I'm correct about that."

She looked away and nodded. “I needed her.”

“Why not talk to me about this?” He was yelling now. The calm, protective Laurie she knew had morphed into someone bitter and full of indignation. “I’ve asked you countless times over the years. I wouldn’t have minded.”

“Wouldn’t you?”

“No! I love you. I knew you had a dark past. Do you know how many fucked up scenarios I’ve envisaged over the years – about what happened to you or what you did? ‘What is it she won’t she tell me?’ I used to ask myself. And the whole time you’re still talking with your old social worker. Does she call you Tahani?”

“No. Nadia. That’s who I am.”

He got up from the couch and loomed over her. His arms hung down by his sides, but she could tell his upper body and jaw were rigid with tension. A vein throbbed in his neck.

“When did you last speak to this Diane?” he asked.

She looked up at him. *Please don’t ask me that.*

“When?”

“A few days ago.”

He nodded as if he already knew the answer and then hit her with the cruellest smile she’d ever seen. It was like he despised her. Like he didn’t even know who she was.

“I’ve got to get some air,” he said, and before Nadia could form a reply, he’d grabbed his keys off the kitchen island and stormed out.

Chapter 22

Nadia padded through the hallway towards Andrew's door. She was still shaking after Laurie's abrupt departure, struggling with a mixture of anger and guilt. It wasn't the first time he'd walked out after they'd had words, but unlike the other times, she knew this row was entirely her fault. She should have told him about her past years ago. It would have been hard but he would have understood.

But it was easy to say that now.

Still, he'd be back once he'd calmed down. This was how Laurie operated. When things got too much for him he left, and didn't come back until he'd regained his composure. Usually, he'd go to another room or for a walk in the garden and it was rare he'd leave the house altogether but not unheard of. Most of the time, Nadia thought it admirable he had the wherewithal to remove himself from a situation rather than exacerbate it. Other times she hated him for acting so unresponsive and cold.

She grabbed Andrew's door handle to stop her hand from trembling and took a moment to compose herself. Once satisfied she wasn't about to burst into tears, she knocked on the door, just gently at first, then a little louder. There was no answer. She pressed her ear up against the wood but couldn't hear any noise coming from the room beyond. Andrew usually had his headphones on, so he could listen to music or his computer games as loud as he wanted. Twisting the door handle, she eased the door open and peered through the crack.

"Aww. Baby."

She opened the door fully and relaxed her shoulders. Andrew did indeed have his headphones on but was fast asleep on his bed. He looked almost angelic lying there with a slight smile on his face. It was only a quarter past eight. But he often stayed up late playing his Nintendo and every so often it would catch up with him. Nadia made a mental note to have a word with Laurie about their son's computer game usage. Not today, of course. Probably not this week, either. But soon.

She tiptoed across the room to the side of the bed and carefully removed Andrew's headphones, holding them to her ear to listen. It was some modern pop song she vaguely recognised, a female singer over an electronic backbeat. It wasn't obscene to her ears, but these days pop music all sounded the same. But that was what growing old did to you. Art became a foreign entity, something to be wary of and misunderstand. It was the way of the world.

She switched off Andrew's music player and headphones and placed them on the bedside table before turning back to her son and cupping his face in her palm. Her little boy. Her baby. She'd protect him forever, she told herself, keep him wrapped up in her love if that's what it took.

But of course, it didn't happen that way. Children become teenagers and teenagers become adults. Andrew was currently straddling that messy, difficult grey area between childhood and adolescence. She knew that place all too well. If she could live it for him, she would do it in a second. Negotiating life as a confused thirteen-year-old was hard, even without a campaign of hate focused on you. But that was the way of the world, too.

"Sweet dreams, my darling," she whispered, retracing her steps towards the door. Once there, she paused and watched her eldest son for a few moments longer. Then she turned out the light and headed back into the kitchen.

She'd already called Melissa and told her what was going on, and she'd been more than happy to put the twins up for the night. So now there was only one thing to do. Her phone was lying face down on the kitchen island. Before her brain talked her out of it, she snatched it up and scrolled through the contact list until she found *Customer Service Line.* It was the name she'd saved Diane's number under when she'd first joined the cult of iPhone and had never bothered changing it when moving from model to model. She thought the name rather silly now and the stuff of spy movies, but she was younger back then, and the memory of what happened was a lot fresher in her mind. To the young Nadia, it was a way of keeping their relationship, and Diane's link to her past, a secret.

She tapped the call button and held the phone to her ear as the dialling tone purred. It rang twice. Then a third time.

"Come on Diane," she muttered. "Pick up."

She leaned over the kitchen island, feeling the cold granite through the thin material of her dress. There was still no answer. She straightened up and lowered the phone, about to hang up, when a voice came on the line.

"Nadia! How are you?"

She rolled her shoulders back and placed the phone against her ear. "Hi, Diane. I'm okay, thanks." She heard herself and laughed. A bitter laugh. Who was she trying to kid? "Actually, I'm not okay. Not one bit. It's been awful."

"Oh, shit. What's happened?"

The warmth and concern in Diane's voice were all it took. Nadia let out a wail of emotion and burst into tears. "My h-horse," she stammered. "My beautiful Tudor. Th-They weren't satisfied with hurting him. Now they've poisoned him. He's dead. I'm scared, Diane. Because what's next? I don't know what to do."

Diane went quiet as though she was thinking. "Have you called the police?" she asked.

"They left about an hour ago. I told them I thought Stacey poisoned Tudor and was exacting revenge."

The line went quiet again. She could almost sense Diane doing a silent 'Hail Mary' to herself, the way she had done a few times when Nadia was still Tahani and looking to her for guidance.

"What else did you tell them?"

"As much as I could. As much as I dare. I told them about me and Stacey. And about Zoe Evans. I told them what Stacey had said to me in the court corridor and that I think she's living up to her promise."

"Did you mention me?"

"Not to the police. But Laurie knows about you now. He wasn't happy finding out I'm still in contact with you. But there are a lot of things he's found about me today he's not happy about."

Diane huffed. "Gosh, kiddo. I always wondered if this day would come. We have been playing with fire somewhat, haven't we?"

"But I needed you, and you're retired now. What harm are we doing?" Even as she spoke, she knew the answer to that question, but Diane confirmed it anyway.

"We shouldn't be talking about Stacey Wilson. I shouldn't have ever told you she'd gone missing. I'm a bloody idiot."

Nadia sniffed back. "No! You're looking out for me like you always did. I had to know. I had to be prepared." She wiped her nose with her wrist. "I wish I'd been more prepared now."

"Has anything else happened?" Diane asked.

"I don't know," she said. "Maybe. To be honest, I think I'm going mad. I don't know what to believe anymore. I approached someone in town, thinking it was Stacey. I told her to leave me alone. But it wasn't her."

"Oh, love. What a bloody carry-on. Is there anything I can do to help right this minute?"

Nadia walked to the dining table and sat on one of the chairs facing the glass patio doors. She could see the yurts from here and beyond them the patchwork of fields that stretched up to the horizon.

"There is something, actually," she said. "Laurie made a good point before. What if it's not Stacey doing this? What if it's Zoe's dad? He could have found me somehow, and this is him exacting her revenge?"

An image of Mr Jameson's weaselly, unsmiling face flashed in her head once again.

"Doubtful," Diane said. "I don't think Zoe's dad was ever on the scene. I don't remember him being at the trial and all the reports stated she lived alone with her mother."

"But that's not to say he's not found out somehow . . ." she trailed off. Why was she so set on it being Mr Jameson? Was she so desperate to know what was going on she was ready to accept anything? She was jumping at shadows, looking for demons where there weren't any.

"Don't forget," Diane continued, "Stacey has failed to attend her last four supervision meetings. The police and the probation service are out looking for her. If you want a suspect, she still looks like the prime candidate to me. But, Nadia, I'm still not a hundred percent certain this is even Stacey." She made a noise like someone letting a tire down. When she spoke, her voice was low and serious. "How are you right now, Nadia? In yourself, I mean."

She jerked her head to look at the phone screen, not believing what she was hearing. "You as well?" she said, returning the phone to her ear. "Even you think I'm crazy."

"Hey, hey, that's not what I said. I'm just worried about you. You take a lot on, kiddo, you always have. Are you sleeping?"

"I was. Until my world got ripped out from under me."

Diane didn't respond and the gap in the conversation provided Nadia with enough time that she could appreciate this last statement was a tad histrionic. Yet that was how she felt. She'd created the perfect life for herself. She knew where everyone was and what she had to do next. For a long time, she'd been in control of every facet of her world. And now she wasn't. That terrified her.

"Did the police say they'd look into it?"

"Yes. They're going to contact the West Yorkshire police and see what they can find out."

"There ya go then." Diane's voice rose to her usual sing-song rhythm. "If it's a concerted effort, they'll find her. She can't run forever. Also . . . I wasn't going to tell you this but – well, bloody hell, we're here now aren't we – and it might put your mind at rest. There have been sightings of Stacey up in Bradford. Apparently."

A gasp of panic blossomed in Nadia's chest and got stuck in her throat. She coughed to try to clear it. "How is that supposed to make me feel better, Diane?"

"Pardon, love?"

"If she's up there, then that means someone else is terrorising me down here!"

Diane huffed. This time Nadia could sense her rolling her eyes. "I hadn't thought of it that way. Bugger. Me and my big mouth. I'm sorry, kiddo. But try to stay logical, will ya? The police are on it. Let them do their thing."

Nadia sneered. "They think I'm crazy as well. Everyone does."

"I didn't say you were crazy. I was only trying to look at the situation from a different perspective. I'm trying to help you. I'm very sorry to hear about your horse, love, but if someone is messing around down there, the police will find them."

"*If* someone?! So, you don't believe me?"

Diane made a noise like she was going to speak, then stopped herself. She did it again.

"What is it?" Nadia snapped.

"Well . . . Is there any evidence of foul play? With your horse, I mean?" Nadia stiffened, fighting an urge to hurl her phone against the wall. She didn't need this. Diane was supposed to be on her side. "All I'm saying is focus on what you know, not what you're worried might happen."

Nadia closed her eyes and rubbed her temple. She could feel a headache coming on. "Yes. You're right." But then she stood upright, remembering why she'd rung her old friend in the first place. "Listen, Diane, would you be able to look into Zoe's parents for me? Please. I don't need to know much, just if they're still alive. And if so, where they're living now."

Diane inhaled, like a sigh turned inward. "I'll see what I can do," she said. "But I think it's a dead-end. From what I remember of that case, both of Zoe Evans' parents were absolute wastes of space. Her mum was an alcoholic who had about five men on the go at any one time. All of them dodgy, from what I remember. And as I say, her dad was never around. He left the mum when Zoe was small. *But*, I'll ask around and see what I can find out. Hopefully, *that* will put your mind at ease."

Nadia nodded. "Thank you."

"Okay, I have to go," Diane said. "And if I were you, I'd run myself a hot bath and have an early night. Things might look better in the morning. And try not to worry, yeah?"

"Yes. Bye."

She hung up and placed the phone face down on the island. She remained that way for a few minutes, staring into space, but without really thinking about anything. It was a strange feeling.

Like being suspended in time, unable to make sense of anything. Was this what a nervous breakdown felt like?

Come on, Tahani, pull yourself . . . Whoa!

Tahani. She'd not thought of herself as that person for such a long time. But it was understandable, she supposed, given how much of the past was being raked up. She raised her head and tossed her hair over her shoulders.

She wasn't that girl anymore.

That girl was dead.

Forcing herself out of her trance, she regarded the clock on the wall above the fridge. It was a few minutes to nine. A bath sounded good, but she had work to do. The horses needed feeding, and that was more important. Work was better than rest. It took her mind off her problems. She walked into the hallway and slipped her feet into her wellington boots.

Try not to worry, Diane had said.

It was easy for her to say.

Chapter 23

Daisy, Buttercup and Dandelion were all pleased to see Nadia as she entered the stables. That's what she told herself, anyway. Although the stamping of hooves and snorting noises were more to do with the fact they recognised it was feeding time. She did the rounds, shovelling large piles of fresh straw into their stalls and filling their troughs with fresh water. She took a few moments with each of the mares, stroking them and telling them how everything was going to be okay and that she was sorry for all the upheaval recently. They seemed to appreciate it, but she knew deep down the gesture was for her benefit rather than theirs.

As she finished with Dandelion, she turned her attention to the far side of the stables. It was difficult for her to look at Tudor's empty stall, but she hadn't mucked it out since he'd died, and it stank worse than normal. Heath whinnied at her as she walked over there. He was confused, the poor thing. His father and mentor had gone. He was the alpha male now, and he didn't seem to know what to do with his new status.

She reached up and patted his nose. "It's okay, darling," she whispered. "We'll get through this. You'll be okay."

"He's probably spooked with everything that's happened."

The voice startled her. She shot a look over her shoulder and the muscles in her arms tensed. "Mr Jameson," she said, taking in the old man. "You made me jump."

"Did I? I didn't mean to." He was standing in the open doorway of the stables with his hands behind his back. This evening he was wearing a green hunting vest over a red plaid shirt and he'd tucked his beige cargo trousers into thick orange walking socks. On his head, he wore a green tweed deerstalker. He nodded at Heath as Nadia turned around. "It's a good job he didn't eat any of the poisoned feed."

She narrowed her eyes. Had she or Laurie told him the details of what happened? She couldn't remember. The way he was looking at her gave her the creeps. It was like he was playing with her.

"I've told you before – you're not supposed to be in here, Mr Jameson," she said. "The stables aren't part of the glamping site. It's a separate business."

He glanced about him and held his arms out, which she deciphered as him telling her he was only standing in the doorway.

"What do you want, Mr Jameson?" she asked, walking over to him.

"I don't want anything. I was just checking in on the horses. Wonderful creatures, aren't they? Such a shame what happened to your stallion. Are you any wiser about how the toxic material got into his feed?"

She crossed her arms as she studied his face. There were signs people gave off when they were lying, but she wasn't sure what they were. "Not yet. But the police are looking into it. They think it was foul play. Murder."

"Murder?!" Mr Jameson exclaimed and laughed. "Can you murder a horse?"

"Of course."

"I'm not sure you can, Miss Morgan."

"*Mrs* Morgan. And what would you call it if someone fed your horse something they knew would kill them?"

Mr Jameson peered up at her. He had small piggy eyes that were too close together. But did he look like Zoe? She grimaced as she realised it was hard to remember what her old bully looked like. Despite Zoe being the one who'd died, she was still a dark force in Nadia's life. She represented everything vile and wretched about her past.

"Equicide!" Mr Jameson said and looked pleased with himself. "That's the term for killing a horse. I'd say the definition of murder is the unlawful killing of a human by another human. So only humans can be murdered, and only humans can be murderers."

He didn't blink as he said this. Nadia felt the hairs on the back of her neck prick up.

"Do you know a lot about murder?"

"I read, *Mrs* Morgan. That's all."

Nadia swallowed as she remembered Diane's words. Zoe Evans' dad was a waste of space, she'd said, and had left when Zoe was young. The man in front of her certainly didn't appear to have a paternal bone in his body, but he seemed scholarly and had even taken that to the extremes of a pompous bore.

That didn't fit the narrative of Mr Evans. People could change, of course, but not that much.

"Some people do use the word murder concerning animals, of course, as you just did," he went on. "But I feel doing so blurs the crucial distinction between man and beast. We can abuse animals, of course. But we can't murder them."

"Fine. Thank you for the lesson, Mr Jameson. Now, can you please leave me to do my work? I must clean out Tudor's stall and it's getting late." She took a step forward, hoping it would make him retreat to the outside, but he didn't move. "Mr Jameson! Can you please leave?"

Her voice had risen considerably, but she didn't seem able to calm herself. She'd clenched her hands up into claws.

"Hello there! Everything okay?"

Nadia looked past Mr Jameson and was relieved to see Elenore wandering up the track. She raised her eyebrows at Nadia as if in solidarity.

"What a beautiful evening," she called out in her husky French accent.

Mr Jameson turned around. "Oh, it's you."

"Oui. It is I. And it is you," she said, with a smile. "Are you okay, Nadia?"

"Yes. Thank you," she replied as Elenore got up to them and positioned herself in between her and the horrid little man. "Mr Jameson here was just leaving. Weren't you?"

He sniffed and jerked his shoulders back. "I was heading out for an evening stroll, anyway. I only stopped in to say hello. To see the horses."

"Well, now you have, you can go," Elenore said. Her tone was pleasant but forceful, and as Mr Jameson slumped away, Nadia wanted to throw her arms around her.

"Thank you," she mouthed.

Elenore turned, and they waited until the old man had disappeared around the side of the large oak before she spoke. "That man is a pain in the ass, is he not? I found him snooping around in my garden the other day."

"Oh, gosh. I'm so sorry," Nadia said. "Maybe we should start vetting our guests more before we let them book."

It was a light-hearted comment, but as she heard herself say it, the dark undertones hit her and she felt nauseous.

Elenore chuckled. "He is harmless, as they say." She reached up and gave Nadia's arm a gentle squeeze. "How are you? It has been a difficult few days, *non*?"

"You could say that." She bit her lip, wondering how much she should divulge. Elenore was becoming a good friend, but they weren't that close, not yet. Also, she wanted to keep at least some aspects of her life light and simple. She put on a smile. "Did you see the police were here?"

"Yes. And I saw Tom just now. He filled me in on all that has happened. I am so sorry."

It was a strain to keep her smile in place, but she attempted it. "Thank you."

"You look exhausted, Nadia."

"So everyone keeps telling me."

Elenore lowered her chin and pulled a face like a naughty schoolgirl. "Ah. The last thing you want to hear, right? I get it.

Where was Laurie going at this time of night? I saw his car zoom past earlier."

Nadia shrugged. "We had a few words. He said he needed to clear his head."

"Oh? Merde. I should not have asked."

"It's fine," Nadia said. "He told me I looked exhausted, that's all."

Elenore's eyes bulged, and then she laughed. Then Nadia laughed. It felt good. She couldn't remember the last time she had done it.

"Well, I must get back," Elenore said. "I only came up to see how you were. And then I saw that old fool bothering you. Do you need anything?"

"No, I'm fine."

"I tell you what – if Laurie is out 'clearing his head' why don't you come down to the cottage and we can have a glass of wine? It will help."

Nadia was about to put her off when she realised how stupid that would be. The twins were at Melissa's and if she locked the doors for once, she could justify leaving Andrew asleep in bed. And she'd love nothing more than a decent glass of wine and a chat. Something to take her out of her head for a while.

"That would be lovely," she said. "I've just got to clean Tudor's stall out and I'll be down. Half an hour? Is that okay?"

"Perfect, I have a delicious Chablis in. I shall put it in the freezer, so it is ice cold for us." She began walking away down the track but called back over her shoulder. "I'll see you soon."

Nadia watched her for a moment before heading back into the stables. She grabbed the fork and shovel and headed for Tudor's stall, pulling open the gate. The place stank of stale urine. She leaned the shovel against the nearside wall and was about to start forking the straw up into a pile when she noticed something in the corner of the stall. Something scratched into the wood panels that ran around the top level. It looked like words. Squinting to try to read them, she edged closer.

What the . . .?

She stared, open-mouthed, at the message. Because that's what it was. A message.

A message for her.

LYING BITCH YOU'LL GET WHAT YOU DESERVE.

She read the words, uttering them out loud. Then she stepped away, casting a glance around the stables. It surprised her that the overriding emotion she was feeling was rage rather than fear. But this was it now. No more flapping and second-guessing herself. She wasn't going crazy. This was Stacey. It had to be. She was here. She'd come for her revenge.

"Stacey?" she called out, moving out of Tudor's stall and peering into the darkness outside the stables. "Show yourself. Let's finish this."

Nothing happened.

"Stacey!" she yelled. "Come out!"

Still nothing. She felt sick and dizzy. The pitch fork clattered to the ground as a black fog seeped across her vision. Gasping back deep breaths, she turned to leave but stumbled into the side of the stall. She had to get out of here. The ammonia stench was burning her nasal passages.

Staggering out of the stall, she left the stables through the nearest doorway and ran around the side of the building and up the drive towards the house. The cool night air revived her enough that she made it without fainting or throwing up and once inside, she rushed over to the kitchen island and scooped up her phone. The police had talked about lack of evidence and no signs of any break-in, but they had to believe her now. There was their damn evidence. A mission statement from Stacey scratched into Tudor's stall.

You'll get what you deserve.

She'd opened her phone's keypad and was ready to tap in the first nine when the phone vibrated in her hand and began to ring. It startled her, but she held onto it. The caller ID was coming up as *UNKNOWN*.

She answered the call and held the phone to her ear. "Hello?" she said. "Who's this?"

"Mrs Nadia Morgan," a woman's voice said. "My name is PC Rebecca Anderson. I'm from Bodmin Police Hub, part of Devon & Cornwall Police."

Nadia smiled and nodded. "Yes. Great. I was literally about to call you."

"Oh?"

"There's been a development since your colleagues were here and—"

"Nadia," PC Anderson interjected. "I'm not sure what's going on here. I'm a Family Liaison Officer for the highways division."

"What?"

"Is Laurie Morgan your husband, Nadia?"

"Yes." She was already feeling faint, but whatever she'd gone through in the stables was nothing compared to the wave of dread that ran through her now. "What's happened?" she asked.

"I'm afraid he's been involved in an accident." PC Anderson's voice was low-pitched and gentle. Too gentle to be delivering this information. "No other vehicles were involved. We think he might have lost control of his vehicle."

"Is he . . . dead?"

"No. But he is in a serious condition. He's being taken to Bodmin Community Hospital by ambulance."

"Right. Yes." She was looking around for her car keys while she spoke. "I'll go there now."

"Are you safe to drive, Nadia?" PC Anderson asked. "I can have a car come and pick you up. They'd be there in around twenty minutes."

"No. I'm fine," she said, heading down the hallway to the front door. "I'll drive myself; I'll be okay." She was gripping the door handle, about to open it, when she remembered Andrew was in his room. "Shoot!"

"Nadia? What's wrong?"

"Nothing," she said, lowering the phone from her ear and talking into it like people did on reality TV shows. "I've got to go. I've got to sort out my kids."

She hung up and retraced her steps towards Andrew's room and knocked on the door. She felt like her entire body was fizzing with electricity. How did she tell her eldest son that his dad had been in a serious accident?

And that she was to blame.

THEN . . .

5 August 2001

The room was chilly and, except for the table and four grey plastic chairs, one of which she was sitting on, the space was barren of features or fittings. There wasn't even a poster or a sign on the wood-panelled walls. There was a mustiness to the air, and the smell reminded her of that of the library at school.

But this was no library.

She'd expected the policemen to handcuff her to the table when they'd brought her in here a few minutes earlier, but that hadn't happened. She'd not seen a pair of handcuffs since being arrested. At least, she thought she'd been arrested. No one had given her that speech that you always heard on American cop shows, but she wondered if that was just television.

The chair creaked as she sat back and closed her eyes. Until this point, she'd not had any real chance to consider what had happened. Ever since the creek, she'd been in a whirlwind of panic, not wanting to think too deeply about Zoe, or Stacey, or indeed anything. But now, sitting here alone with nothing else to focus on, the horrifying events of two days earlier were all she could think about. She'd hated Zoe Evans. But she didn't want her dead. If she closed her eyes, she could see her standing in front of her, prodding a finger at her. After that, it all happened so fast. Stacey stepped forward. Someone yelled. There was a flash of movement followed by a dull crunching sound and Zoe's expression turned from sneer to surprise. Stacey's plan was that they say she slipped and banged her head, but it hadn't gone that way. The thought of her lying there with blood pouring from her head made Tahani want to curl up into a tight ball. She already knew that image would stay with her forever. Poor Zoe. It wasn't supposed to happen. None of this was. Tahani wasn't even supposed to go out that day.

But she knew what she had to do.

Another image she couldn't shake was her parent's disappointed faces as DC Richards informed her that their only child was involved in Zoe Evans' death. They'd stared at Tahani in disbelief, their usual loving eyes wet with tears. At that moment, she knew she couldn't do what Stacey wanted her to.

She stiffened at the sound of footsteps outside the door. DC Richards had already told her that if she told the truth the court would be more lenient on her. She had to tell them what they wanted to know. She couldn't hurt her parents any more than she already had done.

The door opened and DC Richards entered, followed by DC Stanhope and then a woman Tahani hadn't seen before. She was about her mum's age and had straight brown hair that skimmed the bottom of her jaw. She wore a navy skirt and blazer over a white blouse with a high collar.

"Tahani, this is Diane Chambers," DC Richards said, gesturing at the woman. "She's a social worker who will be acting as your appropriate adult in this interview. Do you understand?"

She stared at the woman. "I think so."

"Hello Tahani," the woman said and smiled. "You can call me Diane. Or Di. I'm here to make sure you understand what's happening and that your well-being is paramount. I'll also be able to answer any questions you might have. But I'm not a solicitor, or a lawyer, or anything like that, so if you'd rather defer this interview until you've sorted out representation, then please say now."

DC Richards made a noise with his throat and Diane glared at him before turning back to Tahani with a smile. She raised her eyebrows as if wanting an answer.

"I'm okay," Tahani told her. "I've talked to my mum and dad and we don't think I need . . . You know . . . What you said . . . representation."

"Not yet, at least," DC Richards muttered under his breath as he pulled out the chair opposite. He sat down and DC Stanhope joined him on the other side of the table. Diane walked around and sat next to Tahani.

"Don't worry," she whispered as she got settled. "Just tell them the truth. It's all you need to do."

"Okay then," DC Richards said, leaning forward and looking Tahani in the eyes. "As you know, you're here because we have reason to believe you were involved in the murder of Zoe Evans. But what we need to establish is how far that involvement goes. Do you understand?"

Tahani glanced at Diane, but she wasn't looking at her. "Yes," she told DC Richards. "I understand."

"Excellent. And have you had a good think about everything? And what else you might want to tell us about the events of Tuesday, the third of August?"

She nodded. "Yes."

"Excellent. Now, for full disclosure, Tahani, I should tell you that Stacey Wilson is being interviewed right now by my colleagues in a room just like this. But she's not telling them very much. And that's not good, Tahani. If we don't get to the truth about what happened, we'll have to assume you're both guilty." He kept looking over at Diane as he spoke. "If the court finds you guilty of murder, then you could get ten years in prison, Tahani. Can you imagine that? Ten years. And yes, given your age, it wouldn't be an adult prison, but some of these kids' units are worse than the adult ones if you ask me. You'd be mixing with a lot of bad people. How old are you? Thirteen. You'd only be twenty-three when you get out, but a twenty-three-year-old that's grown up inside? With no real social skills or education to speak of? Starting a new life after that is going to be damn hard, I'd say."

"All right, DC Richards," Diane said. "You've made your point. How about you cut to the chase?"

DC Richards sat back and stuck his bottom lip out. He was pretending to be confused, but Tahani could see through the act. "I'm sorry, Ms Chambers. I'm sure I heard you saying to Ms Carroll just a few minutes earlier that you *weren't* a solicitor."

"My apologies," Diane said. "But, seriously, the kid has got the message."

DC Richards returned his gaze to Tahani. "Is she right? Have you got the message? Are you aware of the severity of your situation?"

Tahani nodded. She could feel the tears building up in her chest and didn't want to speak in case they bubbled over.

"Who hit Zoe Evans with the rock, Tahani?"

She sniffed. "Stacey said it was the fall that killed her. She banged her head."

DC Richards frowned. "Stacey Wilson isn't a pathologist. Or a police officer. I wouldn't listen to her if I were you. We know the first blow Zoe received was delivered with force." As he said this, his gaze fell on Tahani's arms, resting on the table in front of her. With her thin wrists and slender forearms, they looked even spindlier than usual, especially surrounded by three adults. "It was a fatal blow, Tahani. So, we need to know. Who hit her with the rock?"

Tahani screwed up her face as the tears fell. She imagined her parents waiting for the news. They'd be sick with worry. Her mum had got so thin lately. She didn't need this. Then she thought of Stacey. Of their pact. You didn't break a pact under any circumstances. That was what she'd told her.

Yet breaking your parent's hearts had to be worse. Ten years in prison had to be worse. She slid her arms off the table and crossed them tight across her chest.

"We have our theories, Tahani," DC Richards said. "But it'll help us, and it'll help you too if you tell me now exactly what happened. Can you do that, Tahani? Tell me what happened that day."

She opened her eyes and looked into the policeman's face. "It was Stacey," she whispered. "Stacey picked up a rock and hit Zoe. After that, I can't remember much else. I didn't know what to do. She told me to not say anything and that it'd be okay if we both kept quiet. But I can't . . . I'm sorry . . . I'm so sorry." She sobbed uncontrollably. With her head in her hands, she heard DC Richards thanking her, telling her that was exactly what he wanted to hear.

"It's all right, kiddo," Diane whispered, placing a hand on her back. "The hard part is over now. You're going to be okay. I'm here."

Chapter 24

Nadia screeched the car to a halt in front of the barrier blocking her entry to the hospital car park. A screen attached to the barrier flashed up a smiley face with the word 'parking' above it. She wound down her window and jabbed angrily at a green button until a ticket appeared. She didn't have time for this.

Yanking the paper ticket from the machine she lurched the car forward as soon as the barrier rose, pulling into the first space she came across. She clicked off her seatbelt before she'd even switched off the ignition and, once the car was fully stationary, she grabbed her phone from the passenger seat and leapt out, slamming the door behind her. Weaving through the rows of parked cars she hurried across the tarmac towards the hospital entrance.

The glass doors slid open for her as she approached and she continued through into the reception area, eyes darting around, speed-reading the many colourful signs that said things like *Radiology* and *Cardiology* and *Emergency Room*.

But where was Laurie?

She approached the reception desk with all the grace of a hurricane. "They brought my husband here," she said, spitting the words out. "He's been in an accident."

The woman behind the counter looked at her like she was stupid. "What's your husband's name?" she asked, unfazed by Nadia's disposition. The badge pinned to her navy uniform said her name was *Linda*, and that she was a *Patient Coordinator.* She was wearing thick-lensed glasses that made her look older than she probably was. Her eyes looked enormous as she stared up at Nadia waiting for a response.

"Laurie – *Lawrence* – Morgan. He was in a car accident. The police called me and . . ." She trailed off, Linda wasn't listening and had turned her attention to a computer on the desk in front of her. She typed something in and frowned.

Why was she frowning?

What had the computer told her?

"I can see they brought him in half an hour ago," she said. "They've taken him straight through to theatre."

"Yes. Okay," Nadia said. "So, what do I do? Where do I go? I want to be there when he wakes up."

Linda returned to her keyboard and typed something else into the computer.

Why was she being like this?

Why was everyone always so unhelpful and unkind?

This is exactly why Nadia wanted to escape the world. It was why she'd created a safe space for herself and her family in the countryside, away from cynical people like Linda, and this hospital with its stench of bleach and spectres of death lurking around every corner.

"Is it just you?" Linda asked.

Nadia nodded. She'd woken Andrew and taken him to Melissa and Tom's on her way here. He was scared and angry and wanted to come with her but she'd told him he was to stay with his siblings. They'd had strong words, but she'd been adamant. He could see his dad tomorrow, she'd said, when Laurie was feeling better.

And that wasn't a lie. He was going to be feeling better soon. He had to.

"And you are immediate family?"

"I'm his wife!" Nadia replied. "Nadia Morgan."

"You need ward thirty-nine, the emergency surgical unit." Linda stood up from her chair and leaned over the counter to point down the corridor to Nadia's left. "If you follow the blue signs around this side of the building, then it's the first left. Go down the long corridor and then left again. You'll go across a tunnel over the car park that has windows on both sides. Once on the other side, take the first right and you should see ward thirty-nine in front of you."

"Fine. I'll find it." Nadia set off at pace before Linda could say anything else. She'd found it hard to concentrate on the directions, but she had a rough idea of where she was going.

Her poor Laurie. This was her fault, she told herself as she hurried down the first corridor. If she hadn't been such a secretive horrid person, if she hadn't done such awful things, then they'd never have got into an argument. Laurie wouldn't have stormed off angry and frustrated. He wouldn't have had an accident. Nadia wasn't driving the car, but she'd caused him to crash, just like she'd caused her mum's cancer to return and for her dad to die from a stroke at just forty-nine.

She crashed through the double doors at the end of the corridor and took a left. In front of her was the tunnel that spanned over the car park and joined the modern wing of the hospital that she'd just been in, to the original structure on the other side. She raced along the glass tunnel, eyes focused only on the doors at the other side and pushed through into a large oblong space with three double doors leading off it. The stark hospital smells and the grimness of decay seemed to intensify in this older building. But that was to be expected. This part of the hospital was where people came to be treated for the worst things life could throw at them. Even over the bleach, she could smell death in the air.

She went through the doors to her right and found herself in a dimly lit room with a reception desk in front of her. She approached and pressed her hands up against the Perspex surround to get the attention of the woman behind the counter.

"My husband has been in a car accident," she said. "Lawrence Morgan. He's in theatre now."

The receptionist was thin with white hair and looked about as ancient as the building, but as she raised her eyes to Nadia, she smiled. "Lawrence Morgan. Let me check for you." Squinting at the screen in front of her, she rolled her mouse around, followed by a couple of clicks. "Yes. He's in theatre now." She sucked her lips into her mouth like she was considering saying something else.

Nadia raised her hands to her face and then dropped them down by her side. She didn't know what to do with them. "Can you tell me what happened?" she asked.

The woman, whose name badge read Rita, frowned at the screen. "The police brought him in. They're around still, I believe.

I'll mark that you're at the hospital and waiting and someone will come and speak with you as soon as they're available."

She smiled at Nadia, and her face said, *that's the best I can do.*

"Thank you," Nadia said, looking over her shoulder. "Am I okay to wait here?"

"That would be best," Rita said. "There's a coffee machine and one selling snacks down the corridor over there and the toilet, too, if you need to go. We have a café as well on this wing, but I'm afraid it won't be open until the morning."

Nadia thanked her and shuffled over to the rows of orange plastic seats. There were a few more people here already; a middle-aged couple, who were holding one other's hands so tight they'd made them red; a single man with a shaved head and sad eyes who stared at her as she approached; and an older woman with grown out grey roots who was dabbing at her eyes with a balled-up tissue and didn't look up as Nadia sat two chairs down from her.

Settling into the hard plastic seat, she pulled her phone out of her pocket. After texting Melissa to say thanks and that she'd keep her updated, she switched it off and slipped it back into her pocket. Best to save her battery. She didn't know how long she was going to be here.

She sat back and waited. Minutes ticked by. Then hours. She fidgeted. Used the bathroom and blew her nose. Paced up and down. Offered sympathetic smiles to those around her. Nothing helped.

She was distraught.

Terrified.

The coffee machine accepted credit cards, and she used Apple Pay on her phone to buy a large Americano. It was good and hot but tasted bitter. Maybe everything would taste that way from now on, she wondered. She drank it regardless, wandering up and down the corridors as far as she could go in each direction, arriving at closed doors that required keycards to get through.

Back in the reception area, she tried to stay out of her imagination by reading the posters on the wall in front of her. But it didn't help. Those words, scratched into Tudor's stall, kept flashing across her mind.

YOU'LL GET WHAT YOU DESERVE

No one had yet told her the details surrounding Laurie's accident – only that he'd run off the road and it was serious – but with everything else that had been going on, her brain kept coming back to the same explanation.

Stacey.

She'd done this.

Either she'd run him off the road, or cut his brake cables, or whatever else people did to sabotage someone's car. But it was her. It had to be. She'd killed her beautiful stallion and now she was trying to take her husband away.

Nadia sat upright at the sound of voices and twisting in her seat, saw a policewoman talking to Rita. The old woman pointed at her and Nadia got to her feet as the policewoman walked over.

"Nadia Morgan?"

"Yes."

"I'm PC Anderson. We spoke on the phone. How are you holding up?" Nadia realised she'd imagined her older than she was when they'd spoken earlier. In reality, she was in her mid-twenties and looked to be mixed-race, as well. She had a kind face and cheeks that dimpled when she smiled.

"I'm fine," Nadia replied but didn't return her smile. "Is there any news? Can you tell me what happened?"

PC Anderson shook her head. "Your husband's still in theatre, but the doctors will come and speak to you as soon as they're done." She glanced at the other people sitting around and her affable expression dropped into one more serious. "Do you want to come with me? There's a room down the corridor we can go that's a bit more private."

"Yes. No problem."

She followed PC Anderson across reception and down the next corridor. She stopped outside a door halfway down and, pushing it open, stepped back so Nadia could go in first.

The room was small with three orange chairs standing around a white, rectangular table in the centre. In one corner was a gurney bed with a blue curtain pulled halfway around it.

"Take a seat," PC Anderson said as she shut the door. "No one will disturb us in here."

Nadia did as she was told, placing her hands in her lap. She felt the same way she had done in that police station all those years ago – scared and confused and as if her world was crumbling around her.

"What's this about?" she asked. "Can you tell me what happened?"

PC Anderson sat down opposite. "As I say, he's still in theatre, Nadia. From what I've been told, he's in quite a critical condition."

Nadia let out a yelp and placed her hand over her mouth. "Is he going to . . .? Will he . . .?"

"The doctors are doing all they can. But I'm afraid there's more. There were no other cars involved when Laurie went off the road." She swallowed, allowing the words to sink in. But she didn't need to. Nadia was already two steps ahead of her.

"And?" It felt like the only thing she could say.

"My colleagues who attended the scene have reason to believe Laurie's crash was no accident," PC Anderson said and lowered her voice. "Nadia, they think someone tampered with his car."

Chapter 25

Nadia had been in shock from the moment PC Anderson had called her three hours earlier. But the news someone might have caused Laurie's accident, that wasn't a shock at all.

"Was it the brakes?" she asked.

PC Anderson shook her head. "No. It seems he was driving rather fast, down the country roads near to where you live, and unbeknownst to him, the nuts on his front wheels were loose. The fact it was all of them points to foul play. The nearside wheel came off whilst he was doing sixty miles an hour and he lost control. He came off the road, and the car rolled down an embankment into a field."

"I see." Nadia looked down at her hands. She had them clasped so tightly that the skin on her fingers had turned white. "That sounds bad."

When she looked up, PC Anderson was regarding her with a strange expression. But she could go to hell. How did she know how someone might react to this news? She was in shock. She was terrified.

"Are you aware the police were at our house today?" she asked.

"I've not been back to the station all day," PC Anderson replied as if dodging the question. "Once I do, I'll contact the relevant departments and—"

"I know who did this!" Nadia leaned forward. "The other police officers thought I was just being paranoid; I know they did. But this proves I'm right. Someone killed my horse, and they tried to kill my husband too. You must stop them. Please. You must do something."

PC Anderson's eyes grew wider, but she tried to remain calm. "I see. Well, we do have our theories about what happened."

"Oh?"

"There have been quite a lot of environmental activists in the area," she went on. "I believe Laurie drives a Range Rover, correct? We've had a few similar cases over the last few months of 4x4 owners having their wheel nuts loosened. It's terrible, I know, but there are people out there willing to take risks with people's lives to make their point."

Nadia opened her mouth but shut it again.

No!

This wasn't happening.

On top of Laurie currently fighting for his life on some slab, the police were going to put his accident down to a bunch of eco-warriors.

No.

It was Stacey.

She had to make them see.

"But what about what I just told you about my horse? There's a woman called Stacey Wilson. At least, that's what she used to be called. I'm not sure what she calls herself now. But she hates me. She and I were involved in something together a long time ago. Something bad. She thinks I betrayed her and now wants revenge. She killed my horse, and she sabotaged Laurie's car. I'm sure of it. You need to find her. Please . . ."

She trailed off, seeing the expression on PC Anderson's face. She looked at Nadia as if she'd just been speaking an alien language.

"Nadia, this is an established pattern."

"No. Please," she whined. "You've got to believe me. It's Stacey Wilson. She's written something in my stables. A threat. Get your colleagues to come and have a look. She's out to get me. She wants me dead. I'm sure of it. This is all my fault."

She lowered her head as tears fell from her eyes. What was the point? PC Anderson was a Family Liaison Officer. She had no power to stop Stacey. She was trained to be friendly and calm and to deliver bad news with compassion and empathy.

PC Anderson placed her hand gently over Nadia's. "It sounds like you've had a lot to deal with recently and I'm sorry about that. But until the CSI team has filed their reports, we won't know anymore. As I say, these are all just theories."

No. It's not a theory. It's Stacey.

It's Stacey!

"I get it," Nadia whispered and opened her eyes to the light to stop herself from crying. She wiped the tears from her face with the heel of her palm. "When will I be able to see him?"

PC Anderson looked at her watch. "Not yet, I'm afraid. Even if he gets out of theatre in the next hour, he'll be put in ICU and won't be allowed visitors for the first few hours." She smiled. "I'm sorry for getting you here. I thought things may have moved quicker than they have. Why don't you go home and get some sleep? You can return first thing in the morning."

"Get some sleep?!" The words sounded harsher than she'd intended. "I can't go home to bed, knowing Laurie might . . . I need to be here!"

"I understand. But we don't know how long it's going to be."

She was being dismissive. Like they all were in the end. But that was the police for you. They wanted concrete evidence, or they didn't care. The frustrating thing was that she had evidence. The words carved into Tudor's stall. Surely that meant something. Or would they just say that she'd done it? A crazy woman looking for attention. That's what people thought of her. Even Laurie thought that.

"Can I speak to the other officers?" Nadia said as PC Anderson stood and gestured for her to do the same. "The ones who came out to the stables."

"Yes. I'm sure. At some point." PC Anderson placed her hand on Nadia's back and guided her to the door. "But I think for now you should just focus on the next few hours. Why don't I drive you home and you can at least get a change of clothes and some supplies? A toothbrush, for instance."

She opened the door, but Nadia stopped. "I don't want to go home. I want to stay here."

"You can gather Laurie some supplies together too," PC Anderson added. "For when he wakes up. We can come straight back here if that's what you want."

"Fine. Okay then. But I don't need you to drive me."

"Are you certain?"

"Yes, I think I can make it there and back okay." The words came out more sarcastic than she intended, but she didn't care.

"Well, that's up to you. But please be careful. And if you feel concerned about driving, give me a ring." She pulled a card from her shirt pocket and handed it over. "I'll be on call up to 3 a.m. But you can leave a message any time."

"Thank you."

"And try to stay present, Nadia. The worst thing you can do in these situations is let your imagination run away with you. Laurie is in good hands. I promise."

Nadia nodded, but it was a resigned sort of nod. The nod of someone so broken and exasperated by her circumstance that she couldn't do anything but accept her fate.

And maybe this is what Stacey wanted all along. To make her think she was going crazy. To take her to the edge of sanity and leave her dangling there.

If that was her plan, it was a good one.

It had worked.

Chapter 26

It was almost midnight when Nadia got back to the house. She flicked the lights on as she entered the main space and, after placing her phone and car keys on the kitchen island, headed for her and Laurie's bedroom. It had taken her twenty-six minutes to drive back from the hospital and she wanted to be back there within the hour. In her room, she stripped down to her underwear and went into the en suite bathroom. There, she went to the sink and twisted on the cold tap, splashing water under her arms before leaning over the basin and cupping her hands together to wash her face. The cool water revived her as she hoped it would, but as she stood, she caught her reflection in the mirror above the sink. Everyone was right. She looked exhausted. Her dark olive skin was a dull beige colour and her hair was in desperate need of a wash. A brush, at the very least. She didn't have time for either. Reaching for a can of deodorant, she sprayed herself liberally before heading back into the bedroom and over to the wardrobe. It wasn't a particularly warm night, but she knew exactly what she wanted to wear. She pulled out the red floral smock dress from where it was hanging amongst her other summer dresses and held it at arm's length. She hadn't worn it since last year, but it was Laurie's favourite. It pinched her waist a little, but in doing so accentuated her hips and breasts and she always got a lot of attention from him whenever she wore it. She stepped into it and pulled it up over her shoulders. The three buttons on the back were a pain to do up, especially as her hands were shaking and the adrenaline and panic in her system were making her rush. She managed the first two and left the third. She was looking around for where she'd placed her phone when she heard the front door slam.

Her heart did a somersault. It was Stacey. She'd come for her.

Nadia glanced around the room, eyes searching for something she might use as a weapon. She wasn't going out without a fight. Walking over to the bureau, she picked up the clay money pot that she and Laurie put their loose change in on an evening. It had a good weight to it and although it was cumbersome, she could get a good grip. It would have to do. She moved to the door, not daring to breathe as she peered around the side. Stacey was staring right at her, silhouetted in the doorway to the hall.

"I knew it," she hissed, moving into the main living space. "Well, here we are—Andrew?"

As reason kicked in, so did her faculties. The shadowy figure stepped forward and morphed into the familiar shape of her eldest son.

"Mum. Where's Dad?"

"He's not here," she said, lowering the money pot and placing it down on the bookshelf to her right. "I told you I'd call as soon as there was any news."

"But I saw you drive past Melissa and Tom's house just now. They said it was okay for me to come up here. Don't worry. What's going on?"

She took a deep breath, choosing her words carefully. "Your dad was hurt quite badly in the crash, darling. The doctors are helping him right now, but we can't see him yet. I need you to stay with Melissa and Tom tonight. Tomorrow, all being well, we can all go up to the hospital together and see him."

He scowled at her, full of teenage indignation. "Where are you going?"

"Well . . . back to the hospital. But I'll just be sitting around until morning. I promise I'll come back and get you as soon as Dad's awake. Or Tom can drive you over. I'm sure he'd do that."

"I want to come with you now."

"No, Andrew."

"Why not?"

"Because . . ." She was going to tell him he was too young but standing there under the kitchen spotlights he looked so grown up that she changed tack, ". . . I don't think Dad's allowed to have more than one visitor until he's on a proper ward."

It was a lie, but it placated him. Or so she hoped.

"I want to stay here then. All my stuff's here and I don't like it at Melissa and Tom's. It's boring. They ask loads of stupid questions."

"Andrew!"

"Please."

"No, it's not safe."

"Mum! I'm thirteen. I'll be fine!"

Nadia rubbed at her face. She was so het up; she was practically vibrating. She did not have the energy to argue with him. And Laurie needed her.

"Please, Andrew. Just one night," she tried.

"I want to be on my own. I'll be okay, I promise. I'm not a little kid anymore, Mum."

She gritted her teeth. "Fine. But you lock all the doors after me, do you hear? And you don't answer the door to anyone unless you know who it is!"

"Yeah, sure."

She stared at him. Could she do it?

"Mum. Go. I'll be fine."

She rubbed her eyes. "Right. Okay. But it's late, Andrew, so no staying up playing Nintendo. We're all going to need our energy over the next few days. For Dad. Text me when you're in bed and let me know you've locked up. Okay? I'll keep ringing you if you don't."

"Yes. Just go."

"And the second you wake up, you ring me." She glanced around, frantic. "Where the hell is my phone?"

Andrew stepped over to the island and held up her phone and keys. "Here."

He gave them her, and she pulled him towards her for a hug. At first, he struggled like he always did, but then he let her. "Is Dad going to be okay?" he asked.

"Yes," she said, trying to convince herself as much as him. "Of course he is."

Chapter 27

"Mrs Morgan? Nadia?"

"Huh? What?" She lurched awake, unsure at that moment where she was or what was going on. She glanced around, seeing the rows of orange chairs and the off-white windowless walls. It hit her at the same time as she looked up to see a man wearing a light grey uniform standing over her.

"Good morning, Nadia," he said. "How are you today?"

She swallowed. Her mouth was gummy. "Urm. Sorry." She rubbed gunk from the corner of her eye. "I must have fallen asleep. What time is it?"

"It's just after eight," the man said.

Eight. That was fine. She'd got back to the hospital a few minutes after two. At that time, the journey back had taken her just twenty-four minutes, but it had felt like twenty-four hours. She didn't know what was up or down anymore, but the last time she'd looked at the clock it was six. She hadn't been asleep long.

"I'm Robert Carmichael," the man said. "I'm a surgeon here at the hospital. I've been operating on your husband."

"Laurie!" she said, sitting upright. Her neck was stiff from where she'd been sleeping, but it was the least of her concerns as the entirety of the situation slammed into her. "Is he okay?"

Robert Carmichael was a tall, slim man with shaved grey hair and a long but pleasant face. He smiled, and she took that as a good sign. You didn't smile when someone was dead. Did you?

"Do you want to come with me?" he said, holding out a hand to help her up from the seat. "There's a room around the corner, which is a bit more private."

Yes. She knew it well.

She followed him down the corridor to the small room she'd been in a few hours earlier. Carmichael gestured for her to sit in the same chair she'd sat in then and closed the door behind them.

"Is Laurie going to be okay?" she asked before he even had time to sit.

"Your husband sustained some very serious injuries, Mrs Morgan. There was a bleed on his brain and damage to his spinal cord. He's been in theatre for five hours and we've managed to stop the bleeding, but I'm afraid he sustained what we refer to as a C-6 injury."

"That's his spine?" Nadia said. "But he's going to be fine? He'll be able to walk?"

Carmichael did that thing with his mouth that people did when they didn't know how to respond. A sort of half-smile, half-grimace.

"Oh shit. No! He's going to be paralysed?"

Carmichael still didn't answer.

Why the hell wasn't he saying anything?

"We did all we could, Mrs Morgan. But the type of injuries your husband sustained are what we call life-altering ones. He is lucky to still be alive."

"But he's going to be in a wheelchair?"

Carmichael nodded. "We'll know more when he's conscious and can give us feedback, but it is looking that way."

Nadia gasped. She felt like she was going to faint. This couldn't be happening. This was Laurie they were talking about. Her perfect husband. He was strong and dependable. He could walk.

"We are confident, though, that his paralysis will only be paraplegic," Carmichael added. "That's some consolation."

"Is it?"

He looked down. "Maybe not now. As I say, we'll know more when he's awake. He's still under heavy sedation and we need to keep him in the ICU for another twenty-four hours. But after that."

"Can I see him?" she asked.

"I'm sorry, Mrs Morgan, he's just come out of theatre. We can't really—"

"Please, Mr Carmichael. I've been here all night waiting to see him. I won't stay long. I just want to see him. Please." She started crying, noisy wails of sadness filled the room as snot and tears poured down her face. They were actual tears and it was genuine emotion, but today she allowed them to flow freely rather than fight them.

Carmichael shifted in his chair. He looked uneasy. Dealing with hysterical spouses was probably beyond his remit. In fact, why was a surgeon even giving her this news? Is that how it worked these days? Maybe it was because of the staff shortages she kept reading about?

The tears kept coming. There was so much pent-up grief inside of her that she worried she might never stop.

"Okay, Mrs Morgan," Carmichael said, holding his hand out, letting it hover over her hand. "You can go see him. But only for five minutes. Do you understand?"

She sniffed. "Yes. Thank you."

Carmichael couldn't get to his feet fast enough. "Follow me."

He showed her out of the room and led her down to the end of the corridor. Swiping his keycard down the electronic lock, he pushed open the double doors and ushered her through. Beyond the doors was an almost identical corridor to the one they'd just been in, but this one sloped down towards the end where another corridor intersected it.

"This way," Carmichael said, striding past. She followed him down to the end and they took a left. A sign hanging down from the low ceiling in front of them said *Intensive Care Unit.* The words alone made her shudder.

They got to another set of locked doors that Carmichael opened with his keycard and pushed through into a large square room with two doors leading off on each side. Over to the left was a small reception desk. Carmichael strode up to the counter and waved at a young man with dark skin who appeared from out of a back room.

"Hey, Sanj. Can you tell me what room Lawrence Morgan is in, please?"

Sanj looked hesitant. "He only arrived a while ago."

"I know, this is Mrs Morgan. I told her she could see him. *Briefly.* Don't worry, this is on me."

Sanj nodded and referred to something below the counter, either a sign-in book or a computer screen, Nadia assumed. "Room eight," he said, raising his head and pointing to a door behind them.

"Thank you," Carmichael said. Without saying a word, he and Nadia walked over to the door. There was a long thin pane of glass as big as the doorframe on one side of the door, and he peered through it for a moment before stepping back and opening the door for her. "Five minutes."

Nadia nodded and stepped into the room. She'd watched enough medical procedural dramas over the years to have some idea of what to expect. Everything was how she'd imagined. The monitors, the bleeping machines, the tubes and catheters and plastic bags full of blood and saline. But nothing could prepare her for the shock of seeing the man she loved hooked up to them. He had a mask covering most of his face and a bandage around his head, but the areas she could see were bruised and swollen. His right eyelid was so bulbous and purple it looked like the sort of injury a cartoon character might sustain. Only much less funny.

She remained in front of the door as it closed behind her. She wanted to move closer, but her legs wouldn't take her.

"Hey," she said. "It's me."

The machine keeping Laurie's lungs breathing made a hissing sound. The machine monitoring his heart went beep.

"I'm so sorry, Laurie," she said. "I didn't mean anything I said. I shouldn't have been so defensive with you. I knew you were just trying to help me. Trying to get your head around an impossible concept."

She managed a few steps forward. His right arm was in a cast and they'd put one of those plastic collars around his neck. Apart from a catheter tube that fed into another plastic bag for urine, there were no wires or tubes at the end of the bed. She shuffled over to it and lifted the sheets. She didn't know what she expected to see, but his feet looked like they always had done. He had a bit of yellow callus on the side of his big toe and his nails needed cutting, but that was all. She ran her finger down the arch of his left foot. She flicked his little toe, watching him all the time.

He didn't move. The machines went hiss and beep.

"I was right, though. I know it now. No one's going to tell me different. This was her. Stacey Wilson. But you know what? I'm done letting that bitch terrorise us. I'm done being scared. I've spent my whole life trying to stay positive and not think about the past because I know what horrible things lurk there. But I'm facing it now head-on. I don't care anymore. She will not get away with this. If the police or the probation service can't or won't find her, then I will. I'll find her and I'll stop her. And I swear to you, Laurie, I'll kill her for what she's done to you. To us. I'll kill her . . . I'll . . ." Her words were lost as a fresh wave of sobs erupted in her chest. She rubbed at her eyes and then wiped her nose with the back of the same hand. Lying there like that, with all those tubes and wires coming out of him, Laurie looked broken. He looked like he was dead. She felt sick and angry and more powerless than she'd ever felt. But she'd meant what she'd said. Stacey was the one who was going to pay. She'd find her and she'd—

"Mrs Morgan. Time's up I'm afraid." She spun around to see Carmichael standing in the open doorway. The movement sent her head spiralling. "That really is all we can allow for today. Tomorrow, if we see any positive developments, we can—Mrs Morgan!"

He rushed forward and grabbed her as she lost control of her limbs. She stumbled forward, mumbling something about needing to go home. Carmichael guided her to the floor and wiped the hair from her face. She heard him call for help but pushed him away. She didn't need help. She needed to go home. She needed to escape this thick black cloud that was surrounding her. She'd not slept or eaten since she could remember and her arms and legs felt like jelly, but that didn't matter. Her husband looked like a dead man. He couldn't walk. She loved him. She needed him. And it was her fault he was like this. She had to find Stacey. She had to stop her before she struck again. It was down to her now.

Carmichael was shouting in her ear, and she wished he'd stop. She heard other voices, but they sounded muffled and alien. Where was she? Where was Laurie? The black cloud was all around her now and was lifting her into the air. It felt nice. She felt safe. It was nice to feel safe. She'd almost forgotten what it felt like.

THEN . . .

18 November 2001

The trial for the murder of Zoe Elizabeth Evans was held at Leeds Crown Court and lasted just twelve days. Both Tahani Carroll and Stacey Wilson stood in the dock away from each other and their parents. Each was charged with the murder of Zoe Elizabeth Evans, but they also faced a charge of manslaughter; as well as separate, lesser charges of failing to report a crime and attempting to pervert the course of justice.

From the start, it was a messy and miserable affair. Both girls' solicitors went in hard, each blaming the other girl for leading their client on. Tahani's solicitor, Jeremey Henderson QC – an old man with bushy eyebrows that her dad talked to mainly, in hushed tones – had told her he was going to put across a case of diminished responsibility which would hopefully see her receive a verdict of accessory to murder.

Tahani sat and trembled throughout the whole proceeding. The trial seemed to span on forever and after day three or four, she lost all sense of what day it was. She tried to follow what was going on as best she could, but all the adults had deep, booming voices and scary faces and she often drifted off into her imagination to stop the fear overtaking her. Mr Henderson had also instructed Tahani not to look at the jury, but the fact she'd been told that only made her want to look at them more. They all seemed so stern and terrifying on the occasions that she risked a furtive glance their way. They stared back at her with eyes full of suspicion and, in some cases, hatred.

How could a child do this to another child?

She wanted to shout across the room at them she was innocent. That she'd only wanted to go down to the creek for some fresh air. And like she'd told the police, it was Stacey who hit Zoe. It should be her alone being scrutinized and talked about like she wasn't here.

At one point Mr Henderson mentioned something called *doli incapax*, which Tahani knew was Latin, but didn't know what it meant. It seemed to make for a lot of heated arguments between the two solicitors, however, and they had to approach the judge and even remove the jury at one point whilst they discussed things. It was all very confusing. Scary and confusing.

On day nine, it was Tahani's turn on the stand. Her mum and dad hadn't wanted her to be cross-examined at first, but Mr Henderson had insisted it was the right thing to do. As long as she told the truth, he said, then she had nothing to worry about.

Tahani had been terrified enough up to this point, but being on her own in the cramped wooden box with the whole of the court staring at her was unbearable. She was shaking as the official helped her up on the leather-backed stool they'd had to find her, due to her size, but stopped trembling enough to swear on the bible like they did on television. She made sure she spoke loud and clear and gave the statement the seriousness it required.

"Just tell the jury what you told me", Mr Henderson whispered as he approached. He even smiled at her. It was the first time he had done since they'd met.

After that, it was all a blur. She could have been on the stand for ten minutes; it could have been ten hours. Mr Henderson questioned her first and then the crown prosecutor, a man called Sir Alastair Frances who had even bushier eyebrows than Mr Henderson. He never smiled at her once. He was tall and gruff with loose skin that hung down either side of his down-turned mouth and jangled as he spoke. Each time he addressed Tahani, he would lower his chin and peer at her through his eyebrows. It was a strange way to talk to someone, she thought, and after one session her dad wondered aloud if Sir Alastair was trying to intimidate her. Trying and succeeding, Tahani wanted to say, but she didn't. She didn't speak much between court appearances. She was worn out and scared and didn't really know what to say about anything, anyway. She just wanted it to be over.

She told the court and Sir Alastair what she'd told the police, that Zoe had approached her at the creek and that she feared she would hurt her. She told them that Stacey had picked up a rock and hit Zoe on the side of the head and Zoe had stumbled back into the water. Stace was looking out for her, she said, but she'd not expected her to do anything so extreme. As she spoke, she could see the events playing out in front of her and by the time she'd finished, she was crying. Later, Mr Henderson said that was good optics, but she didn't know what that meant.

"Did Ms Wilson have a history of this sort of thing?" Mr Henderson asked her at one point. "Unprovoked attacks on other children, I mean, sometimes even hospitalising them?"

The question elicited a gasp from some members of the jury that rippled around the court and seemed to anger the judge. Tahani reluctantly agreed that her friend did have history and spoke about poor Brett Hughes.

"Were you scared of Stacey Wilson, Tahani?"

This was a question they hadn't rehearsed, and it threw her a little. She looked at her mum, but she had her head down. She looked at her dad, who met her gaze and gave her a nod.

"Yes," she replied.

As she said this, she could sense everyone in the courtroom staring at her. As well as each member of the jury, there was also Zoe's mum and aunt, and, of course, Stacey. Tahani could almost feel the intense rage coming off her from across the room.

On day twelve, everyone had said everything they wanted to say, and the jury retired for what the judge called 'deliberations.' Mr Henderson told Tahani and her parents to expect a long wait and that in cases such as this one – muddled and complicated, with no concrete evidence to back up anyone's claims – the jury could take days or even longer to reach a satisfactory verdict.

Yet in the end, they took just a day and a half.

The jury was unanimous in finding Stacey Wilson guilty of the murder of Zoe Evans; also finding her guilty of failing to report a crime and attempting to pervert the course of justice. They found Tahani guilty of being an accessory to murder, failing to report a crime, and attempting to pervert the course of justice. She looked over at her parents as they read the verdict out. Her dad smiled at her, but her mum still didn't look up. She looked thin and pale and like the last twelve days had completely broken her.

As they led Tahani out of the courtroom, Diane was waiting in the corridor. She told her she'd done well and that she'd remain in contact with her between now and the sentencing hearing, which would be in a few weeks. It was there in that corridor where Stacey approached Tahani, stepping away from her legal team as they led her past and looming over her.

"You fucking bitch," she hissed. "We had a pact, and you fucked me over. But don't worry, Hani. I'm going to get you. Just you wait."

At the sentencing hearing Tahani got six years for her role in Stacey's death, but as she was only thirteen was told only four years would be custodial – served in a secure training centre outside of Leeds – and the rest would be served in the community 'on licence.'

But Stacey was sixteen and because her crime was so severe, she got ten years. Two of these would be served in a young offenders institute and then she'd be transferred to an adult prison when she turned eighteen. It was a tough and unexpected sentence and Tahani felt bad for her, but in the subsequent weeks and months, she tried not to think about Stacey, or Zoe, or any of the events of that summer. The trial was over. Now she had other problems to deal with.

Chapter 28

"Nadia! Wake up!"

Her eyelids flickered open before automatically closing tight as bright sunshine hit her pupils. She turned away from the light source and let out a groan. Where was she?

"Nadia . . ." The voice went again. She wished whoever it was would go away. She was asleep. Wrapped in her benign blanket of no thought. "I've made some tea. I think you should wake up now."

She opened her eyes once more, and this time was able to keep them that way. Looking around, she realised she was in bed, but it wasn't her bed. It smelled different and the duvet cover was rose pink with a pattern of tiny white flowers. As her consciousness spread, she realised she was wearing a t-shirt she'd never seen before, but still wearing her bra and knickers. Letting out another groan, she rolled over to see Elenore standing at the side of the double bed holding a mug of steaming drink. Nadia could smell the pungent aroma of strong tea but with a hint of honey sweetness, too.

"Morning," Nadia mumbled, pushing herself upright and accepting the mug of tea as she tried to remember what she was doing here. "Thank you. Oh . . ."

Her heart dropped into her stomach as the events of the previous days flashed across her awareness.

Laurie. The hospital. All those machines.

He was . . .

He'd never . . .

What was she going to do now? She screwed her face up, trying to remember how she'd ended up in Elenore's bed. Her last memory was standing over Laurie as he lay strapped to all those wires and bleeping monitors. She remembered feeling distraught, but also new emotions too. Ones she hadn't experienced for a long time. Rage. Determination. She'd wanted to get out of that sterile room as fast as she could and hunt Stacey down. But then her legs had turned to jelly and Carmichael had rushed in. She remembered there was lots of shouting and noise. And had she been in a wheelchair at some point, or was that her mind playing tricks? She also had a vague memory of being in a car, with Elenore driving. But it was all hazy as if she was trying to remember the plot of a film she'd only half-watched many years ago.

"The doctors wanted to keep you in the hospital," Elenore said, perhaps realising she was searching for answers. "You fainted from exhaustion and stress. Do you remember?"

"I think so," she said, bringing the tea to her lips. "It's all a bit of a blur." She sipped at the tea. It was hot and strong and sweet. The sort of tea people made one another in these sorts of situations. In England at least. The fact Elenore, a Frenchwoman, had seen the need perhaps showed how desperate a state Nadia was in.

Her friend smiled and sat on the end of the bed. "You did seem rather out of it," she said. "But you were also certain you wanted to come home. For the children, you said. You gave them my number, and I picked you up. It was very late, so I brought you back here."

Nadia nodded and put on a smile that made her feel disgusting. "Thank you. That's so kind of you."

"Not at all. I am glad to help. It is so horrible what happened to Laurie."

Nadia kept smiling. If she didn't, she was going to cry. She took another sip of tea and looked around the room. She'd visited Elenore's house many times but had never been upstairs to the bedrooms before. This one, presumably the spare room, was decorated in neutral colours, with a bureau and wardrobe the only pieces of furniture besides the double bed.

"Oh, shoot! Andrew. I need to go home." She made to get up, but Elenore raised her hand.

"Andrew is fine. He texted you a while ago and said as much. I saw the message flash up on your phone. Perhaps you should call him, though." She got up from the bed and pulled Nadia's phone out of her pocket, handing it to her. "I'll leave you in peace and then when you're ready, come through to the lounge and I'll make lunch."

"Lunch?" Nadia said. "What time is it? How long have I been asleep?"

Elenore smiled. "It is half-past-twelve. You have been asleep for over ten hours. But you must have needed it, yes?"

"Wow. Yes."

She must have needed it. That was what her dad used to say when her mum complained she got up too late in the school holidays. How she wished her dad were still alive. He'd help her make sense of this horror.

"Thanks, Elenore," she said. "I'll get dressed and be through in a minute."

"No problem. Your dress is in the wardrobe. I hung it up for you and put you in one of my t-shirts. I hope you don't mind."

"Not at all. I appreciate everything you've done for me."

"Bon." Elenore walked to the door and opened it, turning back as she did. "Do what you need to do and I'll see you in the lounge. I was thinking of making egg sandwiches. Is this okay?"

"Perfect."

Elenore shut the door, and Nadia threw back the duvet. She had an enormous bruise on her right knee which she assumed was caused when she fainted. It didn't hurt but it looked nasty. Swinging her legs off the bed and onto the carpet she stretched her arms above her head and swiped the lank strands of hair from her face. She felt like crap, but she couldn't let that slow her down. This wasn't the time for feeling sorry for herself. At least whilst Laurie was still under the care of the hospital, finding Stacey was her priority. Finding her and stopping her. Doing what the police couldn't be bothered to do.

But first, she had to ring her son. As she brought up his name on her phone and tapped 'call', she prayed he wasn't lost in some computer-generated world with his headphones on.

"Mum, how's Dad?" He answered after one ring.

"Erm . . . He was still asleep last night. Resting after his operation. But the doctor said he's stable. We'll know more today, I think." She was trying her best to avoid saying anything that might come back to bite her, but it was difficult. "I saw him, though. I told him we all loved him and that you and the twins were looking forward to seeing him."

"Cool. He's going to be okay, then?"

"Yeah . . ."

How did she tell him? How did she tell her thirteen-year-old son that he could forget about ever playing football in the garden with his father again? And those walks they liked to go on, on a Sunday afternoon, they wouldn't be happening anymore. Laurie was paralysed. He was going to be in a wheelchair for the rest of his life. How was she going to cope? How were any of them going to cope?

"I'm just at Elenore's at the moment," she told him. "I slept here last night."

"Oh? Right."

"I didn't want to disturb you," she lied. "You seemed to want a night on your own and it was late when I got back from the hospital. Did you sleep okay? No problems?"

"Yes, Mum." He said it like a typical thirteen-year-old. As if she'd just asked him the most ridiculous question anyone had ever come up with. "I set my alarm and got up at seven. I've taken new bedding and some eggs down to the yurts and I've done the horses."

Nadia recoiled. She almost removed the phone from her ear to check the caller ID showed it was her son she was talking with. "Are you serious?"

"Yes! I can do things, you know? When you let me. I'm not a kid anymore, Mum. Like I keep telling you."

"Oh, Andrew." She sniffed back an entire year of emotion. Her little boy. Sounding so grown up. "Thank you, darling. I'm sorry if I don't trust you more. I should. And I will. It's not you. It's me." *And it's my own upbringing*, she wanted to say but didn't. Andrew never asked about his maternal grandparents, but she'd always hoped that if he did, she'd tell him as much about them as she could.

Oh . . .

The next thought hit her harder. Would she have to tell Andrew who she was one day? And what had happened?

Maybe if she found Stacey and finished this herself, she wouldn't have to. Clearly, her old friend was close by. She could set a trap for her, lure her somewhere secluded. And then . . . well, then she had to end this. The idea of hurting Stacey, of killing her, even, didn't shock Nadia as much as she thought it would. But she was a wife and mother now. A fierce momma bear fighting for the survival of her family. That changed things.

It changed everything.

"Are you going back to the hospital today?" Andrew asked. "Can I come with you?"

"Yes. Of course." She got off the bed and padded over to the window. Peeling back the curtains, she peered across Elenore's garden to the track and the dense woodland opposite. It must have been there where Elenore had seen the dark figure.

Stacey.

Was she in those woods right now?

She'd always been a rough-and-ready type of girl. Might she be camping out there? Living right under their noses whilst she carried out her reign of terror.

Nadia let the curtain fall closed and turned her back to the window. "Have you eaten?" she asked.

"I made myself eggy bread. Like Dad does it. I'm stuffed."

The words made her heart swell. "You're a good boy, Andrew." As she said it, her voice broke and she had to take a moment before she carried on. "I'll see you soon. Elenore's making me some lunch and then I'll get the twins from Melissa and Tom's and we can all drive over to the hospital together."

Shoot . . .

The words had barely left her mouth when she realised. Her car was still in the hospital car park. And Laurie's car was . . . She cleared her throat. No matter, she was sure Tom or Elenore would drive them and she could drive her car back.

"I'm going to have a shower," Andrew said. "I'll see you soon."

"Okay, darling. And thank you."

He huffed. "What for?"

"For being you."

He laughed, and she pictured him rolling his eyes. "All right, Mum. I'll see you soon."

They said their goodbyes and she placed the phone on top of the bureau. The sunlight was still making itself known through the curtains and the day was already halfway done. She needed to move.

After making the bed, she took off the t-shirt Elenore had supplied and folded it neatly, laying it on the pillow she'd just plumped up. Except for an old fur coat that smelled of musk and damp, her dress was the only thing hanging in the wardrobe. She slipped it off the coat hanger and held it by the collar in front of her. Laurie never got to see her in it last night, but hopefully today he would. She held it to her nose. There was a faint smell of perfume, but that was all. She could get another day's wear out of it. Slipping it on over her head, she did up the buttons and adjusted the material around her waist before heading back over to the bureau. There was still the hospital to call, and she was nervous about what news she might receive when she did. But they had her number down as next of kin, and no one had called or left a message since last night. That had to be a good sign.

It surprised her at how focused and proactive she felt today, considering Laurie's condition, but the long sleep had helped. Or maybe this was what happened when you were pushed to your limits. Either you curled up and let life walk all over you, or you fought back.

She was reaching for her phone when it rumbled into life, vibrating itself across the polished surface of the bureau as the shrill ring tone pierced the air.

Her heart leapt into her throat.

The hospital?

Something's gone wrong . . .

Lifting it, she saw it was Diane's name on the screen. That was okay. She needed to speak to her. Her plan was to lean on her as much as possible, to not let it go until she'd disclosed the name Stacey was now going by.

"Diane, hi," she said, answering the call. "I was hoping to speak to you."

"Is that right?" came the stoic reply. "How are things, kiddo?"

Nadia sucked back a deep breath, preparing for her response. "Not great. Laurie was in a car accident yesterday. He's in hospital."

"Oh my days," Diane cried. "How is he?"

"They think he might be paralysed. I'm trying not to think about it until we know for sure."

"Oh bloody hell, Nadia. Do they know how it happened?"

"His front wheel came off. Someone had loosened the nuts. The police think it was green activists, but I don't agree." She waited for Diane to say something, but she didn't. "I think it was Stacey, Diane. In fact, I'm sure of it. She's here somewhere. I think she's been sleeping rough in the woods next to my house, watching us. The police are useless, they won't do anything. But I'm going to find her. I'm going to find her and—"

"Nadia!" Diane cut in. "Stacey's dead!"

The words echoed through Nadia's skull. She had more to say, but she'd forgotten how to speak.

"W-What?" she stammered. "How? When?"

"I've just got off the phone with Mary, Stacey's supervising officer," Diane continued. "The police tracked her down to a flat in Halifax. Well, more of a squat, really, from what Mary said. I've not had the full story yet, but I thought you'd want to know as soon as I did."

Nadia's mind swirled at one hundred miles an hour. Conflicting thoughts crashed into each other and nothing made any sense.

"But she was here, Diane. She's been—" She shut up as the door opened and Elenore peered around the side.

"Is everything all right?" she whispered.

"Sorry," Nadia mouthed, placing her hand over the receiver. "My friend called. Give me five minutes."

"No problem." She backed out of the room and shut the door.

Nadia waited a second before returning to the call. "Diane, are you still there?"

"Who was that?"

"My neighbour. She's been looking after me." She closed her eyes to get her train of thought back. "As I was saying, I'm almost certain Stacey is behind all this. She even scratched a message into Tudor's stall. A threat."

"I don't think so, kiddo," Diane said almost sternly. "When the police got into the flat where she'd been staying, her body was in a state of decomposition. They reckon she'd been dead for weeks. It was the smell that alerted neighbours something was wrong."

Weeks. But that meant none of this could be Stacey.

"I don't know what to say," Nadia whispered. "I was so sure."

"Hmm," Diane said, as if to say, I told you so. But then added, "The thing is, I'm wondering now whether you might have been onto something, regarding Zoe's family."

"Oh?"

"What I told you was correct. The mother was a waste of space. She's dead now, as it goes. COPD got her in the end, but she had problems with alcohol for the last three decades. And the father was never around. Not even in court. He's dead too now. But I found out from Mary that there's a sister called Helen. She was older than Zoe and would have been an adult when it happened. She moved in with the dad when the parents separated, which is why I didn't know about her."

Nadia turned to the window. "A sister? Do you think this could be her?"

"I don't know. If you ask me, this still could just be—"

"It's someone, Diane! Don't you dare tell me all the horrible things that have happened to my family are just coincidences. No one's that unlucky. If it's not Stacey, then it has to be the sister. What else can you tell me about this Helen person?"

Diane snorted as if she was under duress. Nadia was losing her patience with her.

"Diane! Please! Tell me!"

"She was never on anyone's radar," she said. "You'd have thought she'd have been at the trial, but Mary thinks the parents kept it from her. Or they couldn't be bothered letting her know. They were an odd family. All of them. I shouldn't let it worry you. It's probably nothing."

There were those words again. It was probably nothing. Meaning any thoughts she might have that this Helen person was behind Tudor's death or Laurie's accident was in her head. *Probably.* That one word, doing a lot of heavy lifting.

But maybe everyone was right. Maybe all this was in her head? A mixture of paranoia and her overactive imagination making her believe things that weren't true. She was sure Diane thought it. The police certainly thought it. Even Laurie thought it. And she had been pushing herself to her limits running two businesses and a family. Had she pushed herself over the edge?

Twenty years of guilt and shame had to take their toll on a person. She'd spent fifteen years pretending her life was perfect. That she was perfect. But it wasn't, and she wasn't. She was still the same scared, timid girl she'd always been. Being an adult was just about finding better coping mechanisms for the pain.

On the phone, Diane was still talking, telling Nadia she should concentrate on her family, on being there for her husband. Helen Evans was long gone, she said. She'd never even been around. Her and Zoe weren't close and . . .

"What did you just say?" Nadia asked. "About the sister? About the trial?"

Diane sighed. "Just that Helen was working in France at the time."

"Yes. France." Nadia repeated. "Is that definitely true?"

"According to Mary. Helen Evans was working in a rural town in the south and didn't have access to UK news. It all came as a real shock to her, Mary said. But she stayed in France afterwards. Which is why I very much doubt you have to give her any more thought. She probably washed her hands of the whole thing."

"How old would she be now?" Nadia asked. She felt dizzy and sick.

"She left to live with the dad when Zoe was six and she was sixteen, so she'd be twenty-three at the time of the trial. Forty-five, now."

She said some more things, but Nadia had dropped the phone from her ear. Her hands were shaking as she held it in front of her. "I . . . I've got to go, Diane," she said into the receiver. "I'll speak to you later." She hung up before Diane could respond and stared at the carpet, wondering what the hell she was going to do. Her heart was beating so fast that she felt like it might burst out of her chest.

Older sister . . . Forty-five . . . France . . .

She rubbed at her eyes with the thumb and forefinger of her free hand. This can't be happening. The sound of a creaking floorboard made her jump, and she spun around to see Elenore standing behind her.

"Hello, Tahani," she said.

There was a flash of movement and something heavy knocked the rest of the thoughts out of her head. The room tumbled away as a kaleidoscope of colours flashed across her vision. Her past and future collided in a maelstrom of chaos and confusion as a black cloud enveloped her once more. But unlike at the hospital, this was no warm embrace. This dark void of oblivion was filled with dread and desperation and made her want to scream. But she couldn't scream. She couldn't do anything. She thought of Tudor. She thought of Laurie, lying in the hospital with tubes sticking out of him. She thought of Andrew and the twins.

Then she didn't think anything at all.

Chapter 29

Nadia reeled, instantly awake as an intense smell of ammonium carbonate invaded her nasal passages. She shook her head. It hurt like hell. She felt a sharp pain over her right eye and instinctively raised her hand to feel for any bumps or cuts.

What the . . .?

Her arm wouldn't move. She shifted her weight to try again, but something was holding her back. She tried to stand, but this was impossible, too.

What was going on?

Where was she?

She struggled some more before the world swam into focus and she saw Elenore standing in front of her, holding a small blue bottle.

"This stuff works better than I expected," she said and smirked. At least, it looked like Elenore, but it didn't sound like her. Her French accent was gone and in its place an accent much closer to Nadia's own – well-spoken, with traces of Yorkshire in some of the vowel sounds. She stepped back and chucked the blue bottle on the floor. "That's one thing Hollywood got right."

As Nadia's awareness spread, she realised she was in the workshop attached to the side of Elenore's house. Another attempt at raising her arms brought the realisation that Elenore had tied her to the chair. It was one of the wooden chairs usually found in the kitchen. Probably the same chair Nadia had sat on many times, whilst drinking wine with her friend. Who she now was almost certain was Helen Evans. Zoe's older sister.

"It was you," Nadia said. "You did this. Tudor, Marge, Laurie . . ."

Helen grinned. "I'm good, aren't I? It took you all this time to realise. But I'm so glad that stupid bint Diane Chambers let it slip just now. What a dramatic moment in our story, don't you agree? I couldn't have planned it better myself."

Nadia glanced around, searching for an escape route. Her hands were bound around her back with each wrist tied to a spindle of the chair-back rather than to each other. Her ankles, too, had been tied to a chair leg on either side. Helen had used blue plastic string, the sort Nadia had used for the washing lines in the bottom garden. It was thick and durable and seemed to tighten the more she pulled. Elsewhere in the workshop, standing along the side wall, was an old workbench. Sitting on top of it was Nadia's iPhone. It was the only thing she could see that might help her. But there was no way she could reach it. In the far corner of the workshop, on the opposite side of the wall to the door that led into the house, was a metal cupboard. The doors were open and Nadia could see it was empty. In front of her stood two more dining chairs facing the one she was on. Helen saw her looking and moved over, positioning herself in between them.

"Don't worry, all will be revealed. *Tahani*."

"Why do you keep calling me that?" she said. "My name's Nadia."

Helen chuckled silently to herself and pointed a bony finger at her. "You're a good actress, you know that? But don't for a second think I haven't done my research. I've been tracking you and Stacey Wilson for the last year."

"You killed Stacey?"

She frowned, as though Nadia had hurt her feelings. "Of course. On one of my 'trips up to London to meet my solicitor.'" She made the quotation marks in the air with her fingers. "She was a real mess when I found her. Broken. Destitute. Addicted to heroin. It didn't take much for me to finish off the wretched cow."

Nadia raised her head. Her mind was racing fast, trying to come up with a way of escape.

"She was moaning something terrible at the end," Helen went on. "She blamed you for it all, you know? Saying anything and everything to get me to stop. But I didn't. I wouldn't. Although I had to kill her much quicker than I'd intended, which was a shame. I'd wanted it to be slow and painful. But there you go . . . Life!" She leered at Nadia, a manic grin spreading across her face.

"It was awful what happened to Zoe. And I'm so sorry," Nadia said. "But it wasn't me. I would never hurt anyone. Zoe and I didn't get on, but I didn't want her dead."

"But she is dead. Isn't she? And you walked away. Left her bleeding out in the creek. Do you know what water does to a body, even after twenty-four hours? I saw the photos on your mate's computer when I broke into her house. My poor kid sister, bloated and pale, her skin like wet paper bags. You did that to her. You and Stacey."

Nadia lowered her head and chewed on her top lip, trying to focus her thoughts. She'd already hung up the call to Diane when Helen hit her and, for all Melissa and Tom knew, she was still at the hospital.

But Andrew knew she was here. She'd told him she'd return to the house soon. Would he come looking for her if she didn't show up? And what would Helen do if he did?

"You did all this to get back at me?" she asked. "You moved all the way to Cornwall and bought a house? Why go to so much trouble? And if you've been tracking me for a year, why wait this long?"

The answer, of course, was because Helen was sick and twisted, but Nadia felt it would be useful to keep her talking.

"I wanted to make sure I had the right person," Helen said, with a casual shrug of her shoulders, a hang-up from her time living as Elenore. "I hadn't planned on moving down here. But as I was researching you, this house came on the market and I thought, why not? I can be nearby while I work out what to do with you. I was going to kill Diane that day – when I broke into her office – but I thought better of it. It might give the game away before I'd even started. But I'll have my revenge on her, too, don't you worry. If I have enough time, that is."

Nadia met her gaze. "Time?"

Helen sat on one of the two chairs opposite and let out a deep sigh. "Two years ago, I was diagnosed with a frontal lobe glioma. They operated, but it came back almost straight away. After that, they told me there was nothing they could do but prolong the inevitable for a year or so." She crossed one leg over the other and leaned back. "The knowledge you're going to die changes a person, I think. But rather than making me wallow in my fate, the prognosis gave me a new lease on life. It made me appreciate what was important. And understand what aspects of my past needed reparations. I wasn't a decent sister to little Zoe, you see. She looked up to me but I wanted nothing to do with her. I didn't even say goodbye to her. So, when the doctors told me I was on my way out, I knew what I had to do." She laughed and gestured around her with open hands. "And look at this! I did it! Stacey is in the ground where she belongs. Your husband is going to be a cripple for the rest of his life. And you . . . well, we'll get to you soon enough."

Nadia struggled with the ties on her wrists. The right one felt looser than the left and with time, she might free it. But it would take some effort, and the harsh twine was tearing at her skin with every movement.

"Did you like my accent, Tahani?" Helen asked, getting up from the chair. "And my portrayal of Elenore? I lived in France for some time, and I speak the language, so it came relatively easy for me. But I was rather proud of myself all the same. All that crap about dead husbands. I think I missed my calling as an actress!"

"You're crazy," Nadia muttered but regretted it as soon as the words were out of her mouth. The last thing she wanted to do was rile Helen even more.

But she laughed. "I have been told some symptoms of my condition are a change in personality and behaviour." She shrugged. "Who knows? I could be crazy."

"What are you going to do to me?" Nadia asked, yanking at the ties.

"Isn't it obvious? I'm going to make you pay for what you did. As soon as I knew there'd be no real comeback for me, it was like a beautiful epiphany. I wanted to make Stacey suffer more than she did, but in her place, you'll do. I mean, with two dead animals and a broken husband you already are suffering, aren't you? But it's going to get a lot worse, I'm afraid." She flashed her eyes at Nadia. "I can't tell you how much fun it was, making you think it was Stacey messing with you all this time. You fucking fool. You fell for it better than I ever hoped."

Nadia sniffed. "Please, Helen. I'm sorry about what happened to Zoe. But it wasn't my fault. Please, let me go. I understand you're upset and that you're not well and I'm sorry about that too. But killing me won't solve anything."

"I'm not going to kill you, Tahani," Helen said, smirking as she did. "At least, not yet. I said I wanted you to *suffer*. Like my parents suffered. Like Zoe suffered. Like I'm suffering."

"Don't you think I've suffered enough? They locked me up for four years and during that time, both my parents died. My mum's cancer returned because of all the stress and my dad would never have had his stroke if it wasn't for me. I did that. I killed them."

"Yes, you get everyone killed, don't you, Tahani? Your parents, your cat, your prized stallion . . . Laurie was lucky to survive the accident, but he's going to need someone to wipe his arse for the rest of his life, so I'm not sure *lucky* is the right word." Her smirk grew wider, but then her expression dropped. "And you got my little sister killed. Stacey might have hit Zoe with the rock, but she did it for you. Didn't she?"

Nadia sobbed. "I'm sorry. I'm so sorry. Please, I—"

"Are you sorry?" Helen snapped. "Are you, Tahani? Or are you saying anything you can think of so I'll let you go? The problem is that didn't work for Stacey, and it won't work for you."

She wandered over to the workbench and picked up Nadia's iPhone. Walking back over to her, she shoved it in front of her face. Nadia flinched, expecting to see a horrific photo of Stacey on the screen. But Helen was just activating the facial recognition software to unlock the phone.

"What are you doing?" Nadia asked as Helen wandered away. She leant back against the workbench and tapped at the screen with both thumbs.

"I'm pretending to be you while I text Melissa," she replied as if it was obvious.

"Melissa?"

"Why, yes." She glanced up from the screen and frowned. "I'm telling her you've asked Elenore to collect the twins. I'll find Andrew later, but for now, this is what's happening."

She turned and yanked open one of the workbench drawers. Reaching inside, she lifted out a large hunting knife. The sight of it made Nadia's heart almost stop. Helen held it up, and the serrated blade shone as it caught the light.

"These are for your children," Helen said, waving the knife at the empty chairs in front of her. "You're going to watch me kill them in front of you, and there's nothing you can do about it."

Chapter 30

Helen Evans stared at Nadia with wide, unblinking eyes. Taunting her as she struggled with the ties around her wrists and ankles.

"Do you think you're going to get away with this?" Nadia said.

Helen snorted. "I don't need to get away with it, *mon amie*, fem. As long as I make you pay for what you did, my work here is done. Even if the police catch up with me, I'll be dead before I stand trial." She stuck out her bottom lip. "They do say the most dangerous people are those with the least to lose."

"If you want me to pay for Zoe's death, then focus on me. Leave my family out of it." She lowered her head as tears rolled down her cheeks. "Please, not the twins. Not my babies. They're innocent."

"You have to suffer, Tahani," Helen said. Her voice was cold now. "Like you made my family suffer."

"My name is Nadia," she replied, weakly. The initial burst of energy she'd felt when Helen had administered the smelling salts had long since faded and she had a splitting headache. She'd been yanking against the ties around her wrists since she became conscious, and the sharp twine had cut into the thin skin around her wrists. The pain was the only thing keeping her alert. She had, however, created some slack in the ties, but wasn't sure if she'd loosened the knot or had simply stretched the plastic a little. Either way, her wrists and ankles were still bound to the chair. She rolled her feet from side to side to try to work them free, but it was useless.

"Your name is Tahani Carroll," Helen responded. "That's what they called you when they found you guilty of being an accessory to my sister's murder. That's who you are, a spineless, evil bitch."

"Fine! Kill me if that's what you have to do! But leave my children alone!"

Helen waved the knife at her. "Don't worry. I'll make it quick. But you are going to watch me do it and—Ah! Here we go!" Her face seemed to light up as Nadia's phone chirped to signal there was a new message.

Nadia gritted her teeth, putting all her strength into her forearms as she pulled at the sharp, unforgiving rope. In front of her, Helen made a show of reading the text, then chuckling to herself as she tapped out a reply and pocketed the phone.

"Game on," she said with a flick of her eyebrows. "Melissa is giving the brats their lunch, but I can collect them whenever. Elenore is driving them up to the hospital to meet you there. Isn't she a good friend?"

She walked over to Nadia and bent down so their noses were almost touching. "I have to leave you for a few minutes now, but I advise you not to try anything stupid. Because remember, I'm going to have your kids with me. And this big knife." She straightened up. "Besides, there's nowhere for you to go.

The garage door is double locked and I'll lock and bolt the house door behind me. I suggest you sit tight and I'll be back soon with the main event."

She sauntered over to the door that led through into the house. In the doorway, she turned and looked Nadia up and down, shaking her head. "You thought you were home dry, didn't you? Living down here with your husband and kids, under a different name. I bet you didn't even give my little sister a minute's thought since you moved here. Everything was going so well for you before I turned up. But that's life, Tahani. It's shit, isn't it?"

Nadia didn't answer. She just ground her teeth together and carried on, twisting her hands free. They were numb with pain and her fingers and palms were sticky with blood. But she couldn't stop. She couldn't let this vindictive psychopath hurt her babies.

Helen stepped into the house and closed the door behind her. As the key turned in the lock, Nadia peered around the space, looking over both shoulders in case she'd missed anything. But there was nothing. For a second she wondered about screaming for help but thought better of it. Helen was unhinged and had nothing to lose, and Melissa and Tom's house was too far down the track for them to hear her cries.

It would take Helen around thirty seconds to walk to Melissa's house, but double that, walking back up the track with Edward and Emily in tow. Add on a few minutes for small talk with Melissa and Nadia reckoned she had around five minutes to do what she needed to do. Which was . . . what? Escape? Find something to use as a weapon? Get into the house somehow and call the police? They were all valid ideas, but who was she kidding? She was weak and dizzy and still tied to this damn chair. Her head was throbbing so intensely from where Helen had hit her it was affecting her vision.

But she had to do something.

She was desperate.

She had to try.

With a grunt of effort, she pushed back against the chair before leaning forward again. The movement created some momentum and as the chair rocked back she felt the front legs lift off the floor. It wasn't enough to tip over, but as she rocked forward, her feet touched the floor and she pushed off to create more force. Her stomach flipped over and a surge of adrenaline flooded her system. She was so close to the edge, but the chair rocked back once more onto four legs. She tried again, kicking out with her feet and lurching back with her upper body at the same time. The chair teetered on two legs for a moment, but then the balance shifted. She was going over. Screwing her face up, she tensed every muscle in her body, bracing herself for the impact. She was falling backwards for what seemed like forever and no time at all before the chair hit the ground and a sharp pain shot up her arms and down into her fingers. A deeper, heavier pain burst into her skull as her head connected with the concrete floor. She'd been leaning forward to lessen the impact, but it was intense all the same. She felt it in her sinuses and in the roots of her teeth. Yellow and white flashes shot across her vision.

But then everything stopped.

Everything was still.

She opened her eyes. The room looked as it had done a moment earlier. She sucked in a deep breath. Her arms were going numb, crushed between the floor and the back of the chair. Grimacing with the pain, she raised her head to examine her legs. They were still tied to the chair, but in this new position, she could work the rope down the chair legs and with a flourish of new energy, she unhooked the ties from the bottom of the chair. Her legs were free. Now, with more momentum at her disposal, she heaved herself over to one side, toppling over so she was on her knees with her head pressed against the floor and the chair on her back. From this position she was able to get to her feet and, twisting and wriggling as if she was conducting an ancient war dance, worked her hands free from the ties around her wrists.

"Yes!" she gasped. "Come on, Nadia! You can do this!"

She lowered the chair to the ground and inspected her arms. The skin around her wrists was torn and bruised and looked to be burnt in places, but she no longer felt any pain. Pain was for another time. She rubbed her bloody hands on the front of her dress and thought about rubbing some on her face as well. It might freak Helen out when she returned and provide Nadia with an advantage. But then she thought of the twins. The next few minutes were going to be hard enough for them. Seeing their mum covered in blood would only add to that trauma.

But she was free.

She could fight back.

Helen was clever, but she'd made a fatal mistake. She hadn't counted on Nadia's determination and what a mother would put herself through to protect her children.

She was still making that mistake.

A sound from the inside of the house alerted Nadia. She hurried over to the workbench and yanked open both drawers, hoping to find something inside she might use, a hammer maybe. But except for a box of small screws, there was nothing. More noises drifted through from the house. The sound of a door closing. Voices. She glanced around. She'd knocked the two empty chairs over in her struggle. Moving fast, she picked them up and placed them in the same position as before, sitting on her chair and placing her arms behind her back as a key turned in the lock. She lowered her head, letting her matted hair fall over her face as the door opened.

"It seems you've got a reprieve," Helen sneered. "For a few minutes at least."

Nadia lifted her head. Helen was alone. The twins. Where were the twins?

"What do you mean?" she asked.

"Mrs Perfect down there has decided to give your brats some ice cream after their lunch. She said she didn't want to disturb them and could I wait ten minutes. Fucking meddling bitch. But no problem." She closed the door behind her but didn't lock it. The hunting knife was still in her hand. A shiver of nerves ran down Nadia's spine as she readied herself.

For the children, she told herself.

And for Laurie.

"You'll have to sit tight a while longer, *Tahani*," Helen said, giving the 'h' the guttural back-of-throat-sound, the way her mum used to say it. She was mocking her, but it only added to

Nadia's resolve. "I told Melissa I'd get my coat and head back in five, once they're finished. If she won't hand them over then, I'll kill her as well. What's another life? I doubt she'll want to live here anyway, after what's about to happen. An idyllic setting, marred by a glut of grisly murders. Awful business." She grinned. "But don't worry, Tahani. Everything is still going to plan. All this means is you and I can chat for a while longer. How nice for us both."

Chapter 31

Nadia raised her head and stared at her captor. She was ready to move. Ready to swing the chair at Helen's head. But she was standing in front of the door, over ten feet away. She needed her closer.

"What do you want to chat about?" Nadia asked.

"Maybe chat isn't the right word," Helen replied, stepping forward and brandishing the knife. "You know I've never killed a human with a knife before. Plenty of small livestock, when I lived in France, pigs and lambs mainly. But not an actual person. You see, with Stacey, I wanted it to look like a suicide. In case they found her body early. So, strong tranquillisers and a rope tied to the doorframe were the obvious choices. But now here I am, doing it the old-fashioned way and perhaps I should practice my knife skills before I slit your children's throats. We don't want me making a hack job of it, do we? That would be awful. For everyone involved."

Nadia tensed her whole upper body to keep any intrusive thoughts from forming around that image. "Please," she said. "Don't hurt them. It's me you want."

"Yes. It is. It's you I want to hurt. But I don't just want to hurt you physically. I want to cause mental and emotional and spiritual pain as well." She held up the knife and eyed it lustily. "But maybe we can start on the physical pain while we wait. What do you think? You could stand to lose an ear. Or an eye. It would be awful for your kids to see their mummy all cut up and mutilated. But then, they wouldn't have to see it for too long."

"You don't have to do this," Nadia said.

"You didn't have to leave my sister to die."

"She was already dead. I was a young kid. I was terrified and confused, probably traumatised. I didn't know what I was doing."

"Yet you stood up in court and told the jury it was Stacey who killed her. You knew what you were doing then?"

"It was Stacey!"

"It was both of you! But you did everything you could to get out of it. Do you think four years in a secure unit is ample justice for what you did? At least Stacey did her time. Twenty years in prison." She shook her head, an expression of rage twisting her features. "I regret not making that bitch suffer more than I did. But she had no family or friends, you see. I had no leverage. Plus, I was new to the revenge business. Not so anymore though, hey? The cat, the horse, your husband's accident. Quite an impressive body of work, if I say so myself. I'm rather proud of what I've achieved. My legacy. And all the while, you thought it was Stacey. You really are a gullible idiot, Tahani."

She took another step closer. Nadia tensed. She had one shot at this. "Zoe certainly thought so," she said. "She hated me. She was a vicious, racist bully and made my life a living hell. She made me scared to go to school."

The words fell out of her mouth easily, but they didn't land. Helen just smirked at her the same way her younger sister had done on the many occasions she'd appealed to her to stop. But these people didn't stop.

"Doing this won't bring your sister back," Nadia said.

"Very true," Helen replied. "But it will make me feel better. I was a terrible big sister to Zoe in life, but maybe I can be a decent one in death. If my last act is to kill those responsible for her murder, then I—"

Nadia sprung up and swung the chair around with every bit of strength she had left. She was holding it with her right hand, and as she brought it around on its trajectory, she grabbed hold with her left too, giving her swing more power as she smashed the chair into Helen's side.

She cried out and stumbled into the wall. Nadia followed her, raising the chair and swinging it at her head, knocking her over. One of the chair legs snapped off and clattered to the ground as Nadia lifted the splintered chair for another go.

But she paused.

Helen was laid out on the concrete floor of the workshop. She wasn't moving.

Nadia straightened up, peering around the space and stretching her eyes wide to allow her brain to catch up. She felt woozy but fought against it.

Turning around, she headed for the door to the main house. She was almost there when she heard a grunt and let out a scream.

A hand had grabbed her ankle.

No!

She kicked out to shake her off, but in doing so, she tripped over. Hitting the concrete floor with a thud, she twisted around to see Helen looming over her. Her eyes were enormous and blood was running down her cheek from a gash on the side of her head. It looked nasty, but it hadn't stopped her. It had barely slowed her down. In one hand, she gripped Nadia's ankle. In the other hand, she held the hunting knife.

"No. Get away . . ."

Helen chuckled to herself. She'd altered her grip on the handle so the blade was facing down and with a victorious grin, she raised it in the air.

"Go to hell!" Nadia cried, kicking out with both feet. Her right connected with nothing but air, but as she bicycled her legs, her left foot caught Helen square in the face. The ferocity and directness of the blow seemed to surprise both women. Nadia gasped. Helen let out a guttural cry and let go of Nadia's ankle. She was free. Nadia lurched towards the door, barging into it with her shoulder and falling through into the house. Once inside, she got to her feet and slammed the door behind her. Trembling hands skirted the door frame for bolts or locks, anything to keep Helen out. But except for an old yale lock, there was nothing. Nadia flicked up the metal switch which dead-locked the mechanism, but she knew it wouldn't hold Helen for more than a minute to two. If she still had the key in her possession, even less.

Nadia glanced around her. She was in the utility room and the air was cooler here than in the workshop. She sucked in some deep breaths to get her mind back into focus.

What did she do now?

She could run to Melissa and Tom's house, but the twins were there and with Helen still in play, she couldn't risk it. Melissa and Tom were lovely people but were what she'd call gentle souls. They'd be very low on the list of people she'd want on her side in the event of a knife-wielding psychopath attack. If she brought Helen to their door, she might get them all killed.

She could already hear Helen scrabbling at the door so pushed through into the main body of the house. It sickened her to think of how much she'd shared with the woman she'd thought of as her friend in this house. They'd never talked about her past, but she'd talked often with Elenore about her life here in Cornwall, about how much she loved Laurie and her children. How much she needed them.

It had all been fuel to the fire for this evil woman.

"Tahani! Get back here!" Helen's voice echoed through the house as Nadia entered the kitchen. She glanced around, searching for a knife or similar. There was nothing in sight. She opened the drawers under the worktop but found the first full of nothing but old bills and the next scattered with rusty keys and bags of loose change.

Where the hell did she keep her knives?

Footsteps in the hallway told her Helen was close. There was one knife's location she knew of all too well. The one Helen was holding in her hand. Nadia left the drawers and raced over to the door. She found it unlocked and yanked it open, buoyed slightly by the breeze that whipped around her bare arms and legs as she stepped outside. She headed for the track and veered left, heading towards her house. Even though she'd never been into physical activity, and hated sports at school, she was a fast runner. If she could get to the house before Helen caught up with her, she could lock herself inside and call the police. Helen Evans' reign of terror would be over, just like that.

With the thought spurring her on, she quickened her pace, heading around the bend in the track and running straight into Andrew.

No! Get away!

"Mum," he yelled out. "What's going on?" She grabbed him and placed her hand over his mouth.

"Quiet," she whispered. "We're in danger." She glanced over her shoulder. Helen had yet to appear, but she'd be close behind her.

"What's going on?" Andrew said, lowering his voice as he pulled Nadia's hand away from his mouth. It was then he saw the blood on her hands and wrists.

"I'm okay," she told him. "But I need your help. Elenore isn't who we thought she was. She's a bad person. It was her who killed Tudor and tampered with Dad's car. She's dangerous."

Andrew screwed up his face. "Why would she?"

"I'll explain later," she said, throwing another furtive glance over her shoulder. "I need you to run back to the house. Now. As fast as you can. Once you get there, lock all the doors and windows and then ring the police. Tell them they need to get here fast, and that your neighbour has a knife and is trying to kill people." She saw the terror in his eyes and grabbed him by the shoulders. She needed him to understand. "I'm sorry to put this on you, Andrew, but I need you to be strong. Say those exact words to them. It'll get them here quicker."

"Come with me," Andrew said, moving away but grabbing at her arm as he did. "We can ring the police together. We'll be safe."

Nadia stared into his eyes. That was what she wanted, too. But she couldn't risk it. Being anywhere near her children was too dangerous. Helen was on the rampage. She had to draw her away from them.

"Listen to me, darling. I'll be fine," she said, squeezing his shoulders. "But I need you to be brave. I need you to do this for me. Now go. Quickly." She pushed him away, relieved when he turned and ran back towards the house. She watched him for a moment before she heard Helen's voice booming up the track.

"You can run, Tahani," she yelled. "But this is already over. I'm going to kill you and everyone you love. This is what you get! This is what happens!"

But it was okay. Andrew was almost at the house. Another ten seconds and he'd be safely indoors. He was safe and the police would be here soon. If it was soon enough for Nadia to survive the next ten minutes, she wasn't sure, but she was no longer thinking about herself. Her entire body was tight with nervous energy. As Helen appeared from around the side of the big oak tree at the end of the track, she set off, running at her as fast as her legs allowed. Helen saw her and braced into a fighting stance. Her face and hair were covered in blood and she was holding the large hunting knife up and ready. She looked more terrifying than ever. The steel blade shone in the late afternoon sun.

"Come on, bitch!" Nadia yelled at her. "Let's finish this. Me and you."

She kept on, running towards her fate, but at the last minute, she deliberately misstepped and swerved around the side of Helen, who threw her arms up and screamed. It sounded like the last throes of a dying animal.

"What's wrong?" Nadia called back as she headed for the woods. "Too slow? Too slow, like your miserable sister? You're both as pathetic as each other. That bitch deserved everything she got. And soon you'll be dead, just like her."

The words prickled the back of Nadia's neck. In normal life, she wasn't the sort of person who would ever dream of saying something so horrid and spiteful. But this wasn't normal life. All bets were off when you were fighting for survival.

And the words had the desired effect.

"I'll fucking kill you," Helen cried, setting off in pursuit of her.

That's it, follow me . . .

Nadia had no plan other than to get that evil woman away from her kids and her home. Helen may have invaded her life, but she wouldn't let her take it from her. This was the life she'd imagined for herself every night, as she lay in bed in the secure training centre. It was the life she'd focused on, to keep from falling into total despair. If Helen Evans killed her in the woods, then so be it. But her children would be safe. The horrors of her past wouldn't taint them. Not now. Not ever.

Chapter 32

Nadia could hear Helen gaining on her as she raced through the woods. She was running faster than she'd ever run and her lungs burned with fatigue, but Helen was dogged in her pursuit. If Nadia was to survive until the police arrived, she had to think clever. She was prepared to sacrifice herself if it meant her children lived, but that didn't mean she had a death wish. Edward's and Emily's smiling faces flashed across her mind as she pushed on, zigzagging around trees and heading deeper into the woods. She'd lost two parents by the time she was seventeen. She hated to think of her children having to deal with that sort of grief. It changed a person. And the twins were so young. It would ruin their entire childhood. And their father in a wheelchair, too. What would become of them all if she died? What would Laurie do? It hurt her heart to think about it. She gritted her teeth and ran on.

The further she ran into the woods, the taller the trees became and the thicker the leaf canopy above her head. A few more steps and the sun and sky were all but blocked out. Here, a chilly gloominess descended over the woods. It seemed fitting. If this was a scene from a film, these were the exact conditions one would expect.

Stealing a glance over her shoulder, she saw Helen was only about a hundred metres behind her. Not far enough. Up to this point, Nadia had been sticking to the path, worn down over many years by dog walkers and hikers. But doing so meant Helen had been able to tail her. Now she needed to throw her off.

The fronds of tall ferns slapped against her cheeks and low branches scratched at the skin on her arms and neck as Nadia leapt from the path and into the leafy undergrowth. She could only see a few metres in front of her and led with her arms, swiping branches and leaves out of her path as she went, moving in a wide arc to further disorientate her pursuer.

After a few more minutes of thrashing through the dense vegetation, she came out into a clearing and stopped to get her bearings. Panting, she stretched her arms back to expand her lungs, surveying the clearing as she did so.

In front of her, on the other side, there was a gap in the trees and the grass below was worn down to dirt. It was more overgrown than the one she'd followed into the woods, but it was a path, nonetheless. It led somewhere. Nadia had always had a good sense of direction and she surmised that if she followed this new path, it would come out down the side of Melissa and Tom's house. Could she make it back there before Helen realised where she'd gone? Would the police have arrived by then?

She froze, focusing all her attention on her hearing. Off in the distance, she could hear police sirens. Andrew had done it. Good boy. But she could also hear the swish of leaves in the undergrowth behind her. Helen was still on her trail.

Nadia ran across the clearing towards the gap in the trees. Her legs throbbed with exertion and a deep stitch in her side cut her in two, but she ignored the pain as best she could.

Pain was for another time.

And it would soon be over. One way or another. Helen wasn't going to get her children. She'd failed. She'd made the mistake of—

Nadia cried out in pain as the ground rushed up to slam her in the chest. Something had grabbed her ankle. She rolled on the wet grass, winded and confused, but looking back she saw her leg was sticking out of an old rabbit hole, her foot bent around at a weird angle. Forget about pain being for later. It was here right now. It felt like her ankle had been set on fire. Snorting through the agony, she grabbed hold of her calf and twisted her foot out from the rabbit hole. It was swollen and bruised. She tried to wiggle it. It hurt like hell, but she could rotate the joint and didn't think it was broken. But whether she could run on it was another matter.

Shuffling on her bum over to the nearest tree, she grabbed hold of a low-hanging branch and pulled herself up. Putting weight on the ankle sent a sharp burning sensation soaring up her leg into her pelvis. She tried again. It was torture. There was no way.

But Helen was getting closer. Nadia could hear her grunting as she barged through the undergrowth. Another few seconds and she'd reach the clearing. After that, it was game over. She was going to die here in these woods. Sliced open like a piece of meat. One last insult from a member of the Evans' family.

No. It wasn't going to happen.

She had to keep going.

Half-hopping, half-skipping, she moved away from the tree and headed for the path. She'd only gone a few steps when she lost balance and stumbled onto her bad ankle. The pain tore through her like a runaway train and she fell to the ground with a shriek. Tears filled her eyes, and she blinked them away as she tried to get up on all fours. She felt like a desperate animal as she shuffled towards the gap in the trees, slow and awkward but determined. It was the only way she was going to escape Helen's wrath.

Or maybe not.

"Oh, dear. What a shame."

Nadia looked around as Helen appeared on the other side of the clearing. She regarded her fallen prey with mad, greedy eyes.

"No. Please . . ." Nadia gasped. But she knew it was useless. There might have been a time when Helen Evans could have been reasoned with, but that time had gone. Revenge and that vindictive disease had ravaged her mind and any sense of reason.

Helen stepped closer and waved the knife at Nadia's foot. "Hurt yourself, have you? That is bad luck. Just when you'd almost got away. It's almost like fate itself wants you to pay for what you did."

Nadia lowered her head, hoping it would make her look subservient and timid enough to buy her some time while she scanned the ground for something she might use. A stick. Or a sharp rock.

"It's not the way I planned things," Helen said. "But you'll die now, knowing your children will be next. Mark my words."

"The police are on their way," Nadia said, peering up at her. "Listen. Sirens. They're almost here. It's over, Helen. Don't do this. I am sorry about what happened to your sister, but it wasn't my fault. None of this was my fault!"

"Who cares?!" Helen screamed. "Do you really think the local police are going to send a firearm unit? Do they even have a firearm unit around here? I'm going to march down to that wet bitch's house and slice them all up. Her and her drippy husband, along with your twins and that fat waste of space, Andrew."

Nadia sniffed. "You can't, they won't—" She stopped as she saw something in the trees behind Helen. As she realised what it was, she involuntarily let out a gasp but coughed to cover it. Time stopped as she waited to see if Helen had noticed.

"They won't what?" she spat and shook her head at Nadia. "You'll say anything to save your skin, won't you? But you can save your breath." She held the knife blade in front of her, gloating as she saw the apparent fear spreading across Nadia's face.

But it wasn't fear. It was trepidation. There was a big difference.

"Killing me won't bring Zoe back," Nadia said, keeping her eyes on Helen but shifting into her peripheral vision so she could take in the whole clearing. "And it won't save you. My mum died of cancer. It's a horrible disease. And it's awful that the doctors can't do anything more to help you. But is this really the way you want to go out?"

"I am avenging my sister's murder." Helen's voice was cold and monotonous. Gone was the mocking joviality of a few seconds earlier. "I don't care what happens to me. The police can arrest me once I'm done. I'll turn myself in. I can already sense I'm on the way out, anyway. I'm doing this for my family before it's too late. So now it's time for you to get what you deserve."

Nadia held her breath as Helen stepped forward and flipped the knife handle around in her grip, holding it out in front of her. One slash of that blade and it could be all over. She tensed, not daring to move. Helen chuckled to herself.

"You really are a pathetic fucking bi—Ooof!"

She lurched over to one side as Andrew appeared behind her and hit her around the side of the head with a thick branch. Dropping the knife, she toppled over onto her knees, but Andrew wasn't done. His face was rigid with emotion as he swung the branch at the back of Helen's head and she dropped to the ground like a dead weight.

"Andrew," Nadia gasped, raising her arms to her son as he ran over to her. He hugged her tighter than he ever had done.

"Mum. Are you okay? Did she hurt you?" He was crying. So was she.

"I told you to stay in the house."

"I called the police like you said. I told them everything you said, and that they needed to get here as soon as possible. I think I can hear cars pulling up now. They're here. It's going to be okay. But I couldn't just sit there, could I?"

He leaned back to look at her, but she pulled him close again. Over his shoulder, she could see Helen's fallen body. The gash on the side of her head had opened further and thick crimson blood was seeping into her already matted hair. She wasn't moving. She might even be dead.

"You're a good boy, Andrew," she said. "And this was very brave of you, but it was also very stupid as well. You could have been seriously hurt."

She stiffened at the sound of voices from the woods beyond the clearing, and then the crackle and beeps of radio receivers. The police were close by. If Helen was dead, she'd tell them it was her who'd hit her.

"You were in danger, Mum," Andrew said. "I had to protect you, didn't I? I had to."

She smiled and held onto him as he tried to pull away. "And you did, darling," she whispered. "You saved me. You saved all of us. Thank you."

Chapter 33

Six months later . . .

Nadia placed the two plates of scrambled egg on the table and called out across the room. "Laurie, Andrew. Breakfast."

Emily and Edward were already at the table, slurping back spoonfuls of soggy cereal and chattering to each other about what film they were going to watch that afternoon. Being so far away from the nearest big town, going to the cinema was a rare treat for them, but since Laurie had finished his recent physical therapy sessions, he and Nadia had agreed that Saturdays should be a family fun day. As well as the cinema, they'd recently watched a matinee show of *Beauty and the Beast* at the open-air theatre outside of Bodmin.

"Smells good," Laurie said, wheeling himself in from his new office. They'd created it out of the spare room that up to six months earlier had been a dumping ground. A halfway house for items they didn't use or need but couldn't bring themselves to get rid of. With Andrew's help, Nadia had taken seven boxes to the local tip. It felt good to get rid of the old rubbish and create a fresh new space. But it was what she'd been doing her entire life.

"It's only eggs," Nadia told him as he got himself up to the table and she helped wheel him into position. "I was hoping to do some smoked salmon with it, but I must have forgotten to buy it."

Laurie looked up at her. "This is great. Thank you."

"My pleasure." She ran her fingers through his hair. He was still her handsome husband, the man of her dreams, but life had been hard for the two of them these last six months. After being discharged from the hospital, Laurie had been depressed and distant for many weeks. On the few occasions he did speak, he was snappy and bitter, telling her he wished he'd have died in the car crash, and that his life was over. The doctors and counsellors reassured Nadia that this was a typical response and that, with the right treatment, Laurie would see light at the end of the tunnel.

There'd been three rounds of paraplegia rehabilitation sessions to date, and with each round, Nadia saw an improvement. But they weren't there yet. The doctors told Laurie not to pin his hopes on ever walking again but through repetitive, task-specific exercises, they hoped his lower body mobility might improve over the long term.

In the meantime, they'd spent some of their savings making the house as accessible as possible. Except for his old office, up in the roof space above the children's bedrooms, the house was all on one level, so once they'd cleared out the spare room it was only a matter of getting a wheelchair ramp and some additional equipment for the bathroom. Regarding that area, it was still rather awkward for both Laurie and Nadia. But they loved each other. They'd get through it.

"Are you not eating?" Laurie asked as Nadia sat beside him at the table.

"I had a piece of toast before I did the horses. I'm not hungry." She tilted her head to one side and watched as he tucked into his food.

"Daddy, what film do you want to watch?" Emily asked.

Laurie swallowed back a mouthful of eggs. "What are my choices?"

"Err . . . well, I want to see *Super Pets* but Eddie wants to watch *Minions*," she replied. "What do you want?"

"Both sound good to me," Laurie said. "But a more important question: are we getting popcorn?"

"Yes!" The twins shouted back in unison.

"Great."

Nadia sat back and smiled to herself. They'd been through so much in the last year, but it had only made her appreciate her family even more. Helen Evans had tried to take them away from her, but she'd failed. Because love was more powerful than hate and resentment, and it always would be.

Helen was dead. But it was the brain cancer that got her in the end. The police arrived in the clearing as she was regaining consciousness and took her away. With nothing to lose, she'd admitted everything, but Nadia still had to attend some awkward interviews where the police had shone a harsh light on her past. Helen died in a hospice a few weeks after being charged and never stood trial for killing Tudor or Marge or for causing Laurie's accident.

But that was the end of it. She could finally lay Tahani Carroll to rest. Along with Stacey Wilson, Zoe Evans and Nadia and Gerry Carroll, her mum and dad. It was over. The past was back where it belonged. Never to be thought of again.

"Mummy, can Daddy take us to the cinema just us three?" Edward asked out of nowhere.

Nadia felt the tension coming off Laurie. "Not yet, Ed," she said. "Daddy still can't drive. But one day, maybe?"

Edward sniffed and looked at his bowl. "Can I play in my room?"

"Yes, of course."

"And me?" Emily said, dropping her spoon into her bowl.

"Yes, go play."

The twins slipped off their chairs and ran past her, disappearing into the hallway that led to their bedroom. Nadia watched them go and then turned back to Laurie. She could tell Edward's question had hit him hard. He could be having the best day, but then something like this happened, and it knocked him into a real slump.

"Are you okay?" she asked, eyes searching the side of his face for a sign. "He wasn't thinking . . . He's only six. We're all going together so . . ."

She trailed off as Laurie sucked in a deep breath. She worried he was going to cry, but he held it together. "I'm sorry," he said. "It's just . . . shit."

"Yes. I know it is," she whispered. She rested her hand on his, but he didn't move. Sometimes she wondered if he blamed her for what had happened. Maybe he should. If it wasn't for her, Helen wouldn't have loosened the wheel nuts on his car and he wouldn't have crashed. But then, if it wasn't for her, he wouldn't have his children. He wouldn't have had the past fifteen years.

She lifted her hand and placed it on the table as silence descended between them. At times like this, she also wondered if this was her penance. After everything that had happened, maybe she didn't deserve the happiness she'd enjoyed. Because all of this, the nice house, the handsome husband, the beautiful kids, it was too good to be true. She'd been a timid, self-conscious girl from a rough part of Bradford, confused about who she was, what she was, and where she fitted into the world. On top of that, she'd been involved in a tragic and horrific event that had ruined many people's lives. Whether she called herself Tahani or Nadia, she didn't deserve this life. People like her didn't get to have a happy ever after.

She looked at Laurie. He'd only eaten half his breakfast but was now staring out of the window the way he often did these days. Maybe this was her lesson. Don't expect a happy ever after. They don't exist.

"Sorry, Mum. I was in the shower. Is it still warm?"

Nadia looked up to see Andrew had appeared on the other side of the table. He was wearing his black hoodie and his hair was wet and slicked back. It made him look a lot older than his thirteen years.

"Scrambled eggs. Nice," he said, sitting down and reaching for the pepper. He applied it liberally to his food before pausing and peering across the table. "Are you two okay?"

Nadia smiled. "Yes, we're fine." She nudged Laurie as subtly as she could.

"Are you coming to the cinema with us this afternoon?" he asked.

Andrew looked at Nadia. "I thought you'd said . . .?"

"It's fine," she told him. Then, to Laurie. "Andrew is going to a party tonight. I said he could spend the afternoon here to get ready."

"Why do you need all that time?" Laurie asked.

Nadia went for his hand again, grasping hold of it tight this time. "Come on, Laur, you remember what it was like being young."

"You've changed your tune."

Nadia sighed but didn't reply. Laurie wasn't expecting a response and she wouldn't know what to say even if he did. Instead, she sat back in her seat and closed her eyes, letting the warm sun filtering through the window calm her soul. She inhaled and exhaled a few times, telling herself that today would be a good day if she decided it would be. It was a worthy idea but was rarely that simple. Some days, she had to really work at it.

She still had her reservations about letting Andrew attend teenage parties. But he was a sensible boy and thoughtful with it, and over the last six months, he'd more than proved he was mature enough to deal with whatever life had to throw at him. And on top of that, he wasn't her, and she wasn't her parents. It was important to give your kids some leeway. Otherwise, you risked forcing their hand and making defiance their only option. The occasional party was okay, she reasoned. As long as Andrew kept his phone on and maintained contact with them. Parenting was about mutual trust and after everything they'd gone through together, she trusted her eldest son to make good choices.

Just like she had done.

THEN . . .

3 August 2001 (That day)

Tahani stepped backwards as Zoe approached her. The girl's eyes were red and puffy and she bared her teeth at her like a wild animal. Tahani had never seen anyone look so full of hatred in all her life. She'd certainly never seen it so close and directed purely at her.

"Leave her alone, Zoe."

Stacey's deep voice broke the silence, and Zoe visibly tensed. This was it, Tahani thought. What she'd been waiting for. Stacey was older and tougher than Zoe. She was going to step in and tell her to get lost.

"Piss off, Wilson," Zoe muttered. "This is between me and her." She lunged at Tahani, slamming her shoulder into her chest. Green fields turned to blue sky as she hurtled backwards and landed on the ground with a dull thud. The impact knocked all the air out of her and for a second or two, she didn't move. She closed her eyes, wishing this was all a dream, that she was back home in bed.

"Stacey," she cried. "Help me."

She opened her eyes to see her friend waving her arms in the air, telling Zoe to stop. But that wasn't enough. Why wasn't she stopping her?

"Get up, you ugly mongrel bitch," Zoe spat. "I've not finished with you."

With effort, Tahani pushed herself up onto her elbows. Stacey was still standing a way off and Tahani looked at her, pleading with her eyes. *Help me!*

"Please . . . Help!"

Zoe loomed over Tahani. Her face was bright red. "I told you, Wilson. Stay back."

And that's when Tahani realised. Stacey was as scared of Zoe as she was. And she wasn't going to help her.

"I said, get up," Zoe spat. "I swear I will fucking kill you if you don't get up. Do you hear me?"

Tahani scrambled away from her and as she did, her right hand touched something hard, about the size of a tennis ball.

"Stand up!" Zoe screamed, spit flying from her mouth. "Fight me, you pathetic bitch! Me and you, right now. Come on." She was enraged and wasn't going to stop.

As Tahani sat up, she heard her dad's voice in her head, telling her she should stand up for herself. She had to. No one else was going to do it.

She took a deep breath as the green panorama of the creek shifted to tunnel vision. It was just her and Zoe now. As she got to her feet, she looked past Zoe to see Stacey was still standing behind her. They made eye contact, and it was as if she knew what Tahani was thinking.

No, she mouthed. *Don't.*

But what right did she have to tell her what to do? She'd stupidly believed she was her friend. But Stacey didn't care about her. She wasn't her friend. She was alone in this world. No one was coming to save her.

"Right then, bitch," Zoe said. "Now we see what you're made of . . ."

Before she'd finished speaking, Tahani swung her arm, smashing the sharp rock she'd picked up into Zoe's temple. The blow jarred Tahani's arm, sending a shock wave into her shoulder, but she kept hold of the rock and swung it again, hitting Zoe in the same place but with much more force. This time she heard a sickening crack and felt the splinter of bone. It shocked her, but she held her nerve. As she stepped away, Zoe shuddered and made a strange whining noise that seemed to come from deep inside of her. Then her eyes rolled back into her head and she fell backwards into the creek, smashing her head on a large rock sticking out of the water.

"Fucking hell!" Stacey cried. "What did you do?"

Tahani stared down at Zoe, feeling a flush of pride in herself that she'd stuck up for herself. Finally. But confusion quickly replaced those feelings, followed by fear. Zoe's eyes were open, but she was just staring up at the sky. Blood poured out of the wound on the side of her head, mixing with the clear water of the creek and turning it a pinkish red. It was scary and disgusting but kind of beautiful too, Tahani thought.

"Hani!" Stacey said, walking over to Zoe and kneeling next to her. "What are we going to do?"

Tahani blinked. "What do you mean?"

"She's dead!" Stacey said, getting to her feet. "You've killed her!"

"What?"

"Look at her. She's not breathing, and her eyes have got that weird look in them. Like my gran's had when we found her last year. She was just sitting in her chair staring at the TV even though it wasn't on." She puffed out her cheeks. "Bloody hell, Hani. This is mental."

"She was going to kill me," she said. "You saw that. She said as much."

Stacey looked back at Zoe. "I'm not sure the police are going to see it that way, mate. Here, give me that rock."

She grabbed it out of Tahani's hand before chucking it across the creek. It landed in the deep part of the stream in front of the bridge with a satisfying splash.

"All right, listen to me," Stacey said, turning back and hunching down to look Tahani in the eyes. "Zoe was pushing you, and she slipped and fell. Understand? She banged her head on a rock and even though we tried to help her, she wouldn't wake up. That's our story. If the police ask why we didn't report it, we'll say we panicked and were scared. It won't go down that well, but it's not too bad. Do you understand?"

Tahani screwed up her nose. She was still trying to understand a lot of things. "The police?"

"Yes. The police. In my experience, they always find you, in the end. This is why we need a plan. We need to make a pact. We stick to this story and we don't say anything else. Do you understand?" She grabbed Tahani's shoulders. "Hani! Do you understand what I'm saying?"

"Yes. I understand," she said.

"Okay, let's get out of here."

Stacey grabbed Tahani's wrist and led her up the embankment, away from Zoe's lifeless body. As they walked through the lush green fields, the grim reality of what had just happened enveloped her like a black cloud.

She'd killed someone.

And the worst thing was she didn't even feel that bad about it. That thought alone made her feel sick. She must be in shock. That had to be it.

Otherwise, what did that say about her?

What did it make her?

Neither of them spoke until they'd reached the main road and even then it was only a few mumbled words of encouragement from Stacey. Her telling Tahani not to worry. That if they stuck to the pact, all would be well. And maybe it would be. But what were her mum and dad going to say?

As they walked along the snicket that ran down the back of the new estate and came out at the far end of their street, she stole a glance at Stacey. She was rough and wayward and already well known to the police. It wouldn't take much for them to believe she'd killed Zoe.

Tahani swallowed down the ball of fear that had been stuck in her throat. She hated she was even considering doing this, but she had her parents to think about. She couldn't let them down. It would kill them. She had to save them from the pain of thinking their daughter was a murderer. And if that meant Stacey Wilson took the fall for her crime, so be it. Zoe Evans' death was her fault, anyway. She should have stepped in to help. She should have been a better friend.

About the Author

M.I. Hattersley grew up in Yorkshire, UK, and has spent the last couple of decades balancing creative work with a long list of mind-numbing day jobs. He's toured Europe with a rock 'n' roll band, trained as a professional actor, and founded a theatre and media company. He now writes psychological thrillers and domestic suspense novels, drawing on years of experience with intense people and unpredictable situations.

About Embla Books

Embla Books is a digital-first publisher of standout commercial adult fiction. Passionate about storytelling, the team at Embla believe our lives are built on stories – and publish books that will make you 'laugh, love, look over your shoulder and lose sleep'. Launched by Bonnier Books UK in 2021, the imprint is named after the first woman from the creation myth in Norse mythology. Embla was carved by the gods from a tree trunk found on the seashore; an image of the kind of creative work and crafting that writers do, and a symbol of how stories shape our lives.

Find out about some of our other books and stay in touch:

X, Facebook, Instagram: @emblabooks
Newsletter: https://bit.ly/emblanewsletter